THE ROMANCE OF EOWAIN

PREVIOUS WORKS

in the

MATTER OF MANRED SAGA

Hedge King in Winter

A Merchant's Tale

The Romance of Eowain

FORTHCOMING WORKS

in the

MATTER OF MANRED SAGA

The Wedding of Eithne

Heron's Cry

Join the mailing list at mdellert.com/blog/mailing-list/ to receive more information, news, updates, and special promotional offers on these and other exciting new titles coming soon from Skylander Press

THE ROMANCE OF EOWAIN

THIRD TALE IN THE MATTER OF MANRED

Michael E. Dellert

2016

SKYLANDER PRESS

New York, NY

Cover Illustration by Saša Ristović-Ritza
Cover and Interior Design by Glen M. Edelstein.
Map Design by Cornelia Yoder.

Dellert, Michael E. 1970–
Romance of Eowain, the / Michael E. Dellert
p. cm.
ISBN 978-1-944400-04-0
1. Fantasy. 2. Heroic Fantasy. 3. Romance. I. Title.

Printed in the United States of America
First Edition: July 2016
1 2 3 4 5 6 7 8 9 10

For Jean Lee:

Always remember to forget
The friends that proved untrue.
But never forget to remember
Those that have stuck by you.

I will remember.

For Sara and Jenn:

A day lasts until it's chased away but love lasts until the grave.

And always, for Kaitlin and Hannah.

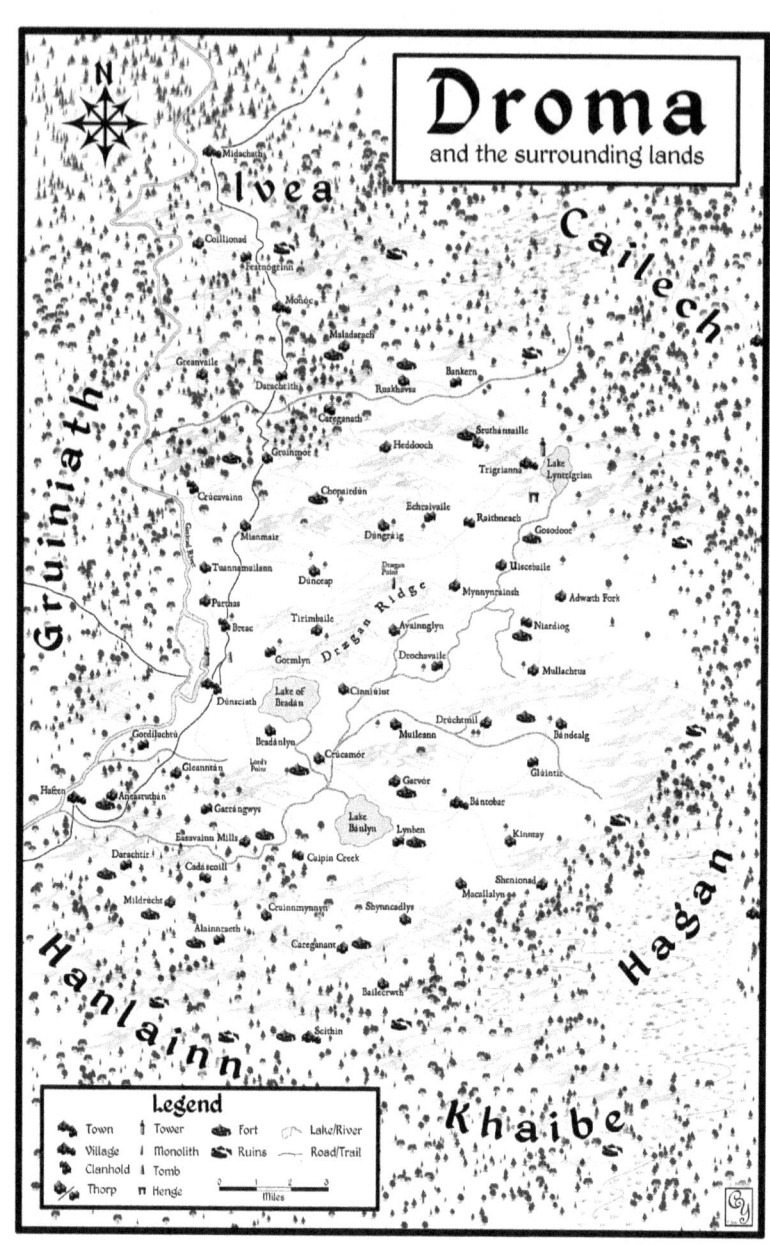

MAP OF DROMA AND THE SURROUNDING LANDS

CHAPTER ⊕NE

FATHER GRUMBLED THROUGH the rain. "I made a promise to the priestess once. She was a wild ban-drymyn hermit-sister of the mountain woods then. She told me I was to save your hand from marriage until the appointed time, but that you'd always hold your ancient right of choice. Whatever fate the ban-drymyn sister saw in you as a child, I don't know, but that was the *geas*, the obligation that came with you into this world. I had to do what was right, by the Gods."

"But I barely know the man, Father."

"You had the chance to meet with him."

"For a mere ten-day, Father. For three days of which, I was a hostage to this Cael the Viper fellow."

"He rescued you himself, amid a number of great troubles in his kingdom. The *coelbreni* and the drymyn favor him. He wrote you those letters, I know you favor those." He shrugged. "He seems a likely enough lad."

Beneath her cloak, the Lady Eithne of Dolgallu clutched the stained and crumpled packet of correspondence. Within were vellum sheets, marked with black *coelbren* runes on leathery white calfskin. She thought of the last one she'd received.

Spring must truly be here, for the first great caravan of the year has arrived today from the south. They fly the flags of a great Narician trading family, and come with goods from Sasana, Aukriath, Thradamír, Picari, and many other foreign lands besides.

Her horse stumbled over another rock in the rutted trail. Her hands went to the pommel to steady herself.

The steed recovered and settled once more into a less kidney-punching rhythm.

Not for the first time, she thought of home. She'd never seen such an event, a great caravan of Foreigners from distant lands. Her tiny village at the foot of the snow-capped mountain of Ydrys was remote, isolated.

Could it be seen from there?

She craned her neck to look east, but the trees were too thick. She couldn't even catch a glimpse of its snowy heights.

And what's my future to be, Great Ydrys? She turned forward again in the saddle and pursed her lips.

The mountain Ydrys had a fell reputation, it was true. Yet it was known that Ydrys the Giant watched the course of the stars and the Wanderers of the Night from his seat upon its summit. Her people still called upon his name as a great astrologer and diviner of old.

What it's always been, I conjure. She knew it wasn't her fate to remain among her secluded mountain people. She'd always known. Blessed by the Ancestors with good crops despite the rough highland countryside, her people were a tough, grim folk, and Eithne missed them fiercely.

She clutched at the epistles beneath her cloak.

Three months ago, she hadn't even known of the existence of this Lord Eowain of the Donnghaile, now hedge-king of the Droma tribe.

That was when the first messengers began to arrive, seeking out marriage opportunities for then-Lord Eowain, the worthy candidate for a small tribal kingship.

She'd since visited briefly with him in person. Her family, some of his family, and the Drymyn Order of priests and priestesses favored their union. Most recently, they'd exchanged correspondence.

> *Which brings me to the matter of our own betrothal. My aunt is certain it will be*
> *all for the good, bringing an end to the feud between our families. My brother—*
> *indeed, all of us—look forward to the peace on our borders when we have the*
> *Cailech tribe wedged between the hammer and anvil of our two tribes. And my*

Lord-Drymyn seems to think our marriage is ordained by his wooden coelbreni
and fated by the gods (though to what purpose, I cannot imagine).
Yet what of you? When you departed here, you had still not yet agreed to our
betrothal, and so my aunt, my brother, and my minister urge me to woo
you now in letters and know your mind on the matter.
But who will teach a soldier the words that would
recommend his suit to a gentle heart like yours?

The staccato drum on the hood of her cloak kept her close company. The last three days had brought middling showers, a farmer's rainfall. It had since abated, a light but persistent drizzle, which was improvement in her opinion.

Eithne ventured to draw back her hood for a look about. *We must be getting close now,* she thought. The rolling hills rose from the river valley, thick with bare-branched trees that showed the first green of breaking buds and little else.

The trail took a torturous route through a defile but rose more gradually than some of the land about them. A rill of water tinkled as it ran nearby.

She wondered, *Could I not have found love at home?* It didn't matter, she knew. She'd tried. But it seemed each time she might have found love and happiness, she'd been reminded of her fate.

She had an ancient right as a young woman to refuse any suitor arranged by her family. It was a right given by the Gods to free-women everywhere, command of themselves and the dignity of their own bodies. And everyone and her mother, all her life, had sworn she wouldn't be denied her freedom of choice.

That didn't stop her family from presenting—or denying her—to eligible suitors.

She'd been held close all her life by Father. Bedraggled with rain and clearly miserable, Father nevertheless kept a stern watch on the woodlands. And her.

She thought even if they had not left on this journey dressed like masterless warriors, their several days on the trail would certainly have made him look the part. Water ran down the ill-used round steel helm in rivulets and dripped from the nose guard. His featureless wool cloak proclaimed nothing of his origins and loyalties. Unshaven, he looked as if he hadn't known a bath for above a month.

Father grumbled. "Eithne, you must agree to this marriage."

"No matter how much the men of Dolgallu talk of women's choice in the matter of marriage, you have left me with little, Father." She crumpled the missives in her fist, under her cloak and away from the rain.

"You know our ways. The blood of our families must be nurtured, not squandered away."

Indeed, she'd never been permitted to love those she counted closest as friends. Marriage was a sacred trust. The blood of the people of Dolgallu was a gift to be passed down from family long gone to those yet to be remembered.

The drymyn claimed it was all according to some plan only the Gods knew and at which the drymyn only guessed with their oracles and prophecies. She was but one of the vessels for that blood in that generation of the world.

To her other side rode the strange old wild woman of the wood known as Alva Damar. The ban-drymyn who had laid this geas upon her and her father at the moment of her birth.

Smallish and dark, her long black knots tumbled, with a shock of white hair, from beneath her own hood. Her face was gentle and tired with years of care. But after so long on the trail with her, Eithne knew she was tougher than the leather mountain boots she wore. She was armed, armored, dressed as a man. The studded leather cuirass, short hunting bow, and plain broadsword were formidable.

The small, swarthy woman shook the rainwater from her hood. "It is the way of our Ancestors, lass." Together, the old ban-drymyn and her father might be any pair of lordless lieutenants, or deserters from any of a hundred border skirmishes. "You knew this, always and already. This is true of the men as well. There must never be any unsanctioned mixing of blood."

Eithne indeed knew it well. All decisions on matters of love were approved or rejected by the council of family elders. Their will in that, above all else, was not to be thwarted.

She felt herself grimace in a most unladylike fashion. "Aye, ban-drymyn. So it has always been. My right to a choice in the matter of my own marriage has always been subject to your authority, hasn't it?" The hermit woman from the mountain woods measured and recorded the family blood-lines of her village. Through their strange harmonic geometries, the *coelbreni* runes and the celestial forces and portents assigned to them, Alva had determined that marriage was advisable and not forbidden to that man in that time of the world.

"And so I am sent away to live among so-called 'civilized' lowlanders, with their horses and their steel and their trade." She felt a flash of anger. *And why shouldn't I be angry?*

She clutched the letters again and recalled Eowain's closing advice to her in his final missive:

> *I must beg you, take the utmost care! Matters in Droma have become still more treacherous. Twice, Cael the Viper's bandits have struck.*
> *A fifth young child has been abducted...*
> *...a rash of terrible and monstrous creatures that seem to have descended upon us...*
> *...a monstrous vermin, big as a pony, erupting from the earth...*
> *...a terrible bear along the Trigrian trail north of our Drægan Ridge...*
> *I bid you, whatever dangers the Cailech present (and they are formidable), be wary of still further dangers. Have your father bring his hardest men to keep you safe.*

At the three points of the triangle around herself and her companions rode three others a-horse, two men ahead and one other behind. Escorts and bodyguards. They wore jacks of leather sewn with rings of steel, and bore both swords and spears.

Her father wanted to attract no undesirable attention, traveling with women in such a small company through uncertain lands. Five men on foot marched both ahead and behind their company, similarly armed and armored.

Among them traveled her two maid-servants, Breda and Cuneen, dressed like the men, as was Eithne herself.

Somewhere ahead of them, she knew there were five more men who scouted their way, alert for bandits and robbers. Their vigilance had helped avoid several unwelcome encounters already. She had to trust them to do so again if the need arose. The damnable rain made it difficult to hear any forewarnings of danger. She remembered what Eowain had written on the topic of her route.

> *As for the Cailech, I shall put it abroad that your arrival is expected at Trígrianna during the dark of the moon. But I beg you, take the longer, southern way, through the lands of the Hagan and north again to Scíthin. The Hagan king is friendly to us, and his lands are generally at peace right now. I believe the south is the safer and more fortuitous route.*

Down from the mountains to the Mórraith River they had come, then turned south as Eowain advised and passed through the kingdom of the Hagan tribe. The Hagan were allied to her betrothed, but going as they had through Hagan territory was a round-about way to travel.

Surely, no road can truly be called 'safe' now. Eithne didn't doubt the straighter way through the Cailech hills had become too treacherous. The Cailech king knew of her impending marriage and was not one to sit idle while his enemies aligned against him.

But even Eowain's Hagan ally might not be trusted where a noble maiden worth a ransom was concerned. So they had traveled in secret and without announcement.

Her chestnut-coated horse lurched once more. She was too well-bred to curse aloud, but five days and more on the trail had frayed her temper. "It seems we'll never get there." She regretted it instantly. She could hear her own petulance. *But by the Gods, I'm tired of this interminable—*

There was movement ahead on the trail.

A man in brown cloak and leathern cuirass stepped with open hands from the brush.

One of our scouts, Eithne realized. Father's hand went to his hilt. The woman Alva wicked rain from her bowstring.

Two other men then stepped from the brush. A young drymyn acolyte, a lad of about fourteen, as she judged from his face and his brown robes.

The other was a mystery to her, a young man about her own age, in a stern leather vest of foreign design and warm woolen robes of good color and quality. He pulled back his hood. His hair was black and knotted behind his head. His black moustache and the goat's-beard on his handsome chin were oiled and curled, his leather breeks torn and stained with rain and blood. He wore a broadsword low upon his hip, a leather sash buckled across his chest, and bore the gear and wondrous demeanor of the explorer.

The scout said a few quiet words to the sergeant at the van of the company, and the acolyte and the strange man were passed back to them.

The acolyte bowed. "My Lady." The acolyte slapped at his companion, who bowed belated and bemused.

The young lad went on, "I am the acolyte Adarc," in a good clear lowlander tongue that Eithne understood well. "I'm the disciple of Medyr, Lord-Drymyn and Councilor to His Grace, King Eowain." He rose and indicated his companion. "This is the merchant Corentin son of Winoc, of the Aukrian merchant-house of Pelan."

The strange man bowed. "*Gôljan, qêns gûdakunds.* The greeting to the noble and beautiful woman of the mountain." He bowed to her father and to the ban-drymyn at her side as well. "*Gôljan, thiuda gûdakunds.* The greeting to all you people born of nobles." She didn't understand all his words, and doubted anyone else recognized his foreign manner of speech.

The acolyte put a hand on the merchant's forearm to quiet him. "My lord, my lady, the King bids you welcome to his kingdom of Droma." He gestured to all the forest ahead of her.

Then pointed north. "But sure and there's a nest of monstrous vermin not far from here, my lady. Bugs big as ponies, sure and they are."

The merchant nodded. "They spit the globs *ôgjani*—you say terrifying, yes?—the globs terrifying, that burns the flesh from men. And, I dare to say, the flesh also of the *gûda*-maiden like yourself."

"Stop that." The acolyte seemed cross with the merchant.

"*Hwas?* Am I so wrong?"

The acolyte motioned up the trail. "My lady, we have to go carefully. The fort at Scíthin lies but a mile farther on."

✝

EOWAIN CAME UP from the brook for evening prayers, after a happy day's hunting.

Booths had gone up in the great triangle of the horse-fair. Along the river front from the ferry to the corner of the enclosure, pavilions and wagons gathered where the road veered toward Padarn's shrine.

A wooden jetty stood upstream from the ferry, where the riverside stretch of gardens and orchards began. Banners snapped in the chill wind. A rain that wouldn't fall threatened instead.

By river, by road, afoot through the forests and over the border from Gwynfor, traders of all kinds made their way to Dúnsciath.

Subsistence goods the men of Droma grew, or bred, or brewed, or wove, or spanned for themselves the year round. But once a year they came to buy the luxury cloths, the fine wines, the rare preserved fruits, the gold and silver work.

To those great fairs came merchants even from Mêndevos and Doviath. They'd trickled in already, led by Aukrian traders a week earlier. Shippers with Narician wines, shearers with the wool-clip from Gwynfor, and clothiers with their finished goods: gowns, jerkins, hose, town fashions come to the country.

Not all the vendors have yet arrived, Eowain reckoned. Most would appear in the next fortnight, and set up their booths during the longer spring evening, ready to sell.

But buyers had arrived in purposeful numbers already, hungry from a perilous winter and bent on securing good beds and food for their stay.

Eowain sat a moment upon his horse to watch the pageant. His Lord-Drymyn rode near on a small pony.

Called Medyr of Droma, the Lord-Drymyn was the chief priest of his kingdom and Eowain's royal tutor as a boy. He wore his hair long, braided and knotted from his pate to his shoulders, but across the crown and temples it was shaved from ear to ear.

Medyr observed with philosophical detachment: "Yes, the world and his wife will be here, either to buy or sell. This is what your aunt Rathtyen's downriver schemes bring upon us—a plague of merchants."

The Lord-Drymyn rubbed his chin. "Do you see anything there to concern Your Grace?"

Eowain took it all in with a new sense of gravity. "I've never seen it so lively before. It bodes well. We've scavenged down to the bottoms of barrels for cabbages, even in my own hall." He thought of his Aunt Rathtyen. "Perhaps you've misjudged her, Lord-Drymyn. Maybe my aunt isn't so wrong? With more coin from trade, we can buy green grain and preserved meats from the farms in Larriocht, where spring comes earlier." He thumped a wagon of grain-bushels and salt-bricks in the market. "We can use the profits from our share of the taxes and tolls to stockpile supplies for the King's Company."

Medyr agreed. "Last year, the town of Uisneach was under seige all through July and into August. Small hope getting buyers or sellers past that and upriver for any such business." He shrugged. "I had my doubts even about this year. But it seems trade's well on the move again. Our chief-holders are hungrier than ever for what they missed a year ago. It'll be a profitable fair, I conjure."

Eowain dusted an early spring fly from the hide of the curl-horned ram across his pommel. "We may be fighting off crossing attempts all along the river front this summer. I want the granaries filled and supply lines organized before the season grows late."

The Lord-Drymyn nodded. The King's roe-buck lay across the pommel of his own pony. Flies didn't trouble him. "I'll speak to the Lord-Captain, Your Grace."

Eowain put his gloved fist to the heart of his boiled leather hunting vest. "Gratitude, Lord-Drymyn." But something then troubled his sight.

The great courtyard of his fort seethed with visitors, servants, and grooms. The traffic in and out of the stables flowed without cease. To Eowain's hall had flocked all the gentry of the tribe, and of neighboring tribes too, lordlings, warriors, yeomen, with their wives and daughters. They took residence in the overflowing guest-halls and awaited the three days of the annual high-spring fair, when King Eowain would be wed.

Yet Eowain's sight found a rider that had entered at the gatehouse and walked his horse through the throng toward the stables.

Behind the rider, a brown-robed acolyte and two retainers on rough-coated ponies followed. One retainer with a crossbow slung at his saddle.

In perilous times, no man would undertake a long journey without provision for his own defense, and a crossbow reached further than a sword. But it was a weapon only newly-come to Droma, a Foreigner weapon lately smuggled in to supply dissidents and bandits against his own succession.

So it was their master held Eowain's eye, even if it was at first that the man had also brought an archer with him for security.

The master of those men was perhaps Eowain's own age, a year or two more than twenty. He both wore a sword and looked as if he could use it. He rode on a dark bay with the ease of one well-trained to the saddle. In the spring heat he'd shed his short riding-cotte and slung over his lap. His black hair was pulled back and knotted, while his moustaches and goat's-chin were carefully oiled and curled.

Eowain sent a groom through the throng. "Have that man to me for any news."

Eowain was king of a large tribal palatine where his writ ran, and no other. But he was yet unaccustomed to the throne, crowned mere months earlier, and the matter was far from settled with his cousins.

"Tnúthgal has the coin and the will to supply bandits with smuggled Foreigner weapons. A man openly bearing such a weapon raises a number of questions, don't you think?"

Medyr cautioned him. "Don't do any obvious discourtesy to the man and his retainers. News is expected, Your Grace."

"Better still, to hear for myself then what the man knows."

The rider scarcely waited to dismount once he'd heard the groom's message. He thrust his way through the crowd to Eowain and did the appropriate reverence.

Yet it was the acolyte that traveled with him who presumed to speak. "Your Grace, I am Adarc of Triath, acolyte to the Lord-Drymyn, sir."

He nodded to his master Medyr, then indicated the kneeling man. "You may remember Master Corentin, son of Winoc the Merchant, from Aukriath."

Medyr frowned at him. "You're that merchant's son? That went to Trígrianna?"

"*Ja*, the same, my lord-drymyn." The merchant's son rose.

Adarc cleared his throat. "From the Lady Eithne of Dolgallu, Your Grace: Greetings and reverence to the King of Droma, health and good fortune. I'm to inform Your Grace that the Lady is safe arrived."

Eowain let out a breath he hadn't known he was holding. That she was safe in Droma was a relief, though with all the fighting and banditry of recent weeks, such safety was hardly to be counted upon.

"She sent word to tell you, after giving thanks at several local shrines in the neighborhood of Scíthin, she regrets to say she is insulted, Your Grace. By the Lady Gluintír, at the very shrine of Padarn and upon his feast day."

Eowain winced. *Oh no.*

The Lord-Drymyn narrowed his eyes. "And when will she be here, Adarc?"

"The Lady Eithne will arrive in Dúnsciath the day after tomorrow."

THE FOLLOWING MORNING, Eowain in his hall received petitions and passed judgments. Commoners and lords alike presented grievances, seeking their King's justice. Eowain did his best to be even-handed, with the Lord-Drymyn Medyr beside him to advise him on the precedents of their tribe's common law.

Then the merchant and the acolyte were brought forward. Eowain had received good reports of their travels since their arrival back at Dúnsciath. "We've heard tales of adventure against monstrous vermin and terrible bears. We thank you for your courage and the services you've done our kingdom."

The merchant and the acolyte did another reverence in gratitude. Then the merchant clapped his hands. One of Eowain's own scouts—joined by the merchant's tall, brawny Foreigner—bore between them into the hall a basket overflowing with some rank animal's hide. Another servant carried an iron-bound case.

The merchant flourished the magnificent hide of gleaming black pelage from the basket. "This was the fur of the bear *mikil-skaftjan*, greatly made by the Gods, *ja?*" It cascaded to the floor between his hands, and shone in the torchlight. "The House of Pelan would like to offer it as a gift to the great king who is called 'Eowain the Bear'."

Then the case was held open to reveal precious gems. "Won on our adventures through your countryside, Mighty King. Another gift for you, Your Grace, as a sign of the esteem in which the House of Pelan holds Your Magnificence."

Eowain was grateful. Such a beneficence would go some way to depleting the tribe's treasury.

Eowain's chamberlain, with an appropriate apology, ventured into the hall and awaited permission to interrupt. "Your Grace, here in the great court is your cousin Tnúthgal, with a delegation of northern chief-holders, asking leave to speak with you. They say the matter is urgent."

Eowain allowed his black, level brows to rise a little, and indicated that Tnúthgal and his worthies should be admitted at once.

Relations between Eowain and his cousin, if never exactly cordial—that was too much to expect, where their interests so often collided—were always correct. Their skirmishes conducted with wary courtesy. Eowain had an idea why Tnúthgal and his cronies were there, and scented battle, but sought to give no outward sign.

The men entered the hall in a solid phalanx, no less than ten of them. His eldest cousin, Tnúthgal son of Ferudach, third in the line of Donnghal, led them. He was a portly, vigorous man not yet forty, bearded, brisk, and dignified. He had a river-holding to the north, above Dúnsciath, with good farmland and horses, and was aware of their excellence and his own worth.

For this occasion, he'd put on his best, and made an impressive figure, as clearly he meant to do. Several of those grouped at his back were well-known to Eowain: Bran the Handsome of Maladarach, Fionnguine of Greanvaile, Eigneachan of Careganath—men of substance, every one.

"You are welcome, gentlemen. Cousin," said Eowain. "I would introduce to you the Master Corentin of Aukriath, newly-returned to us from his recent adventures."

Tnúthgal considered the Foreigner up and down, then did him as little honor as courtesy allowed before the chamberlain ushered them aside.

The abrupt arrival of his cousin irritated Eowain, and insulted him in an underhanded way. The merchant had been presenting him with gifts after all. Yet he restrained himself and waved to Tnúthgal. "Speak, cousin. You'll have attentive hearing."

The ten made their reverences gravely, spread their feet, and stood planted in a battle-square, all eyes alert. Eowain concentrated his own attention on them, and hoped he had much the same effect.

Tnúthgal lowered his head.

Eowain thought of the wild ram, before he clashed horns with his rival.

"Your Grace," said Tnúthgal, "We've come to speak of this 'spring fair' of yours. During the busiest season for trade on the High-King's Road and the river, when we might do well out of tolls on carts and pack-horses and man-loads passed along the road or the river to reach the fair, we must levy no charges, neither murage nor pavage. All tolls belong only to the King. Goods coming up the Gasirad by boat tie up at your jetty, and pay their dues to you. We get nothing. And for this privilege, you pay no more than thirty-eight bronze drychids, and even that we must distrain from your tenants in our holds."

"No more than thirty-eight drychids!" Eowain raised his brows a shade higher. "The sum was appointed as fair. And not by us. The terms of the charter of the Airthir Federation have been known for many years."

"They have, and been found burdensome enough. But bargains must be kept. We've never complained."

Not yet about this, anyway, thought Eowain.

Tnúthgal went on. "Bad years or good, the sum's never been raised. It falls hard on us so pressed as we are now, to lose the best tolls of the year. Just this winter, Droma was under siege by bandits above a month. A scourge from which we still suffer, I might add." There was a murmur of agreement from the assembled lords. "We have only defended ourselves after great damage to walls, and to the great neglect of roads and trails."

And whose fault is that? Rumor had long implied that Tnúthgal himself had supplied the bandits with arms and comforts. Eowain's hold on his throne was undermined by his cousin's encouragement of their depredations.

"Despite our efforts," his cousin went on, "there's still great need for work on them. It's costly labor, after all the winter's losses. Not half the dilapidations are yet put right. In these troublesome times, who knows when we might be attacked again? The traffic of your fair pass through our streets. They'll add to the wear and attract more banditry, while we get nothing to make good the damage."

"Come to the point, cousin." Eowain kept his tone tranquil. "You are come to make some demand. Speak it out plain."

Tnúthgal bridled. "Your Grace, I will! We think—and I speak for all the holds along the High-King's Road—that in such a year we have the best possible case to ask that the throne should either pay a higher fee for the fair, or, better by far, set aside a proportion of the tolls on goods, whether by horse-load, cart, or boat. Hand over this to the hold-chiefs, and we'll restore our defenses. A tenth share of the profits would be most welcome, and we should thank you for it. It is not a demand, with respect—"

Eowain saw the look in his cousin's eyes. *Annwn-fires and bloody damnation,* he thought.

"—but an appeal, Your Grace. We believe the grant of a tenth would be nothing more than justice."

Eowain considered the phalanx of stout men before him. They'd all been men of the King's Company once, in younger days. Some still were. They were none of them openly armed, but he took for granted they knew how to use their belt-knives to terrible effect. Granting this boon would put more ready coin in their hands. Coin they might use to finance further rebellion. "Do you, now? All of you?"

Some of the southern chiefs looked away, but Tnúthgal answered him. "We do. And all our tenants too. There are many who voice the matter rather more—forcibly—than I have done." His hand stayed deliberately away from the hilt of his belt-knife. "But we trust in your fellow-feeling, and await your answer."

The faint stir that went around Eowain's hall was like a great, cautious sigh. Most of the courtiers, guests come early for the fair, looked on wide-eyed and anxious. Younger ones shifted and whispered, but warily.

Eowain leaned forward, rested right elbow on knee, and put his hand conveniently near the sword resting against his throne. "A decision has been made on this now, within the past month, since the bandit siege of which you complain. His Grace King Murdach of Aileach confirmed to us our ancient charter, with all its grants in lands, privileges, rights, and titles, just as they were held aforetime. Do you think he would have countenanced such a grant, if he hadn't held it to be just?"

Tnúthgal sneered at him. "I don't conjure for a moment that the thought of justice entered into it. I make no murmur against what His Grace of Aileach chose to do, but it's plain he held Droma to be a hostile tribe, and most like still does hold it so, since your father garrisoned the tower and held it against him. But small say we of the land-holds ever had in the matter, and little we could have done about it. The tower declared for the usurper, and we had to put up with the consequences. Now your father is dead and safe out of reach, while we pay the price. Your Grace, is that justice?"

The rebellion of Eowain's father had been several years ago, and Murdach, after a brief exile, had since been restored to his throne. But Tnúthgal raised it now to serve a purpose, to put it once again into the public ear that Eowain's father had committed treachery.

"Is that justice, Your Grace?"

Eowain replied without haste. "We are considering, are we not?" He leaned back. Then, "No," he said, and raised his voice peremptorily when Tnúthgal would have resumed his arguments. "Say no more! We've heard and understood your case and we're not without sympathy. But the spring fair is a right granted to the throne, on terms we did not draw up. It's a right that inheres in me not as a man, but in this throne. In my passing tenure, I have no authority to change or mitigate those terms in even the smallest degree. It would be an offense against King Murdach's Grace, who has confirmed the charter, and an offense against my successors, for it could be taken and cited for precedent in future years. No, I will not set aside any part of the profits of the spring fair to your use, I will not increase the fee we pay you for it, and I will not share in any proportion the tolls on goods and stalls. All belong here, and all will be gathered here, according to the charter." He saw half a dozen mouths open to protest so summary a dismissal. Eowain rose in his place and put a chill in his voice and his eye. Lord-Drymyn Medyr put a hand on his shoulder. "This audience is concluded."

Some among the delegation who would have tried to insist. Tnúthgal, however, had a better notion of his own dignity. He made a deep and abrupt reverence, turned, and strode out of the king's hall. His defeated company recovered their wits and marched just as haughtily after him.

CHAPTER TWO

FIFTEEN MEN OF FOOT—in jacks of hard banded-leather strips, or ringed-coats of leather and steel—assembled in his muddy courtyard. They bore the black, gold, and red banner of the Gwynnn clan.

Eowain had told her father to bring his hardest men.

By the look of them, those certainly fit the bill. Short and swarthy, with black hair and hard-gleaming eyes, they bore shields, swords, maces, spears, and hunting-bows with confidence.

"After all those letters you wrote back and forth, you don't know what to say?" Lorcán shook his head. "Compliment her eyes." He grinned. "I can't remember the last time I saw you this flustered, little brother."

"When Medyr first proposed this arrangement, I had my doubts, but I knew my duty." Eowain turned away. "But then when I met her—?"

"Rescued her from bloodthirsty bandits, you mean?"

"That wasn't my fault—."

Lorcán put up the three fingers of his hand to stop him. "You don't have to tell me."

Eowain shook his head. "But I tell you, when I met her, with that red hair and those fierce green eyes, I loved her. Like I was thunderstruck."

Lorcán slapped his younger brother's shoulder. "Right. It had nothing to do with the fact you live like a damned monk. When are you giving up on that girl—What was her name? The one in Larriocht?"

Eowain looked back through the tower window. "I never imagined myself as a king. I thought I'd have more choice when it came to marriage."

Lord-Drymyn Medyr knocked at the door. "You have as much choice as any free man, where the oracles of the Gods are concerned."

Eowain waved down his advisor. "I wish you would stop going on about all that. There's reason enough to wed her without you mixing the Gods into things."

Lorcán scowled. "With her estate and her rights to the fur trade? Our aunt's keen the lady be granted a charter to start a trading interest. To improve relations between Droma and Ivearda, don't you know."

"I do know, in fact." The Lady Rathtyen, dressed in the black mourning gown of a widowed country lady, had crept up behind them all. "And the Lady Eithne is certainly right to be upset by this insult. The Lady of Gluintír is such a tiresome old hag."

The Lord Ciaran rode forward unhelmed with three cavalry-men on sturdy mountain horses. He and his three men each wore a mailed coat of leather and iron-rings, and carried shields, spears, and long, plain swords.

Along with Ciaran was an old, small, dark drymyn-woman. The merchant had told him about her, though he knew little. She was somehow—Eowain wasn't himself quite sure how yet—involved in the case of their marriage. Her knotted hair spilled from beneath her hood in a shock of white.

Then a fair horse, a whole copper-red shade of chestnut, came forward. Strong and with good wind, by the look of it. Sixteen hands high, and on its left foreleg from hoof to hock, a white stocking.

Astride the handsome horse rode a small, helmed warrior, dressed like the other horsemen in a mailed coat of leather and iron-rings, and bearing arms and armor with every bit as much confidence.

The warrior pulled off the round steel helm, and there was Eithne, red hair bound up in a tight bun. Her green eyes flashed.

Eowain put the best face on it. "Lady Eithne, Lord Ciaran! Welcome back to Dúnsciath. Lady, please, let me help you—."

Eithne swung her leg over the rump, and planted both feet firmly on his courtyard.

"—Dismount." Eowain stood with his hand awkwardly unused. "Your arrival is like sunshine amid gloom, my lady." He leaned in to kiss her. She turned and offered her cheek.

Eithne had taken up a place in front of Eowain in his hall, like any other petitioner. Courtiers, guests from abroad with nowhere better to be, lined the walls.

She'd demanded to bring a formal grievance before his open court. It was her right, as a traveler in his lands. The legal obligations of a king on the matter of hospitality were clear in the ancient texts.

The Lord Ciaran, the strange old drymyn-woman they'd brought with them, and the merchant and acolyte stood as witnesses to her testimony.

Guards and other servants moved through the crowd. Beside his throne, Medyr and Lorcán stood with him to hear the news of the treatment she'd received at Gluintír.

The court had already heard of her arrival in Scíthin, the chilly reception from his cousin Ninnid, and her tour of the shrines in that part of Droma. "Yes." He nodded for her to go on.

"There we were," continued Eithne. "In Gluintír, on the very feast day of holy Padarn, at his own blessed shrine. We'd traveled from Scíthin early, and arrived right at the moment of dawn. I watched the sun rise over a clear view of your kingdom for the first time." She looked him in the eyes. "It's a magnificent land, no question. Rolling grassland hills, two large lakes, the forests to the south, and that great ridge of land that looks like a dragon sleeping on the hills. It was a breathtaking sight."

But her brow furrowed. "Then who comes into the shrine but the Lord and Lady of Gluintír themselves. I've yet to make their acquaintance, not wishing to wake their household so early when there was such a beautiful sunrise to be enjoyed."

Eithne explained how, after a few moments of idle greetings, the Lady Gluintír had said, "I've so looked forward to meeting you. When I'm with one of your people, I'm always reminded of the virtues of the Droma."

Before Eithne could frame a reply to that strange statement, her husband had wagged his head. "Don't listen to her, dear. I imagine meeting us all together must be very intimidating."

Then, once again before Eithne could consider a response, the Lady Gluintír muttered, "I certainly hope so."

Eithne opened her hands to Eowain on his throne. "Well, Your Grace," she went on. "As you have heard, she was already as loathsome to me as a toad, to speak to me in such a manner."

Eowain put his forehead in his hands. He had no particular love for the Lord and Lady of that far-away settlement. They were stingy with their winter taxes, and had left him to make up their shortfall. *What has that old windbag gotten me into now?*

"If that were not enough?" Eithne paused. "Then the Lady of Gluintír screwed me in my place with a stern eye and said, 'So. You are to be our King Eowain's bride then?'"

Medyr hovered forward. "And how then did you answer, my lady?"

The whole council leaned in.

Eithne flashed them an angry glance. "'I am, madam,' I told her. And she says to me, 'Oh, so it is you. I thought it was a man wearing your clothes. Well, I suppose looks aren't everything.'"

With eyes wide and shocked, Eithne looked to his courtiers for their sympathy, and found it. Even Lorcán groaned beside him.

Over the grand hearth, the great twelve-point rack of a magnificent Great Elk hung. His father had won that trophy. He thought for a moment about his roe-buck antlers and curled ram-horns. He hadn't enjoyed a hunt like that in a long time.

But he turned back to the matter at hand. "So what would you have me do?"

"Well, I wouldn't presume to insist upon any one course of action Your Grace might consider—" She dropped a wry curtsy. "But I have a few suggestions."

Medyr muttered on his other side: "How did I know she would?"

†

LATE IN THE NIGHT, a rider from the southeast hammered at the tower door with news for the king.

Before dawn, Eowain rode out with four men, fitted for war, grim looks upon their faces. They spoke to no one and rode southeast at a gallop.

When he and his companions returned without a word near sunset on horses and mules laden with mysterious cargo, tongues began to wag.

That night, Eowain's hall was bright with candle and firelight. The invited lords and ladies arrived in their finest gowns and tunics. They mingled about and drank small beer. They speculated on where Eowain had been all day, and what he'd been doing.

Rumors surrounded the mule train they had brought with them as well. The mules had each been laden with sacks and chests, and their burdens brought quickly and quietly into the tower. Yet neither Eowain nor any of the staff or guards in the fort had offered even a hint, neither for love nor money.

The Lady Gluintír sniffed. "One can only guess. Gods know, there's been trouble enough on the eastern marches." She helped herself to the sweetmeats of candied fruit and sugar-covered nuts going around. "Why, just the other day there was some kind of terrible hundred-footed vermin tearing up the borderlands. Bigger than a horse, I heard, with steel plates for hide and burning spit. Terrible business." She pinched her fingers together in front of her mouth. Then she snapped her fingers. "It was the very day 'that woman' arrived, in fact..."

Eowain, with Lady Eithne on one arm, and her father, the Lord Ciaran, at his side, came into the hall.

Eithne wore floor-length skirts in tartans of black, red, and gold. Upon her fingers were three golden rings, and upon her sash a jeweled brooch of wrought silver. An astonished murmur went around the hall, for surely that jewel alone was worth as much as seven cows or more.

Eowain, in kilted tartans of green, gold, and white, and a sash over his shoulder displayed the white curvilinear river-salmon of his clan, led Eithne to one end of the dinner board. The guests came to their seats. Eowain offered his bride-to-be the chair at his right hand, then invited the assembly to sit. Her father was given the place to the king's left.

"Thank the Gods," Lady Gluintír was heard to whisper. "All this unbridled joy has given me quite an appetite." As the assembly made itself comfortable, servants went around with wine.

Three rounds of cheerful thanks to Gods, Kings, and Soldiers went around the hall, and everyone drank.

Then Eowain tapped at his cup. "My bride," he announced, "has somewhat to say."

She put her hand on his, then raised her cup of wine. "To the good men of Droma and their fine ladies, I thank you for this warm reception after so long a journey. I am a feeble substitute for the entire Gwynn family—"

Lady Gluintír sniffed. "Yes, but you mustn't be hard on yourself, dear. You're better than nothing, I suppose."

Eithne's eyes narrowed. She raised her cup. "To the Lady Gluintír," she began. The lady's face flushed for expected flattery. The assembled courtiers raised their cups. "For the welcome I received to your thorp, I despise ye."

There were startled second glances at her from around the table. Lady Gluintír put a hand to her breast.

"I think, my lady," continued Eithne, "that your offense to me was no accident, but a trade."

Lady Gluintír's mouth and eyes went round.

Eithne waved to the assembled lords. "You are a general offense, madam, and every man here should beat you."

"What is the meaning—?"

Eithne folded arms across her chest. "Your hospitality is as dry as biscuit after a long journey."

"Are you quite fini—"

"Silence, Madam!" Eithne's eyes flashed greenly. "I am hardly begun!" She collected up a dangerous calm. "You are a shynn-mark'd abortive, rooting hog, and as loathsome as a toad, venomous and ugly. It's a wonder the sun ever shines in Gluintír, for in truth, your face is not worth sun-burning. The very tartness of it would sour grapes."

"Why, you—"

Eithne put her fists on the table and squinted at her. "Could I but come near enough such beauty as yours with my nails, I would find that scratching could not make it worse. You are unfit for any place but Annwn." Eithne stood and sniffed. "Even there was never so ugly a fiend as you will be."

Lady Gluintír searched about the table for some ally. She found none. The lords and ladies of the court had found great interest in their place at the table before them.

Eowain produced a dagger decorated with a dark yellow schorl in the hilt. Lady Eithne took it from him, and admired the jewel and its setting as she went on.

"There's no more faith in you than in a stewed prune." She took the dagger, raised the point to her target. "If you ever again speak to me, upon the next tree shall you hang alive until famine clings from ye."

There was silence at the table.

"Now. Out of my sight. You infect my eyes." She put the point of the blade into the wooden board with a vengeful thrust.

Eowain raised his hand. The two guardsmen at the tower door came forward. "You will escort the Lady Gluintír to the outskirts of the village and give her an ass upon which to ride home."

"But— But it's raining! And— And there are bandits abroad!"

Eowain agreed. "Then I suggest you ride quickly, my lady." There was a scuffle as the guards took her elbows. Her husband, his shock overcome, gave her a stern rebuke before them all. She protested all the way to the courtyard. The guards followed them.

Eowain took Eithne's hand. "And if there are any others who think the Lady Eithne deserving of further insult, let this be lesson—and warning—to them all." He looked them over each and every. The lesson seemed to be well-taken. Cousin Tnúthgal, face dark with anger, nodded to him.

Eithne took a long deep breath, regained her composure, and resumed her seat. She leaned close. He smelled the dizzying scent of mountain lilacs on her. "That," she whispered, "was supremely satisfying." She squeezed his hand. "Thank you."

He felt a rush of pride. Pride in her, for the courage to stand before his court and avenge her insult. Pride in himself, for the courage to permit it. *Indeed,* he thought. *She's made of steel, this one.*

The feast went on without further incident. Fresh-roasted ram, acquired by the king's own hand, was the centerpiece. Wine and ôl flowed. Before long, the warrior-chiefs boasted sodden recollections of glory.

At last, someone ventured the question: "Your Grace? Where have you been all day? What tale have you to tell?"

The room soon went silent. Eowain felt awkward and on the spot. Eithne squeezed his hand and encouraged with a smile. "Go ahead, tell them."

"Raiders have preyed on farmers and the occasional spring tradesmen who use the Scíthin trail most often. They've paralyzed trade through the area," he said. There was muttered agreement around the table. This was nothing new to them.

"Early this morning, I received a report. Lord Ailill of Easavainn Mills said he'd sniffed out the bandit's camp. He was going to lead a band of volunteers from his village to deal with the threat directly." Eowain could feel the anxiety that rose from the assembled chiefs. "I feared they might need help and rode out at first light."

"With naught but four men," added Lorcán.

"Aye, four of the strongest men of Droma," agreed Eowain. He went on to tell how he arrived at Easavainn Mills only to find their lord's adventure had already ended in disaster. "Ambushed. Fifteen men, killed on the Scíthin trail. The mood in Easavainn Mills was grim, I tell you."

Eowain led his men on from the thorp and up the road. They went on foot, disguised as common travelers, and intended to draw out the bandits. But at first, the only souls they found were a team of sawyers, driving two wagons of wood from their camp. Eowain despaired the bandits had packed up and left.

But then, "A harsh voice ordered us to halt as my men and I neared a bend in the road. Three archers came partly into view through the brush on the hillside above us. Brigands moved in from cover to our rear and closed off our retreat. Two more bandits stepped onto the road ahead."

He recalled the skirmish that left three bandits dead on the trail. "The archers and their leader turned tail and ran. Led us a merry chase into the wooded hills around Caipín Creek."

There was a narrow defile there, where they were pinned down by another rogue archer while the villains scrambled up a rope ladder and over a rock wall.

One of Eowain's men wounded the archer, but the villains pulled the ladder up after them. "So, I tell you true, we scaled that wall. Fifty feet tall, it must have been, and slick with rain, but up we leaped, like mountain rams." He winked as he popped a morsel of his prize ram into his mouth.

He and his men went on. They tracked the villains down a narrow roe-buck track. They avoided not one, but two deadly traps, then fell afoul of a third and a fourth. "Branches fixed with daggers slashed out at us from the wayside!" He gestured to the deep gash on his cheek, now stitched and smeared with dried cow urine, to ward off fever. "One of them caught me here—damn near took out my eye!" He rose and pulled aside his tunic, showed another deep gash. "And this one near took out my liver!" There were moans of concern from the gathered crowd.

"By now, my blood was all a-fire with battle-lust, and we chased on. But we rounded a corner and the cowards let loose a slide of rocks upon us from a nearby stony bluff." He presented black, blue, and purple bruises on his arms, back, and legs as badges of courage.

"So it was we came at last to the bandit camp. Abandoned it was, in a clearing near the stones of an ancient tower. The crumbled ruins were buried by an old slide of jumbled stones and dirt, overgrown with brush and saplings. In the clearing, their campfire smoldered, deserted and littered with the remains of a meal. There was no sign of the brigands. But then I heard it, like many harp strings plucked."

Eowain went on to tell of the final battle, with snipers in the trees and no less than a dozen more bandits with whom to contend.

"But there was a wicked sorcerer among them. He chanted foul incantations and urged them to courage. All adorned with feathers he was, with the claw of some fell beast hung from a cord about his neck. At last, it was just me and that vile conjurer. He pulled back his hammer for a mighty blow, but I skewered him," and Eowain demonstrated the fatal thrust of his spear. "He vomited forth his blackest heart's blood, and died with an abominable curse."

With the sorcerer dead, he and his men had ventured into the old ruin.

"There we found it, the bandits' hoard. Hidden in an old library in the tower cellars. All told, we returned with four mule-loads of loot the bandits had purloined from our people." Eowain thumped his fist on the board and took his seat again.

The cheering was exultant as the courtiers praised their king. "Eowain the Mighty! Eowain the Bear!" they shouted. He felt his heart swell with pride. Cups were raised to his courage.

But the Lord-Drymyn leaned past Lord Ciaran and whispered, "What of Cael the Viper, my lord? Or the kidnapped children?"

Eowain felt his exuberance vanish at the name. The smile on his face felt like wood. He raised his cup to a reveler down the board, but whispered stiffly, "No. Neither the children nor the damned bandit chief."

Medyr nodded, but said nothing else.

CHAPTER THREE

EITHNE'S MAID, BREDA, gave Eowain a wink as she refilled his earthen cup with ôl. The fire pit in the center of the common room provided warmth. Smoke rose up to a hole at the peak of the thatched roof, through which not enough of it escaped. The day had been uncommonly warm and the roundhouse was steamy, close, and acrid.

Eowain and Eithne sat together on a bench in the common room of the tribe's old royal roundhouse.

Aunt Rathtyen had lived there ever since his father had gifted it to her, to compensate her for the loss of a husband, after his new stone house in the Aukrian-style under the tower was built.

The walls were made of stout oak logs, the roof of thatch. The floor beneath their feet had been paved with flag-stone and covered in fresh rushes.

Eowain sipped at the ôl to soothe his smoke-parched throat.

A fickle game lay between them. The square board was patterned with a round, chequered circle. Eithne played the white stones, and had control of the center and the king-stone.

He played the black side. His goal was to penetrate her defense or prevent her escape from the board.

Eowain told her of his day's business. "Of course, after last night, Lord Gluintír came back this morning to present his complaint—"

"You mean his wife's complaint?"

"Aye, one and the same. She was, as he put it, 'aggrieved' by the inhospitable treatment she received in my hall." He placed a black pawn stone on the board.

Eithne puckered her face. "Lady Gluintír should have considered that before treating me so inhospitably herself." She countered his stone with a white one. Another avenue to the center closed, but at least she'd been distracted from building a route of escape to the perimeter.

He couldn't help but agree. "Apparently, the satirists are on our side. I'm told the story of last night's feast is already told, and we are the heroes. If satirists have as much power as a-foretimes, perhaps she'll develop a festering boil on her nose." He appraised the board. *Where should I move next?*

Eithne laughed. "It could do nothing but improve her looks."

"And perhaps teach her to keep a civil tongue in her head, before someone cuts it out."

"They must not have gotten far if he was back this morning?" She sipped at her own cup of *ôl*. "It's a long day's ride to Gluintír, I know."

Eowain nodded and placed another black stone on the board.

"It would serve her right. She's as odious as a barnyard animal herself." She placed a white stone on the board, ignoring his last move.

What is she up to? If he could just control the center—

He was glad that matters between them had thawed. Since the feast, she had been in better humor.

The clack of knitting needles spoiled his concentration. The woman that had accompanied Eithne on her trip, Alva, was sitting on a bench across the fire. It would have been unseemly for Eowain to have been alone with his prospective bride, of course.

But she's an odd duck, isn't she? Eowain had it from Medyr that she was a reclusive ban-drymyn, one of his Order's priestesses. Medyr was surprised she'd come out of her mountain hermitage at all. The old woman was shortish, with a dark complexion, her face leathery with many fine wrinkles. Her robes were shapeless, and she was so lean as to be nearly lost within them. He wondered if they weren't borrowed from a woman twice her size. She had two long needles and was cable-knitting black, red, and gold woolen yarn together, into what he could not yet tell.

She glanced up at him from under the shock of white in her otherwise knotted black hair, and held his gaze. Her features were practically vulpine, with hollow cheeks and a long, lean nose. Her eyes pierced like those of a hungry wolf.

Eowain felt a bit of a shiver and turned his attention back to Eithne and the game. "Otherwise, my day was fairly quiet. One of my patrols did spy a bandit scouting party along the eastern border, but lost them in the Cailech hills when they passed the border stones. And they found a herd of cattle in that area and brought it back, thinking it strayed from the nearest settlement." He placed another stone, to cut off an avenue for her escape.

Her serving girl, Cunneen, brought willow tea and hot water for Eithne.

"Hadn't it?" Eithne put a white stone to her lips.

"Hadn't what?"

"Hadn't the cattle strayed?"

He shook his head. "It seems not. The headman wasn't missing any cows." He shrugged. "I'm inclined not to look too deeply into it so long as we came out ahead by a herd."

Eithne cast her eyes down. "The honest thing to do would be to find their proper home and return them to it."

"I suppose it would be. But if they're not ours, they must be Cailech cattle. They weren't branded, and might have come from half a dozen settlements on the wrong side of our eastern border. If I sent men back with them, they'd as likely be attacked for thieves as hailed for honesty."

"I'm sure you know best." She put the stone down, capturing one of his black pawns.

"Please don't do that."

She smiled at him with a hint, he thought, of mockery. "Why not? It's perfectly legal."

"You know what I mean."

"I'm sure I don't, my lord."

"I don't always know best. Don't tell me I do if you think differently."

Eithne's green eyes seemed to twinkle in the firelight, and her pale, rose lips twitched with humor. Then she looked away to the fire. "You might not like me so well if I do, my lord."

"I like you well enough already. Honesty shouldn't hurt that." He turned his attention back to the board. She'd scuttled his attempt to contain her.

"Fair answer from a fair king." Her brow furrowed in thought a moment. "Perhaps send a messenger to the Cailech king, describing the cattle and your desire to return them to their rightful owner peacefully?"

With another stone, he penetrated into the inner circle, one step closer to seizing the king-stone. "And why should I? Is it our fault the Cailech can't mind their cattle better?"

"No, my lord." She turned him out again from control of the center as another white stone captured his pawn. "But it might prevent a raiding party coming over your hills in search of them."

"Hmmm." That hadn't occurred to him.

They had chatted like that for hours, and never quite came around to the subject that pressed on his mind. With a black stone, he thrust recklessly against her defense. "Lady—." He glanced at the old ban-drymyn and her knitting. "Lady, please. From our missives, there are still many questions left unanswered."

"Such as what, Your Grace?" She placed a white stone and thwarted him.

"My lady, I have not lied to you. The children of Droma have lost—or no longer have time to learn—skills that should be a credit to our country. They grow like savages—like soldiers who meditate on nothing but blood—surrounded by swearing and stern looks, ragged clothing and everything unnatural. It's to reverse all this, so we can once again become as we were, that we are brought together. Therefore I demand to know why gentle peace shouldn't banish these troubles and bless us once more." His next black pawn blocked a path to the edge for her.

She put another white stone to her lips. Firelight shone in her green eyes. "Do you love me, Eowain?"

His eyes seemed caught there on that white stone, like a hooked fish in the river. Yet he could still sense the rest of her around that stone, the mountain lilac scent of her, the glitter of a stray ginger hair in the firelight.

Frustration and desire moved through him like coursers vying upon a track. His fist tightened. "I said so, dear Eithne. I'm not ashamed to repeat it. I know we are thrust into this, but could you love me?"

She mused a moment. "I can't tell." Her eyes narrowed and she smiled.

"Well can any of your neighbors tell me?" He gestured to Breda the maid. "I'll ask them."

"What is love, Your Grace?" She set her white stone on the board. "Can love be won? Earned? How?" She shrugged. "Or is love merely an unimportant emotion?" She nodded to the ban-drymyn. "Some would say one shouldn't seek it in an arranged marriage, where Gods and portents are concerned." She tilted her head to one side, with a wry grin on her lips. "Challenge."

"What?!"

"Challenge, my lord. I believe you are defeated."

He looked at the board. By tradition, once challenged, he had but seven moves in which to win the game. He calculated all the possibilities.

Sure enough, she was right. In but five more moves, she would forge a path to the circle's edge, and there was nothing he could do to stop her. Shaking his head, he spread his hands apart. "I concede, my lady. You have won."

She smiled like a cat with a mouse in its teeth.

There was an awkward silence while they each searched for something more to say.

Eowain pulled at the collar of his tunic. "Strangely warm today, isn't it?"

"Oh, very," replied Eithne. Her eyes glittered at him. "Though we still have snow and ice in Dolgallu, so I'm afraid I really don't know." The long white fingers of her hands smoothed the black and gold tartan of her skirts.

Then her eyes grew round, and her smile vanished.

Upon the fickle board, a spider, long-legged and unhurried, stepped this way, then that.

Eithne grew rigid, then stood abruptly. "I—" She looked down and away. "Breda. She'll need my help. In the kitchen."

He remembered something she'd written in their correspondences. "Spiders frighten you?"

Her chin rose and she waved dismissively. Her eyes darted back to the fickle board as the little creature explored the scene of their battle.

With his strong right hand, he ushered the protesting spider to the edge of the board, into his waiting palm. He trapped it then, felt its panicked feet scurrying over his skin as it sought escape from crushing.

He rose from the table with his hands clasped gently before him, walked to a window, and blew the spider away and out into the night.

Eowain turned back. Her green eyes regarded him curiously. "You are safe, my lady."

She bowed her head. Her cheeks colored in the firelight, and her lips parted as if to speak.

"The hour grows late, Your Highness." His aunt emerged from the kitchen with Eithne's father.

Eithne frowned and pursed her lips.

"Apologies for the interruption," said Aunt Rathtyen. "We have a busy day tomorrow, with wedding plans and such."

He rose to leave and offered her a kiss.

Across the room, Alva's knitting needles clicked and clacked.

She offered her cheek.

EOWAIN DIDN'T SLEEP well that night.

He sweated through his linens and kicked off winter blankets before sleep overtook him.

River-gnats buzzed.

"Your Grace, forgive me, sire, but you must come at once."

He blinked into the face of his chamberlain, a stout, matronly woman with iron-grey hair bound up into a tight bun.

Doesn't she ever sleep? He rubbed his eyes. "What is it? And what's the hour?"

"Just past sixth hour, Your Grace. And best you see for yourself." She held up a robe and averted her gaze.

He'd pulled off his night-shirt in his sleep. He helped himself into the robe, cinched the belt about his waist. Already, the morning was as warm as any summer day. *Yet we had snow just a few weeks ago.* The vagaries of springtime perplexed him. "Very well, what is it?"

She led him to the nook of his bed-chamber and pulled the wooden shutters away from the arrow-loop. He blinked in the bright dawn sunlight. He could see over his fort and across the hill upon which it stood. Pennons flew from staves. Horses stamped. Men in armor moved about the business of camp.

Men who weren't his own. He squinted at the pennons. "Whose banner is that?"

"Explain it to me again?" He'd heard it twice. A third time wouldn't make it any clearer, but Eowain asked anyway.

"You can't hold the wedding here." The Lady Corchen, Ban-Drúmór of Iathrann, one of the four highest officers in the Drymyn Brotherhood, and chief priestess of all the land, stood before him in his hall.

Her thick hoary mane, like his Lord-Drymyn's, was shaved from ear to ear across the front of her head, and worn long and braided down her neck and past her shoulders. Her charcoal-grey robes were decorated with spirals, triskelions, and other mystic, curvilinear patterns.

To her left was the strange old woman Alva Damar. Gone was her clicking needlework. Now, she stood in the formal robes of the Order and glared at Eowain with those vulpine features.

That gaze unsettled him. He looked back at his exalted guest.

"Why not?"

Corchen waved her hand. "That's not important for you to know. Suffice it to say, the omens aren't good."

Eithne squeezed his shoulder. "I'm already deep in our wedding plans." She looked to the ban-drymyn Alva with furrowed brows. "What's the meaning of this? We're not to be married, then?"

"No, by Ceugant, I never said that." Lady Corchen shook her head. "You must be married. Just not here."

"I see." Eowain didn't, but let it pass for the moment. "So where then?"

"The Vale of Thaynú."

He goggled at her, he was sure. "But that's nigh on fifty miles away."

She seemed unperturbed. "I know. I've just come from there."

He felt indignant. The wedding wasn't for the Drymyn Order and whatever mysterious agenda they had in mind. Their brothers and sisters weren't supposed to get involved in politics.

"Why shouldn't I get married right here on the sacred stone of my tribe? Why in Abred should we all travel through two weeks of difficult, hostile terrain?"

"Because it's a ritual that works for the good of your tribe, which is really the primary concern."

"But my political position here is—." He didn't want to say *insecure.* "Complicated."

"If you don't follow the ritual, specific to you in this moment, your tribe will suffer. Reject this course of action and plague, disaster, famine, and foreign invaders are all possible consequences." She spread her hands and shrugged. "I doubt your situation is more complicated than that."

Then she allowed for his counter-argument. "Of course, you can reject the ritual. You stand to lose not only what you personally value, but you'll be responsible for the misfortunes of your tribe as well."

Eowain crossed his arms over his broad chest. "And it's worth the risk of rebellious kinsmen in my rear echelon and attack by rival tribes? Why? What could possibly be so dire?"

Her manner grew cross and irritated. "Would you like to undergo the rituals and ordeals necessary to be initiated into the priesthood? Would you like to spend twenty and more years studying the ways and philosophies of the ancients? Because that's the only way you'll get more of an answer than you've already been given. If you are married here, the omens are not good. That's all you need to know."

"Medyr!" He turned to his Lord-Drymyn, who had stood quietly nearby with his head down throughout that audience.

His tutor had a pained look on his face. "I can only advise you heed the Ban-Drúmór's warnings, Your Grace. She's the high-priestess of my Order. I can't gainsay her. I have neither the authority nor the experience."

Eowain felt agog at the mad idea. They'd have to travel north into the mountain foothills. Into the countries of Ivea and Thuitre, where the Chremthainn clan ruled.

The Chremthainn had been on-again, off-again enemies of the Droma kings for centuries. They'd only just been pacified once more. Eowain knew that the hot blood of rebellion simmered in their veins, no matter what oaths they all unwillingly mumbled under the lash.

"Isn't there any other way? Couldn't we sacrifice a few bulls and a heifer or something?" The grim look from his advisor, and the Lady Corchen's impassive face told him the answer. "This is madness, you know. You're going to get us all killed."

Corchen shrugged once more. "Mayhap. If you're killed in route, you'll die a noble warrior's death, and events will proceed along a different tangent." She fixed him with a long bony finger. Between the fingers of another hand, she raised a *coelbreni* tile, burned with the sign of *Oir*. The broom-tree sign meant *strife on the borders*.

"But if you choose to live, you have two choices. Follow the advice of those who have access to sources of information you aren't in a position to understand, or accept full responsibility for the events that follow rejection. If you flout the will of the Gods, your life will be the least of your losses."

TNÚTHGAL SAT—DESPITE the rain—a-stride his horse along the High-King's Road. The entourage of the Lady Corchen proceeded past him. She'd arrived in Droma early the previous morning, stayed the day and the night, then turned around to return north. He wondered what business she'd had at Dúnsciath that couldn't have been served as well by a single messenger.

A score of men a-horse, twice their number a-foot, jangled by with armor and weaponry. Not that the Lady needed such protection. To harm her would have condemned a man to damnation, removed from the wheel of life and cast into a pit of fire and darkness, never again to be reborn.

Tnúthgal himself had only a small guard. This was the easternmost edge of his own lands, and he felt secure enough.

Down the road to the south, commoners and free-men alike turned out to cheer. The Ban-Drúmór's presence itself was a blessing. She waved benisons over the crowd as if she tossed out candied nuts to children.

Further south, Eowain's tower overlooked the river and the trees of Tnúthgal's lands. *I was so close this winter,* he thought. *If only that fool Cael hadn't attacked Ruakhavsa.*

Eowain's victory over Cael's bandits there had forced Tnúthgal to withdraw his "protective forces" from what might have been a successful siege of Eowain's tower if events had gone differently.

So he'd tipped his hand too far already. He had to be careful. Treachery did not trouble him, so long as it didn't seem like treachery. His brother, Ninnid, had a claim to the throne as well and might rally against any imperfect succession.

Caerrhthyrs, his chamberlain, stopped a seeming peasant.

"I've a message for the lord. From Béobeirid."

Tnúthgal knew there was no such person. It was a word in the Old Tongue. It meant "viper." As in Cael the Viper.

"Let him through." Tnúthgal watched the procession. The Ban-Drúmór's own steed would be even with him soon. "Yes, what has our friend to say?"

"It's not what he has to say. It's what I think you want to tell him."

"Oh? And what's that?"

"Word from Dúnsciath has it that the wedding's been moved."

"Moved? Moved where?"

The man nodded toward the procession. "The Lady Corchen insisted. The ceremony's moved to the Vale."

"The Vale of Thaynú? That's fifty miles away, through the heart of Chremthainn country. Why—?" He bit off the question.

The man sniffled. "Seems like it's bad omens or something to have the wedding here."

Tnúthgal didn't need to imagine the whys and wherefores. No matter why, if it was true, Eowain and his precious little harridan would be abroad for at least a week, probably two. In dangerous territory. Any of a number of unlucky mishaps might befall them...

It's true enough that love is only ever obtained by overcoming great obstacles. He thought of the courtship his late wife had given him. *The world conspires against true love.*

Tnúthgal had no misgivings about being the world's chief conspirator. "The reasons aren't important. But you're right, I would appreciate it if you would convey this news to our friend with all haste. Remind him how vital it is to our plans that certain persons should be made incapable of sitting in certain chairs." He slipped a silver coin from the purse beneath his cloak and handed it down to the man. "I trust that will be sufficient to expedite your message."

The peasant took the coin. "Oh, yes, my lord! Thank you, my lord!" He withdrew into the crowd.

Well, that's good news. He shook the rainwater from the hood of his cloak. The Lady Corchen drew even with his position. She raised her hand, sketched signs of blessing and protection in the air.

He bowed and thanked the Gods. *May Echraide smile upon me, and the goddess Thaynú, Mother of All.*

Surely, he thought, the goddesses would understand what he did. It was not for himself that he sought the throne. Trade from downriver would bring Foreigner coin and Foreigner interests to Droma, and that would bring Foreigners and their degenerate ways. The morals of their children and the way his people had lived for generations were threatened. What he did, he did for the whole kingdom.

Tnúthgal could understand his cousin Rathtyen's interest in such things. She'd lived many years in the southern lands, nearer to the Foreigner ship-camp at Difelin. She'd been seduced by wealth and wickedness in the house of her late husband.

If she'd only stayed there when he passed, I should not care. But she hadn't. Instead, she'd brought that corruption north and seduced her nephews.

The Ban-Drúmór and her servants and more guards passed Tnúthgal as he thought. *I can forgive Rathtyen for her wordly weakness. She is only a woman, after all. But the Lord-Drymyn should be beyond such things. And why would the King of the East countenance such an insult to the laws and traditions of our people?*

He had no good answer to that question. The Order was too-often concerned with matters merely spiritual, and short-sighted in politics. *Surely, the Gruin-men over the river have not let the Foreign corruption weaken them.* He had spies over river. The recent reformations in the Order had offended the Gruin-King. That he planned to launch a summer campaign was hinted. Tnúthgal had to settle matters in Droma before that.

With a nicker to his steed, he brought it about. His guards and chamberlain followed. Tnúthgal summoned his chamberlain Caerrhthyrs to ride close.

"You must send word to Toryn the Stout. We must advance our plans. Cousins Ninnid and Eowain must be diverted from our intent. Tell him Gluín Hill is his, but he must move now, and that I trust he will remember our largess of recent weeks."

Caerrhthyrs nodded. "Yes, my lord. I'll see it done."

"And tell Feoras of Mianmair to come to Crúcavainn. Tonight. Let no one see him come or go."

The chamberlain made an obeisance and turned his horse to trot away.

Yes, thought Tnúthgal. *It's long past time to settle matters.*

CHAPTER FOUR

EOWAIN RUBBED HIS head. *So if there are one-hundred thirty-three people, and each person needs five pounds of grain per day, that's...* He scribbled on a sheet of paper with a charcoal stick. *Five-hundred thirty-two pounds of grain.* He wrote that number on another sheet.

And each person needs half a pound of meat and half a pound of vegetables per day, so that's... He scribbled again. *Sixty-seven pounds each of meat and vegetables.* He wrote that number on the second sheet.

Each cavalry horse needs ten pounds of grain per day. We'll have thirty-three cavalry mounts. That's three-hundred thirty pounds of grain. And a draft horse for Rathtyen's wagon, that needs thirteen pounds of grain per day. He wrote that down.

How much grain do two ponies need each day? He guessed at eight pounds each.

There was a knock. His chamberlain opened the door. "Your Grace," she said, "Please forgive the intrusion. Merchant-Master Winoc of the House Pelan to see you. He has an appointment, sir."

"Yes, thank Gods, see him in." Eowain had always detested his maths.

The merchant came in a cloud of velvet robes and aped at aristocracy and bowed. The Lord-Drymyn's acolyte and the merchant's son, who'd given him the bear-skin, entered too, with a Foreigner mercenary behind them.

"Zhank you for seeing us, Dread Sovereign. Your time is precious, zeh point, to it I will come." He put a finger to his ear. "You are planning zeh caravan north? I see it in zeh market, zeh buying patterns of your men, yes? Your miller, he is in short supply of zeh muslin biscuit." The Aukrian merchant shrugged and tugged at his ear. "One hears things. From zeh birds."

Eowain saw no reason he shouldn't know. The kingdom needed to know and there was no better way than by telling the merchant. "In a few days time. Why?"

The Aukrian shrugged. "If it would be alright with you, Dread Sovereign, my son shall accompany you? I would like to send an honest scout with you into the north-hills. To see how matters stand there."

"It's a dangerous journey. Those are the lands of the Fiatach tribes. No friends of ours, save maybe the Gwynn now that Eithne and her father travel with us. There are no roads or trails that can truly be called safe. Hostile tribes and bandits and only the Gods know what else might hinder us. We might not make it." Eowain shook his head. The Aukrian was as cold-blooded as a marsh-lizard. "I wouldn't make the journey myself if I didn't have to."

The acolyte spoke up. "Your Grace, if I may?" Eowain dealt him into the discussion. "I'm to travel with the Lord-Drymyn anyway. The merchant's son and I know each other well. His mercenary and your scout Corvac have also grown close. If I were to travel with he and his mercenary, and the scout Corvac, in the Lord-Drymyn's company, sir? Would that be permissible, sir? The Lord-Drymyn's company would be a shield to them, sir."

Medyr looked in behind them. He nodded with finger to lip, then withdrew.

Eowain considered the merchant and the acolyte. "You understand the risks?"

They agreed they did. "Very well. But you'll have to provision yourselves. Keep it light."

Pleased, they left. Eowain returned with a sigh to his own provisioning. *Where was I?* He looked at his scribbles. *Right, grain for two ponies per day. So then...* He rubbed his head.

If it takes us eleven days to travel fifty miles, we'll need... He scribbled at the first sheet again. *Nine thousand eight-hundred and one pounds of grain?* He looked at the figure and scratched his beard.

He stared at the second parchment. *Is that right?*

Lord-Drymyn Medyr knocked at the door. "Forgive me, may I—?"

"Gods, yes!" He threw down the charcoal stick. "What is it?"

"The Cailech, my lord. A hundred Cailech men, with their women and children, have come boiling across the border at Gluintír."

"What? When?"

"In the early hours after dawn, my lord. They've seized the fort on Gluin Hill for their own, and it seems they mean to keep it."

Eowain marched from the room. Medyr was close on his heels. "How did this happen?"

"I don't know, Your Highness. Our patrols reported nothing. They must have come across the eastern hills in the night."

Eowain remembered the matter of the herd of cattle. In the courtyard, his horse was saddled. One of his servants stood nearby with arms and armor. He started to dress. "What about the garrison at Bántobar?"

"Surprised, my lord. Before they could mount a counter-thrust, the Cailech seized the hill-enclosure."

From the gatehouse, Lady Eithne, her father, and the matron Alva emerged while he strapped on arms and armor.

Damn it. They had plans for another fickle-game. And maybe an answer to his question? Or was this some kind of challenge. "My lady, forgive me. There's urgent business across the kingdom, I'm needed at once." He took her hands in his. "Why does it seem we can never have a moment's peace?"

"Is it serious?"

"Deadly so. The Cailech have seized one of our eastern provinces. I must repel them."

Her eyes grew troubled. "But the journey to the Vale? We have to leave soon if we're to arrive there by Cétshamain-day."

"I can't let this stand until we return. The Cailech can't just seize our territory."

She put a hand on his mailed chest. "Don't you see? It's a diversion." Her voice trembled. "They mean to draw you out. They mean to kill you, and scuttle our alliance."

He placed his hand over hers and leaned in to speak to her. "Of course it is. But if I refuse battle? I'll lose my honor and my throne more surely than my life." There was no question in his mind. The Cailech had deliberately used their wayward cattle as a pretext to seize his territory. Maybe even to overthrow him. There was no way in Annwn he could let that happen. He took her hand from his chest to kiss, but shook his head. "No."

She pulled the hand away. "Damn you! Listen to reason."

Eowain stiffened and drew himself up, lifted his chin. "I am king here, lady. I'm not asking you, I'm telling you. I need to do this thing, so it's going to get done." He put a hand on Medyr's shoulder. "You'll start the journey tomorrow without me, with the Lady Eithne and her party, and all the men we discussed. I'll meet you in two days' time on the road."

Medyr bowed.

Eithne glared at him.

He went on. "Have the chamberlain and the quartermaster prepare supplies for the journey. Don't depend overmuch on the kindness of the Chremthainn. The figures are on my desk. Tell her to check my maths." He nodded to Eithne. "Good day, my lady."

EITHNE POUTED. "WHY does Father trust the drymyn so much in this? Prince's Truth be told, I should've said, 'no,' to all this. He let me be kidnapped, for Brenan's Sake."

Her maid, Breda, shrugged. "He rescued you himself, amid a number of great troubles in his kingdom. The *coelbreni* and the drymyn favor him." She arched an eyebrow. "He seems a likely enough lad. If you know what I mean, my lady."

Eithne harrumphed. "That's what Father said."

Her other maid, Cuneen, stooped to gather a cluster of blooms.

That night, the garden of the Lady Rathtyen was alive with rose-colored water avens, lilac bitter-vetch, eponymously-named bluebells, and the gold bog myrtle.

"Remember when his first missive arrived?" Cuneen caught up with a small bouquet. "Oh, I do. It was so romantic."

Who will teach a soldier the words that would recommend his suit to a
gentle heart like yours?

Cuneen clutched the flower to her breast. Out of the side of her mouth, Breda breathed, "I'd sure like to try."

Eithne scowled at Breda and agreed with Cuneen. In person, Eowain was gruff, war-like, preoccupied with all the daily tasks that came to the desks of kings, high or low. He ordered his council, passed judgments, and pursued bandits in his southern woods. He'd had only a few evenings in their first ten-day to sit together and play at games of fickle. Little enough time to speak of matters between them, where their marital arrangements were concerned. And awkward into the bargain.

Eithne shook her head. "No. Even in his letters, he's a man of war, concluding treaties with idle boasts."

If I could win a lady by playing leapfrog or vaulting into my saddle with my armor
on my back, I could—though you may accuse me of boasting—easily get myself
a wife. But, before the Gods, Eithne, I cannot turn pale on purpose or gasp out
fancy phrases, and I have no gift for clever declarations.
So what do you say to my suit? Do you like me, Eithne? Give me your answer; in
faith, do: and so clap hands and a bargain: how say you, lady?

Breda clucked. "As though he were negotiating the purchase of brood-mare."

"Don't they share the same notion of their blood's dignity that our people have? Doesn't love count for something?" Eithne shook her head.

Cuneen offered her the flowers. "Yet there were other words, my Lady. Hints that maybe Eowain is more than we've seen?"

"Like what?" Eithne wrinkled her nose. "Do, tell us." Cuneen had always been too romantic for Eithne's taste. She'd memorized all of Eowain's missives for her.

A good leg will shrink, a straight back stoop, a black beard turn white, a curly
head grow bald, an attractive face grow wrinkled and a pretty eye hollow. But
a good heart, Eithne, is the sun and the moon, or, rather, the sun, and not the
moon, for it goes on shining brightly forever.

Breda shook her head. "My Lady, can you afford to be picky?"

"Well yes." Eithne bristled. "There it is, isn't it?" A woman of nigh on twenty years, old by the standards of her people to be a fresh, new bride. If she refused this suitor, there might not be another willing to partner with an aged maiden from a remote place in the wilderlands. "Yet why should I agree? What else—not counting warfare and insecurity—does he offer? He's not wealthy. I knew that from the first sight of his court, even if he'd not later written it in his letter."

Cuneen put her finger in the air. "Yes, yes, I remember."

You must find me such an ordinary king that you think I sold my farm to buy my crown.

Eithne shook her head. "No, that doesn't much concern me. Dolgallu is a mean and difficult land. That Dúnsciath and its kingdom and her king are also poor and hard, that doesn't bother me."

"So what is it, my lady?" Breda stooped to pick a blossom as well.

"It's the question of quality, in the end, isn't it?" Eithne didn't like the way it sounded, but there it was. "The matter of the man means a great deal after all, doesn't it? His character and his dignity. How much do I know about him? Is he a good man?"

Breda nodded. "He's never been caught lying, I've heard."

Cuneen agreed. "I heard that too. And he's never been taken prisoner from any field of war."

Eithne rolled her eyes at them. "That's like what Father said of him." She mocked her father's deep-throated voice and thoughtful manner. "He's never been known to break his word or an oath. He's avenged the murders of his kinsmen."

"Don't forget what the bards sing of him." Cuneen loved the bards. "There's that one where he faced and killed a giant ogre of a Gruin-man upon the hill of battle."

"Aye," added Breda. "And the one where he defeated her own kinsman, the prince of our tribe." Breda made a face and a gesture as if ticking a point from a board.

Cuneen made a disapproving gesture at Breda's contribution. "Oh, but there's the one where, roused like a mighty bear from slumber in the winter hills of Droma, he rescued you and defeated the bandit-chief Cael the Viper. And we know that one's true!"

Eithne frowned at her maid. "Yet when he wrote of himself in the letters that followed, I don't know? I had a glimpse into the spirit of the man. His courage in the face of the kingly challenges set before him."

Cuneen sighed. "Remember how modest and humble he was?"

In truth, the most incredible thing I have ever done was to become king. I have been nigh on a month in the office and still, I scarce believe it myself. It was always Lorcán that my father intended to be king after him, and if not my brother, there are a half dozen cousins elder than I and fit for the task. I never expected this responsibility should fall to me, and that my brother had to be maimed into the bargain is twice the sorrow.

"And—" Cuneen thought for a moment. "He wrote of his doubts and the nature of his piety too, my lady."

Of the Gods, I will tell you plain: I do not know that I trust Them. As the Lord-Drymyn has taught me all my life, They are forgetful and take no great interest in aiding any man. And yet, I cannot help at times but be moved by Their presence. In the sunlight upon the river on a quiet day, or in the haunting beauty of a foggy morning wood. Surely, I felt the presence of Echraide, the Goddess my people swear by, when I was crowned upon Her hill. It was as if all my difficulties slipped away and a deep sense of peace came over me, assuring me She would guide my hand as king and man.

She knew what he meant about that feeling one has, in little moments, an awareness of presence unseen. In much the same way, as Eithne lifted the bloom to her nose, the velvety petals in her hand and their scent reassured her.

Life goes on. This was the message the season of Flowering taught.

The thought was bitter to her. *Yes, life goes on.* The evening sun had set and the waning gibbous moon was aloft in the starry sky. The weather was still uncommonly warm, even by the low-landers' reckoning. She removed the woolen shawl she'd brought out with her and draped it over her arm.

"Warm night, eh?"

Eithne's heart clutched and she turned with a start. But it was only the old widow Rathtyen, dressed in her black robes.

Her maids glanced to each other and her. *How much had she heard?*

Eithne relaxed a piece. She'd clutched at her dagger, the one with the dark yellow schorl on the hilt, but let it go. "Yes. Yes, very warm. We still had snow in the mountains when I left. This all seems very..."

"Strange?" The old woman chuckled. "You needn't be afraid to say so. I remember what it was like when I got married. Two weeks in a baggage train, like a piece of luggage, and then found my worthy husband was a creature of his mother's, and there were Foreigners all about. Everything was strange." She took Eithne's elbow and guided her out into the garden, away from the house. Away from her maids.

Eithne let out a breath she hadn't realized she was holding. "Indeed, my lady. It is, as you say, all very strange."

"And why wouldn't it be? You're from a small village in the mountains, far from your neighbors, as I understand it." The old woman looked up at her, face wrinkled and jowly with age and care. "We are not quite so removed from the business of the Five Kingdoms here."

At the edge of the garden, the hill upon which her manor-home stood sloped down to a low dry-stone wall. Over the top of it, the slips and shanties of the fishermen were visible, and across the river to the dark hills beyond. The waning gibbous moon silvered the wide, slow-moving waters.

"You are of the Fiatach tribes, are you not?" Eithne nodded assent. The old woman pointed. "There lies Gruiniath, Fifth-Kingdom of the North. Our Manech tribes came from there, long ago. Exiled, we crossed the river and took this land from your forebears. Burned the hills of your kings, took your lands. We took the Fifth of the East and made it our own."

Eithne felt a twinge of old pride. "Not quite."

Rathtyen smiled at her gently. "No. Not quite. But in every way that matters, eh? Drove your people north and east into the mountains. Sat your kings on your thrones. Forced your knee."

Eithne could not deny that much. There had been war even within her own memory, though it hadn't touched her village. The Manech tribes under Murdach had come into Fiatach and Narada lands and reminded them who the King of the East was. Her cousin, Ardgal, had been confirmed in his place because he had bent the knee. Other tribe-kings hadn't been so fortunate.

"My point is, we did it ourselves once, made this land our own." She pointed back across the river. "The king of Gruiniath, who calls himself High King of the Five? He would do the same again, if he had the wherewithal." She pointed to the north and south. "Your restless people to our north, our own uncertain allies to the south and east." She shrugged. "We are hedged with spears against many troubles here. In such a land, it is no easy thing to be a lass like you."

Eithne knew an attractive, fresh young noble woman was a pawn, not a player, in the politics of the Five Kingdoms. Her bride-price had come high, for it would buy peace on one of Droma's frontiers. But a politically and financially favorable marriage might not prove good in more—intimate ways.

Her would-be husband's aunt, had bartered her marriage. Though she'd been fortunate in her own personal life, she'd surely chanced in her long years to see the wide range of marital fates that awaited highborn women.

Eithne might have been sent north to Naricia, or married off to some cousin in the too-close-related royal house of Sasana. Gods forbid, but she might even have been bartered away to the Foreigners to seal some temporary peace, and been exiled to some windswept rock in the Summer Archipelago.

Instead, she'd been promised to the hedge-king of a small but strategically important tribe. Eithne frowned a bit at that thought. *What value does my love really have?*

"You still have doubts?" The old woman was astute.

Eithne turned as the heat rose in her cheeks. "He seems like a goodly man, your nephew."

"But?"

Yes, indeed, but what? Eithne shook her head. "I don't know. There was the matter at Gluintír—"

"That business with Goleuddydd? Pish and tush! She's a foolish thing. Right you were to turn her out of my nephew's house, the way she treated you." The old woman laughed and slapped a thigh. "And the look on her face when you told her scratching it with nails couldn't improve it? Ha! I wish I'd thought of it years ago!"

Eithne stifled a smile. It had been satisfying, she had to admit. "But hers is not the only such opinion of me about the country. They say—."

"Who is 'they?' 'They' say many foolish things. And you are but a stranger here, with a small company. How well can you know what 'they' are saying?" She made a dismissive fluttering with her hands. "Goodwives' tongues will waggle. Foolish men will say foolish things. The moon will wane. The sun will rise."

Then she fixed Eithne with a bony finger and a wink. "But you and I, we must go on, aye? We are not the common sort of women, are we? The kind that faint and withdraw when swords would clash, eh? Gods know, if we let men run things, there'd be an awful lot more swords clashing."

A faint breeze rose, and brought with it the smell of flowering hart's-tongue and ivy-leaved toad-flax. Eithne nodded in agreement. Her father had not raised her to shirk from any conflict.

"So what is it troubles you, dear? Tell Old Rathtyen."

She desperately wanted someone in whom to confide. But isn't that the very trouble? Eowain was beset upon all sides by men and women who wished not the best for him, certainly not the best for her, but only the best for themselves. His cousins were ambitious for his throne. His lord-drymyn and her own matron, the ban-drymyn Alva, they served the forgetful Gods and the ambitions of their own Order.

Even Rathtyen, kindly old woman as she seemed in that moment, had ambitions for her trading fleet and business down-river in her late husband's lands. If Droma was hedged about with spears against its neighbors, no less was Eowain hedged about with spears against his own people. Whom could he trust? Whom could she trust?

Could she even trust him? Was the love he vouched for her true? Or were his words merely those placed in his mouth by his ministers and his own ambitions?

"What is it, dear? Tell me."

Eithne shook her head. "No, it's nothing, my lady. Just the foolish thoughts of a young girl. Truly, I'm well." She took the old woman's leathery hands in her own. "And I am so glad that Eowain has someone like you standing with him against all these troubles."

Rathtyen raised an eyebrow. "Indeed, I'd do anything for him. He is my brother's son, after all."

Yes, there is that, thought Eithne. Rathtyen's ambitions depended on her brother's sons, and so their enemies were her own.

But Rathtyen also had other allies of her own, didn't she? Men from downriver, investors and business partners. Weren't there Aukrian traders in the horse-fair even then?

Circles inside of circles. Eithne pinched the bridge of her nose. "The hour grows late, my lady." Eithne patted the old woman's hands. "I think I should retire. There will be much to do to-morrow, readying myself for our journey."

"Of course, dear. You should rest. The days ahead will prove difficult."

Indeed, Eithne had no doubt.

CHAPTER FIVE

THE SUN ROSE over the summit of Gluín, more than a thousand feet high. Fiery dawn light framed the enclosure and watchtower there.

More than a hundred Cailech-men, and as many women and children?

It wasn't just a raid. It was a land-grab. They meant to hold the hill and the other three settlements on its compass points for their own.

Eowain's own men had only held Drúchtmil through the quick action of the garrison at Bántobar.

If the Cailech held the hill, there would be a dangerous bulge into Droma. Horse and cattle herds in the midland hills would be easy targets.

But a fight over a mile uphill to the crest of Gluín is no easy task.

"Your Grace, we entreat you!" Crimthann Nine-Eyes, chief of Drúchtmil, was a skinny man of thirty-odd years. The leather cuirass and greaves of his father ill-fitted him.

Behind him were the chief-holders of the other thorps around Gluín Hill. They'd all been at Dúnsciath for the spring fair when the assault came, so they'd escaped injury themselves.

Their lands, however, had surely been stripped bare of treasures since the incursion began.

Lord Gwerfyl of Gluintír whispered to another lord, "Really, after the way my wife was treated, I shouldn't be surprised."

Eowain snapped at them. "Am I not considering the tactical situation?"

Indeed, am I not?

Eowain stroked at his chin. The enclosure and watchtower were up there for a reason. And this was the steepest side of the hill, with part of the way blocked by a six-hundred foot cliff.

The Cailech king's own men weren't on that hill. Only a rabble of farmers, herders, and other tribesmen, with little more than spears, clubs, and short hunting bows.

But they held the heights. Soon they'd entrench themselves.

"Their chief, Toryn the Stout?" Crimthann Nine-Eyes shook his head. "He's a man of some reputation. With a dozen fierce companions."

Eowain had heard only rumor of Toryn. He was like a tree-trunk, they said. And twice as tenacious when rooted.

The Cailech held the other three trail-heads and the settlements near them. He couldn't advance up the hill along one of those trails.

But if he seized the height directly from Drúchtmil? The remaining Cailech would break and run.

By the First Hour, Eowain's men had made little progress. The only trail up Gluín from Drúchtmil was rough and offered good footing, but narrow in many places.

The rough and rocky cliff, coated with mosses and lichens, blocked progress. While not strictly vertical, the slope was severe. He certainly might surprise the Cailech that way, but Eowain guessed only three or four men in ten might be able to make that climb and live to see the top.

He wasn't certain he was one of them.

Aside from the cliff, the rest of the hill was grassy, with slippery morning dew over which to advance.

He ordered his men up the Drúchtmil trail. Archers advanced point to point and offered cover to the infantry that followed.

By Third Hour, attrition had claimed its first victims.

Cailech archers used the heights to improve their range. Eowain's men maneuvered around the base of the hill and looked for advantage.

Eowain's own archers made the Cailech pay for their effrontery. But their range and accuracy were compromised by their lower position.

His men found an opening. From Third Hour, his sorties up the hill began to skirmish with the foe. A troop of Eowain's men narrowly won their first engagement and drove a dozen Cailech-men up the hill.

The second skirmish stalled by mid-day. A dozen Cailech-men held a narrow way between two heights against Eowain's troop. His sortie against their position proved inconclusive.

By Ninth Hour, the third sortie proved a decisive loss. Toryn the Stout brought the full weight of his tribesmen to bear and drove Eowain down the hill with heavy casualties.

Eowain sent away the grumbling local lords. They were alone for the first time since morning.

Lorcán, grimaced at him. "They have us in a bad position."

Eowain examined the map of Gluín on the table in his pavilion. "Yes, brother, thank you. That's very helpful." Carved stones represented his troops and those of the enemy. They stood—inscrutable—on the map. Like the *coelbreni*, they foretold a future he couldn't seem to read.

He moved three stones to the north. "What if we come this way? Would it turn their flank?"

Lorcán scowled. He forked the fingers on his good right hand at the map. "You have these two outcroppings." He waved one finger across the map. "An open field of slick grass runs upslope to them. With a squad of archers on top of each one, they pick our men apart. And bring a handful of squads," he indicated one place, "to reinforce their flank." He stabbed at another place.

Eowain breathed a sigh. "We have to take the hill back. I can't wait for a siege."

"I can't believe Corchen insisted you wed at the Vale of Thaynú. Why not ignore her and hold the wedding here as you'd planned?"

Eowain rolled his eyes and waved his hands with mock-drama. "Dire portents of evil and disaster..." He shook his head. "She's worse than our Lord-Drymyn."

"More dire than getting killed on the way to the Vale?"

"Apparently. Even if she's wrong, our people have reason to doubt and fear, and Tnúthgal another to protest. I don't think Murdach's dismissal of his case has brought an end to the matter."

Lorcán rubbed the back of his neck. "I'm sorry I got you into this, Eowain." He shook his three-fingered hand.

"No, I made my choice when you abdicated. If Tnúthgal is in league with bandits to prey on his own people, I shudder at what sort of king he'd make." Eowain shook his head. "But we have a hill to take. What about this?"

"Isn't that impossible?"

Eowain's words felt grim. "Yes, it is. I'll need ten sure-footed men, with steady hands. And I'll go myself."

TNÚTHGAL CROSSED THE horse-meadow, lantern high. To any spy, out on his usual nightly inspection of the stable. The early spring air was unusually warm and moist.

Smells like rain. He grinned. *That should make Eowain's life difficult.*

His spies said Eowain was repulsed from Gluín Hill by Toryn's Cailech-men. Tnúthgal knew that hill well. He'd fought to hold it many times himself.

The news pleased him.

Eowain would be on the other side of the kingdom all through the next day. He could be there above a month, if Toryn just held the high ground.

That would certainly scuttle his young cousin's wedding plans.

Tnúthgal pulled the wooden door of the stable behind him. The horses nickered in their shadowed stalls. He heard a desultory kick against a plank. That would be Ahern, he thought. A spirited war-stallion with a good stud-future ahead of him.

"It's about time you got here." The shadows of the stable whispered, harsh and cruel.

"It's my time to spend. Don't forget yourself, Cael."

The bandit chief was a long, lean man who sidled as much as stepped into the light. Wrapped in peasant rags and a worn woolen cloak, Tnúthgal didn't doubt he wore a chain mail shirt beneath them.

And Cael certainly had a weapon. "It's you what needs me, m'lord, not the other way round."

Tnúthgal wrinkled his nose. The bandit wasn't wrong. It would take weeks, if not months, for Tnúthgal to replace him. "It's my coin and supplies that keep your men fed and shod, all these months. If you'd done your job at Ruakhavsa, we'd be finished already."

"You're the one that went goose-livered. You could have taken the tower, or come up behind and reinforced me at Ruakhavsa. But you withdrew."

"A tactical withdrawal. Once I heard you'd attacked him head on, through all that snow? I knew you were lost. If I'd tried to take the tower, he'd have proof against me. He'd have turned the siege and brought up his troops behind me."

"You left me and my men to die."

Tnúthgal seized Cael by the collar. "You were foolish. Eowain's young, but he's not stupid and he's not weak. The way to beat him is at night, in his bed, with a stick. Not with that rabble of yours in an open battle."

Cael hissed. "If we'd had the help we was promised—."

"There's no helping stupid, my friend." Tnúthgal pushed the bandit and his protest away. "Enough. Done is done. What news?"

Cael sulked and perched on a hay-bale. "We got five groups of ten men each on the High King's Road. They're dressed like common travelers— journeymen, migrant farmers, like that. As the Lady Eithne moves north, these men join up with her supply train, a little at a time, 'for protection.' But they're each armed and armored under their clothes, see? When Eithne stops for the night, we wait for the sign from your man. He's going to get her away from the throng, right? He can be trusted?"

Tnúthgal nodded. "My man knows his business, I assure you. He'll do what needs be done."

Cael shrugged. "Then that's it then. Your man will get her away from her guards, the lot of my men will start a diversion, and a handful will take her. It'll be easier than when we got her at Trígrianna, I'll tell you what."

Tnúthgal glared at him. "Make sure you keep her, this time."

"Oh, we'll keep her. Can't promise what condition she'll be in when she's ransomed, but we'll keep her this time for sure. We got Eowain running all around the houses looking for us now, ain't we?"

"Indeed." He could imagine his cousin's frustration. "Thirteen raids and six kidnappings in the last two months since Ruakhavsa. Eowain's at his wit's end." Tnúthgal had done everything in his power to weaken Eowain's hold on his throne. He relished the idea of the blushing bride-to-be stolen from under his cousin's very nose.

And he wouldn't restrain the bandit-chief's baser instincts anymore either. He'd been kind to Eithne three months ago, tugged at Cael's leash to keep him from her. But not anymore. *Let her suffer now as she didn't then. Let the kingdom see how little the self-proclaimed king's protection really means.*

Eowain's clients would desert him, his loyal warriors would question him. Tnúthgal's stock would rise. Never mind that fool king Murdach had ruled against his claim. If Droma was to survive the coming onslaught by the Gruin-men, Tnúthgal knew she needed a firm hand on the reins.

His naïve young cousin's need for a bride, and soon after a son, were his greatest weakness. Tnúthgal only needed to keep them apart long enough to see Eithne stolen away, and his own purposes would soon be accomplished.

But could he trust Cael again? The fool had made a muddle of things at Ruakhavsa. Cael had lost the girl once already, and then led his rabble into a trap. He'd let Eowain's bravado goad him into giving up the advantage of his position. Cael's only real success that day was in slithering away before he himself was killed. And it had cost Tnúthgal plenty to hearken together more lawless resolutes to the bandit's banner.

He couldn't trust the law. King Murdach failed him when he dismissed Tnúthgal's suit.

He couldn't trust the kings of Cailech or Ivea. They were a rapacious pair. Once they'd help him unseat Eowain, they were as like to kill him as to hand over the throne.

And aid from the Gruin-men was inconceivable.

That left only Cael and his misbegotten brigands as the only tool still near to hand. Their loyalty to his silver could be counted on so long as the silver lasted.

But his coffers were low, and Eowain's choke-hold on the tolls strangled his ambitions further. He had to bring this matter to an end soon.

Indeed, what choices do I have? Tnúthgal nodded. "See that it's done, then. And don't make a muddle of it."

EOWAIN RUBBED HIS face with the palm of his hand, squeezed the bridge of his nose.

Lorcán's assessment of his scheme as "impossible" had been generous. While to call it "a cliff" overstated the case, the rocky, moss-covered slope was still only several degrees shy of strictly vertical.

Near enough to a cliff for his purposes. A fall would kill or cripple him just the same.

He looked up at the gray sky. *The Gods have promised nevermore to attack with Water and with Wind...* That's what he'd been taught by Medyr. *But the Gods, They are forgetful.*

Whether for absent-mindedness or spite, rain poured from the sky. Rivulets of water trickled between the rocks and burbled in and out of cracks. The mossy scree of the slope was drenched.

It was the gorge at Caipín Creek all over again, only far bigger, and without an archer—yet—shooting at them from above.

I should call this madness off, he thought.

But yesterday's disastrous skirmishes had gained nothing and cost much. Every hour that went by, he lost more trust and loyalty from his cattle-chiefs.

Either way, his men would skirmish the whole day up the trail. He'd lose many lives, and might still not seize the crest. This trouble would drag into another day or more.

Eowain had assigned as many men as he could trust to Eithne's security. He hated the idea that she travel without him into the unfriendly lands, with bandits already known to be abroad.

Yet Eithne's caravan to the Vale of Thaynú, it had to depart that morning to reach the Vale by Cétshamain-day.

And he wouldn't be with her.

He had to bring that occupation of Gluín to an end and teach the Cailech-men better than to try his borders.

He looked up the long distance of the severe and slippery slope. *I have to do the impossible.*

With a deep breath, he set his jaw, swallowed the knot in his throat, and nodded to Lorcán.

Ten men volunteered, good men of his personal guard whose loyalties were beyond doubt. Lorcán found a man clever with knots, and every second man was strung to his fellow by a length of stout rope.

Eowain himself was tied between scar-faced Gaeth and barrel-chested Mahon, two of his strongest. He and each of his ten men wore a round steel helm and a jack of stern leather hung with rings of steel. Broadswords and round, iron-banded wooden shields were strapped across their backs.

The first dozen feet proved how difficult a task they'd set themselves. Six of his men scrambled back down. Gloved fingers slipped on wet lichen. Moss pulled away from the surface when pulled upon. Booted feet lost purchase when loose rock gave way under a man's weight.

But Eowain was determined. The heavy rains were to his advantage, as any watchmen atop the hill would be huddled under cover, confident no one would make that climb who didn't have to. He and his men redoubled their effort, finally found the purchase they needed, and crawled up the slope.

Eowain remembered Lorcán's advice: *Don't look down.* He kept his eyes focused on the next grip, the slope above of him, his next foothold, and the rock in front of him. Rain trickled down his fingers, under his sleeves and along his arms, and tickled at his armpits and ribs.

A stone came loose.

He cursed volubly, his stomach lurched. The errant slate bounced sickeningly away, clacking past his men. Eowain thanked the Gods, *No harm done.*

Onward they went. The morning wore away.

On his left, he could hear men shouting. Lorcán led the Company up the trail, business as usual, to keep the Cailech-men's attention from the slope. To judge by the shouts, he'd made contact. Eowain grimaced at the thought of how many men might be injured or killed for that diversion.

As they climbed, he found the grotto of Padarn, the holy man who had dwelt on the hill in ages past. He had lived there on the cliff side as a hermit.

A shout and a clatter of rock rose behind him. Over his shoulder, he watched one of his men tumble a dozen feet. His fall threatened to take his partner with him.

Eowain's throat knotted.

The man found an outcrop with desperate fingers and arrested his fall.

He dangled for a long, breathless moment. Then he found purchase for his boots and raised a thumb.

Eowain looked at Gaeth and Mahon. Mahon raised eyebrows at him. Eowain let go the breath he'd been holding. Gaeth merely nodded his pock-marked head. Onward they went.

Eowain's fingers strained to hold him to the rock face. His leg trembled as booted toes sought better, higher purchase.

Another shout. Another man slipped.

And pulled his partner loose.

The first man caught a hold, but the fallen partner did not. He jerked the first man from his precarious grip on a ledge.

Eowain watched the two men's horrible crash on the rocks and swallowed the panic that burgeoned in his throat. He'd come more than halfway. He couldn't stop now. But he turned his eyes away from that vertiginous fall to the impassive rock before him, gulped air through his open mouth.

"Your Grace?" The face of Mahon was contorted with fear and uncertainty. *We're all going to die here,* that look said.

Eowain gritted his teeth, forced down the fear. "We can do this." He nodded to Mahon with more confidence than he felt. He remembered something his father once said: *First you do the thing you're afraid of. The courage comes afterward.* He set his jaw, nodded again to Mahon and Gaeth. "We can do this." He looked to each of his remaining men. "We will do this."

The skirmish they heard meant comrades fought and died to cover their climb. Their death would be in vain if they failed their mission. With varying degrees of confidence, they nodded back to him. It was every bit as deadly to fall as they scrambled back down as it was to climb on up, so on they agreed to go.

With grim determination, Eowain forced weary muscles to pull him higher. He struggled with booted feet to find their next hold.

It was just past Third Hour when at last he reached the top.

He needn't have worried about watchmen atop the slope. With the heavy rains and Lorcán's assault up the trail, the Cailech had better things to worry about.

Eowain pulled himself over the crest of the slope, crawled a half-dozen feet from it, and rolled over onto his back. Rain fell uncaring on his face. He breathed heavily and savored it. The rain drops struck at his nose and cheeks, the water ran down his chin.

Beside him, Mahon was on his elbows and knees, head bowed. Gaeth held his head and arms akimbo, letting the rain fall full on his pock-marked visage. His other men did much the same as they finished their climbs.

Eowain closed his eyes and mumbled thanksgivings to the Goddess of Droma. Then he rose, and looked out as the sun rose over his kingdom. There, the lakes, Bradán and Banlyn, glittered. And there was the hill of Garvór. Bántobar and Lynben had their cattle in the hills already.

Eithne had seen his kingdom like this, before she'd been insulted. Had her caravan departed yet?

In their missives, she'd written of her love as a tower to be assailed, and challenged him to prove his love to her telling her openly and honestly about himself.

Hadn't he then done it in fact? He stood on top of Gluin Hill. Had, in fact, scaled it, like the tower of virtue of which she wrote? Was this enough finally?

The blast of horns roused him. It was Lorcán's call to charge. *He's staging a full assault up the trail.* A volley of shouts answered. The Cailech marshalled to repulse him.

"Come, men. We've cheated death already. The rest of the day should seem like child's play." He unslung his shield and his broadsword from his back. "Let's go find Toryn the Stout and show him what the Men of Droma can do."

His eight surviving men drew themselves up, and made ready for battle. Their swords rang from their iron-rimmed shields, signal to their readiness. "Hurrah," they grunted.

Across the grassy summit of Gluín, they trotted toward the cattle-enclosure. Two men atop the watchtower strained west to see the progress of the battle on the trail, and paid no mind to the southern approach from the slope.

Eowain signaled. Two of his men put down the watchmen in the tower with crossbows.

The enclosure itself was a hedgehog of stout, spiked timbers that bristled outward in a circle. Around it, a series of three marshy ditches and grassy embankments forced Eowain and his men down and up and down again before they could flatten themselves unseen against the wall beneath the spikes. Within, the Cailech had gathered all the cattle they had stolen from the surrounding settlements. The cow-stench was thick and noxious. The herd lowed anxiously.

Eowain realized he hadn't really thought through this part of his mad scheme. He'd expected the fall to kill them all long before that. But he led the men in creeping around to the entrance.

A handful of spear-armed Cailech stood before the open way, ready to cover any sudden retreat by their kinsmen and seal the entrance behind them. The men's attention was fixed to the west on the distant shouts and cries of battle on the trail.

Eowain and his men made short work of them. The last to die admitted that Toryn and his company were away down the trail, overseeing the defense.

A quick search of the enclosure proved they had neutralized all the garrison Toryn had left behind.

The women and children must be barricaded in the settlements below.

That suited Eowain well enough. He had no stomach for such a slaughter.

But with the enclosure secured, what next?

The cattle milled around and crowded together in the ankle-deep mud with no pasturage to graze.

The horns of the Cailech carried to him from the west.

A perverse thought occurred to Eowain. "Find torches," he told Gaeth and Mahon.

Soon, Gluín Hill trembled beneath the thunderous hooves of a hundred head of furious milk-cow.

By midday, the battle was won. The Cailech broke, Toryn fled in shame. Eowain wiped the blood from his blade and watched Cailech-men run in every direction.

Lorcán labored up the trail.

"Hoy, brother!" Eowain felt exultant. Surely, this was a battle that would be remembered in hearth-songs for months to come.

"Your— Grace—," panted Lorcán. "We've— had word— from Dúnsciath."

The grim look on his brother's face did not bode well. "What is it?"

"The Lady Eithne— The caravan— They're attacked, Your Grace. Attacked by bandits at Mianmair."

Eowain's stomach dropped. *The Gods,* he remembered, *They are forgetful.*

CHAPTER SIX

THE CLOUDS OPENED to offer the moon's illumination to light his way. The waning moon, half past full. *At least the rains have broken.* Eowain murmured thanksgiving for small blessings.

No matter how he wanted to gallop across the kingdom, he'd been reduced to a frustrating slog on muddy trails, lest his horse stumble.

The messenger had seen the attack himself. The Lady's caravan slogged a morning through the rain. They broke their march at Mianmair after midmorning.

Lady Eithne and her guard went up to the chieftain's house for his hospitality. The Lord-Drymyn remained with the troop.

That's when a fire broke out in the thorp. Three dozen fellow-travelers threw off their cloaks and attacked.

The Lord-Drymyn himself threw the messenger in the saddle, and hurried to seek the Lady's safety. But the messenger knew nothing more, neither Eithne's fate nor how matters had since fallen.

Eowain feared the worst. He'd ridden from Gluin Hill with five men as fast as horses would carry them, but he'd met no other messengers since.

Lorcán would settle matters at Gluín Hill. Eowain trusted his brother and personal guard to catch up on foot at Monóc Hill as soon as they might.

But the rain made a muddle of the trails. The stream fords were swollen. The bridge at Drochavaile was clear—a blessing—but the fastest way around the head of Drægan Ridge was by way of Mynnynrainsh, where heavy rains from Drægan's summit washed out the track.

Sunset caught him only just turned back west toward the Drægan Gorge. Shortly past the Hour of Completion, when any right-minded person had rested their head for the night, he stopped and rested the horses, lest they founder. Only halfway through the Gorge, it was yet three miles farther on to Dúnceap, then three more across Copper Hill to Mianmair.

At least four more hours. He drummed his fist against his knee, but it did no good to ruin the horses.

Three of his men stalked a picket. The others ate a cold dinner of biscuit and water. They were none of them comfortable, abroad in the Gorge at night. The Lord-Drymyn's own acolyte and a small mission of foreign traders had been waylaid there not three weeks earlier. His men all knew the matter of banditry was far from settled. They were grim and watchful.

Eowain paced. The unseasonable heat had broken. The air was near to freezing. His breath misted before him, and frosted the tips of his mustaches.

Despite how little the messenger had known, he could imagine more. The fire and the three dozen attackers had been a diversion. The real attack would have been at the manor house, where Eithne had gone to lunch with Lord Feoras.

Eowain knew this bandit, Cael the Viper, wasn't above kidnapping. No less than six missing in recent months. He'd seized Eithne herself once. It was nothing short of a miracle that Eowain could rescue her, or that she survived the experience at all.

Eowain knew another such abduction would not go so well for her. His enemies would ruin her.

He went tense in every muscle. He wished for a foe on whom to vent his rage. *I'll never forgive myself if anything's happened to her.* He punched one fist into his opposite palm. *So help me, Echraide, I'll see these villains torn to pieces with my own hands.*

The decision to wed Eithne was unpopular with some. Many—including his cousins—had lost close kin to the feud with her Gwynn tribe. It was no easy thing for them to let the matter rest and accept peace. Eithne's insult at the hands of Lady Gluintír had been but the overt symptom of a deeper discontent. *What if they're right? What if marrying Eithne is a mistake?*

He regretted the thought. She'd never asked anything but honesty. Yet their wedding arrangements had put her into danger. Even if the popular wisdom was right, how would he live with himself if she came to harm?

At midnight, he and his men mounted again. On sodden trails under the waning half-moon, they made the best speed they could manage. It was near moon-set before they rode down Copper Hill and into the trees that surrounded Mianmair.

The moonlight dwindled and did little to illuminate the scant dozen acres of the small thorp and its four ramshackle buildings. One of the local workshops was nothing more than burnt, ragged timbers. The remaining two workshops were charred and black with soot, but intact. The round-house of Lord Feoras stood alone on a small rise.

Everything was dark and quiet. Eowain smelled shite and the reek of death before he saw them: five bodies hung by their necks from tree branches on the settlement's outskirts.

There was no sign of Eithne's caravan.

Eowain pointed. Four men dismounted and split into pairs. Each knocked in the door of a different workshop and brought out the inhabitants: a cobbler, a jeweler, and their families.

They knelt in the mud and pled for mercy in their nightclothes. Eowain remained a-stride, and held a torch aloft. "What happened here?"

It didn't take long to learn what they knew. A handful of brigands captured and hanged by the Shield Company. The rest run off. There'd been a fuss at the manor house. After that, the whole Shield Company had marched north on the High King's Road. None had seen Lord Feoras nor any member of his household since.

"What of the Lady Eithne?"

They cowered. She'd gone up to the manor with Lord Feoras. "But we didn't see her after that, Your Grace! I swear it!" The cobbler babbled. "It was the Lord-Drymyn what told us to stay in our houses. Ordered the whole Company to pack up. That was the last we knew of them. By all that's holy, that's all we know!"

"When was this?"

"Just past Ninth Hour, Your Grace. Mid-afternoon."

Eowain cursed. *That was some twelve hours ago, about when he'd first heard of the attack. Is Eithne alive? Has Medyr turned against me?* He snarled at his men. They released the freeholders and mounted up.

He had to assume she was still alive, if they'd headed northward. But was she a prisoner? To the north was Gruinmór and beyond that, Darachrith, whose lord he knew was loyal. Eowain had planned for the caravan to break their first day's journey there, not at Mianmair.

But there was also a side trail to Crúcavainn, where Tnúthgal dwelt. If Eithne were alive and a prisoner, her captors might intend to put her in his cousin's power. She might be there at that very moment, suffering Gods knew what tortures.

He spurred his mount down the trail to the High King's Road. By torchlight, he saw signs that a large company had indeed gone north. The way was wide, but muddy and slow-going. Puddles began to freeze and cracked beneath iron-shod hooves.

It was past the First Hour before they came to the Crúcavainn trail. The sun had risen. To judge by the state of the road, a large party had ridden north from Crúcavainn. They'd joined with or followed the Lord-Drymyn's larger company. None had returned that way to Crúcavainn, nor turned aside to Gruinmór. They'd all gone on north.

Eowain ordered a walking rest. The men and mounts hadn't had a wink of sleep. Eager as he was to catch up with her company, they were nearly spent. The High King's Road passed through forested hills there. Eowain kept a weather-eye to the wood. He didn't want to founder the mounts, then be ambushed.

The nine lords of the north were mostly Tnúthgal's supporters. He didn't know how far he could trust any of them. He was reasonably certain of Lord Darachrith's loyalty, but not by much.

By midmorning, the settlement came into view ahead of them. Set upon the slope of a steep and forested hill, Darachrith's huts stood at the mouth of a yawning iron mine, not far off the High King's Road. Heavy smoke rose from a charcoaler's kilns and the iron-smelter's forge. It flew away over the large thorp on a chill northwesterly that swayed the small branches in the trees.

Lord Feargus, chief of Darachrith and a stout warrior in his middle thirties, rode down from his manor.

Eowain could see from his horse-fair that a great company had camped there. "The Lord-Drymyn and Lord Tnúthgal with their host, they were here last night," said the chief.

"Was the Lady Eithne with them?"

Lord Feargus shrugged. "I couldn't say, Your Grace. I invited them all up to the house of course, but the Lord-Drymyn wouldn't have any of it. Said they'd all stayed in camp together, get an early start. Only your cousin came up for dinner. He didn't stay long." He rubbed at his neck. "I'll tell you this, though. The Lord-Drymyn looked mighty grim. And Tnúthgal was uncommon quiet. It scared me a little."

"They marched on for Monóc Hill?"

"Aye, Your Grace. Left at day break. They're hauling a house-wagon?"

Eowain remembered. "My aunt, Lady Rathtyen. She insists she attend the wedding."

Lord Feargus nodded. "She's one, isn't she? Well, they won't get far. You'll catch them for sure."

He thanked Feargus for the news and accepted fresh mounts, then rode on with his men.

Soon, he rode up on the long baggage-train of mules. The rear guard of Shield Company cheered the sight of him.

Eowain spoke with their sergeant.

"Aye, Lord Tnúthgal joined the company after Mianmair. He's got about a dozen men, Your Grace." The sergeant didn't know what had become of the Lady Eithne. "The Lord-Drymyn and Lord Tnúthgal ride together in the van, though. The Lady Rathtyen's house-wagon is ahead in the middle of the train, sir." He raised his eyebrows.

Eowain saluted the sergeant and rode on. The company was in good order, and traveled just as he'd planned. Most warriors were footmen, with swords, spears, shields and scaled leather tunics. Those cheered him all up the line as he passed.

He spurred his mount by his aunt's house-wagon. It lumbered along the road, but he was eager to learn what business the Lord-Drymyn and his cousin had in common.

Soon, he came upon the bodyguard and mounted elements at the van. Fifteen of Eithne's men-of-foot, with fourteen footmen of his own troops. A dozen other men in his cousin's livery, the white-river salmon under the up-pointed crescent, watched with wary eyes as he rode by.

Then came the score of lancers and mounted archers from his Shield Company in green, gold, and white tartans, and Eithne's own three horsemen in black, gold, and red.

Five more cavalrymen bore the white river salmon under the up-turned blue moon of his cousin.

There at the head of the train was the Lord-Drymyn, astride his pony.

His acolyte walked beside him, as did the merchant and his Foreigner mercenary. On the other side of the road was Lord Tnúthgal astride one of his prized war-horses.

Between them—hands bound—was Lord Feoras of Mianmair. Tied atop a saddled mule, he was led by one of Eowain's young scouts.

Medyr smiled, puffed his clay pipe. "It's about time you got here. My message reached you?"

"What's this about, Medyr?" Eowain reined in. His cousin didn't seem happy, and the Lord Feoras even less so. But Medyr seemed his usual chipper self.

"We were ambushed at Mianmair, as you've heard? Yes? Good. Well, about a dozen bandits tried to seize the Lady Eithne—"

"Where is she?"

Medyr put up a hand. "Safe, Your Grace. With your aunt and the ban-drymyn Alva in the house-wagon."

Eowain slumped with relief.

Medyr pointed the stem of his pipe. "I'll say this, Your Grace: Your bride's no shrinking violet. Between her, the good merchant, and my acolyte, the bandits had no chance."

The Lord-Drymyn tilted his head at Lord Feoras. "I believe the good Lord Mianmair knows rather more of the matter than he's telling."

Feoras glared at Eowain.

Medyr shrugged. "He's been silent as a stone. Rather a stubborn fellow, really." Feoras sneered at the Lord-Drymyn, but remained quiet. "Whatever the case, I thought it best to move on, rather than wait at Mianmair like ducks on a pond. I knew you'd be along." He puffed once more on his pipe. Linden leaf smoke blew merrily in the breeze. "How did you fare at Gluín hill?"

EOWAIN LEAPED FROM his horse and pulled the door to the house-wagon. The three ladies and their servants shaded eyes with hands. "What is it?" His aunt squinted at him. "Why have we stopped?"

"Eowain?" Eithne rose and came to the doorway.

She wore a rust-colored bodice of linen and curvilinear patterns, trimmed in black, and a dress with her red, gold, and sable tartan. Bands of hack-silver encircled her upper arms. A cunningly-twisted golden torc with wolfs-head knobs rested about her slim throat. The scent of mountain lilacs washed over him.

Relief rose in Eowain like the floodwaters of the Gasirad in springtime. He offered his hand. "Yes, it's me."

She put her small hand into his larger one, and stepped down out of the wagon. She held her skirts up out of the mud and took a step toward him. She glanced at her father and watchful guards. "Thank— Thank all the Gods you're well, Your Grace." She dropped a maidenly curtsy.

"I should say the same! I have, in fact. All the way from Gluín Hill. You're unharmed?" One of her sleeves was torn open. A linen bandage showed through the gap. "What's this?"

She waved it away. "Merely a slice, my lord. Nothing to concern yourself. The Lord-Drymyn and Lady Alva were... attentive."

He looked to her father. Ciaran gave him a nod. Eowain took that liberty and inspected the wound. A clean and proper field dressing. He commended the two drymyn.

"We're no strangers to war, away on our mountain." Lady Alva stepped down and sketched a courtesy.

"So Medyr tells me." He appraised Eithne with new eyes. "I heard you took three of the villains yourself with naught but a belt-knife."

She raised her chin. "They caught me unsuspecting last time. I swore on my grandfather's honor, I'd never let that happen again."

He couldn't suppress his grin. "Nor should you, Lady. I am—" He looked to her father, back again, and chose his next word with care. "—Impressed."

His voice sounded gruff to his own ears. He cleared his throat. It wasn't the best word to describe what stirred his blood. He wanted to pull her off into the bushes and embrace her. But it was the most appropriate word he could muster in polite company.

She must have seen something in his eyes. Her green eyes glittered at him. She dropped another curtsy and averted her flushed cheeks. "What of you, my lord? You are— uninjured?"

He nodded. "Aye. Weary to the bone, but well enough for all that. I chased across the whole country after you."

"I wouldn't have worried you so, but the Lord-Drymyn thought it best to send no further message, lest it be intercepted."

Eowain put a hand on Medyr's shoulder. "You did the right thing. You had no way to know by which trail I'd come, or where the brigands would have spies."

Tnúthgal reined his mount to a stop. "It was his idea as well that she should travel in the wagon and in secret, rather than a-horse, as she wanted."

His cousin seemed sour about that. *No doubt, such secrecy does not accord well with your own plan.* Eowain commended Medyr again. "Under the circum-stances, I'm sure it was the wisest thing to do."

Eithne's face grew distraught. "Oh, but now that you're here, my lord, I hope you'll permit me to ride again. I do prefer the open air to the—" Her eyes flickered toward his aunt. "To the close quarters of the wagon. It's so... dark and stuffy in there."

He could imagine the horror. "So long as it please your father...?"

Lord Ciaran agreed it did.

"Yes, it would please me well for you to ride. I shouldn't want to let you from my sight again, now that the matter at Gluín Hill is settled."

His cousin's face remained placid.

"I'm glad to hear that you taught the Cailech a lesson, Your Grace." Tnúthgal's tone was the soul of courtesy.

"Are you sure it's wise the lady travel openly, Your Grace?" Medyr furrowed his brows.

"I'm sure my cousin and I can put ourselves between the lady and any harm that might befall her." He looked to Tnúthgal. "Isn't that right, cousin? You are coming with us all the way to the Vale, aren't you? I'll need your strong arm on the road, and men of my own blood to prepare me for the rite of marriage." Then he added, "I can think of no one I would want closer to me."

Something passed across his cousin's face, but he bowed in the saddle and Eowain lost sight of it. "Of course, Your Grace. I'd be honored."

Medyr struggled with a smirk.

"It's settled then. The lady will ride." Eowain noted the disappointment on his aunt's face. No doubt distraught to lose her captive audience. The relief of Eithne and Alva was palpable.

But, they agreed it was best if the women dressed and armed themselves as men. Eowain left the ladies to arrange themselves.

"Now, let's have some words with Lord Feoras." Eowain rode with Tnúthgal and Medyr back to the van-guard.

As soldiers will do, many of his soldiers took the opportunity to close eyes and catch up on sleep. Eowain saw enough watchful men to please him and give any lurking bandit pause. Between the men he himself had assigned, the lady's own security detail, and Tnúthgal's men, their company must have numbered some seventy or eighty men.

I'll have to arrange more supplies and mules at our next stop. After Monóc Hill, they'd move north into the kingdom of Ivea, where their welcome would be uncertain at best, and supplies not to be counted on. A pause at Monóc would also give his brother and bodyguard time to catch up.

Lord Feoras was still lashed to his horse.

"Cut him down." Eowain felt grim. Scar-faced Gaeth and barrel-chested Mahon pulled Feoras from the saddle. They lashed him to a nearby tree.

Eowain dismounted.

Medyr and Tnúthgal joined him. Eowain addressed his question to them. "What makes you think Lord Feoras knows so much?"

Medyr considered the silent lord. "He's not a cowardly nor a weak man, Your Grace. He served your father in the King's Company, and he's been no stranger to policing banditry. At least, not until yesterday."

Medyr raised his eyebrows and spread his fingers wide. "When suddenly, poof! Away went his own guards on an insignificant errand. Then the lord absented himself on a pretext."

Eowain regarded Feoras. "Sent away his guards and absented himself on a pretext? Then what?"

Medyr brought the merchant Corentin to recall—in his foreign way— how the hall was suddenly empty save for the acolyte, the Lady Eithne, her father, and himself. "It was the kitchen staff. We were attacked by cooks." The merchant sniffed.

Medyr went on. "Neither the lord nor his men materialized to defend against our attackers. We found him after the fact, locked in a cellar. Two of your men battered down the door with a timber to ferret him out."

Feoras sneered. "I told you, I don't know anything. I was as surprised as you. Three of the bandits tried to jump me. I was unarmed. Locked myself in the cellar, it was all I could do to stay alive."

One of Medyr's brows rose on his forehead. "And when we announced ourselves that all was clear?"

Feoras looked sheepish, studied the ground at his feet. "How was I to know you didn't have a knife to your throat? It could've been a trick."

Eowain nodded. "I see." *Yes, I see right well.* That man had put his bride and his advisor and all his men at risk. All the worry and weariness of the last two days boiled suddenly through his blood. "How..." His throat choked on his words. "How— dare you?" The words hissed out.

Tnúthgal raised a restraining hand. "Your Grace, I would counsel—"

"You will counsel nothing, cousin." Eowain moved closer to Feoras. "Why? Why would you betray me?"

"I—" He seemed to realize the dire strait he was in. He swallowed hard. "I swear, my lord. I— I wouldn't betray you. I didn't betray you." He spat at Medyr. "Anyone who says I did is a villain, and a bastard, and a knave, and a rascal!"

Eowain growled. "I've never known the Lord Medyr to say any untrue word. I ask you again and for the last time, my lord. Why would you betray me?" He pulled a long knife from his belt and held it before Feoras's face. "Next time, I will not ask, but take the answer from your screaming tongue."

His eyes flickered from the knife to Eowain's face to the two men behind him. "I— I—." He swallowed hard. "Please, my lords!"

"Do not look to me," replied Medyr. "I have not so much courage as to defy this king."

"Last chance." Eowain pressed the blade to Feoras's cheek. A long, thin line of blood appeared.

"Be merciful, Your Grace. Abate your rage, I beg of you! Abate your rage!"

"I'll carve half a grin on your sniveling face is what I'll do!" Eowain snapped the dagger across his face, splattered red across the green spring grass.

"My lord!"

Eowain whipped Feoras with the hilt of the dagger, punched him in the stomach with a balled fist. Feoras choked twice and vomited.

Eowain pummeled at the man. He couldn't stop himself, even if he'd wanted to. And he certainly had no such desire.

"My lord!" He blinked once, at the small, gentle hand that restrained his arm. Again, at the fair face, the copper-red hair, the green eyes. "My lord, forgive me. That is enough, I think."

Feoras was a bloody ruin before him. Eithne, in riding clothes and a jack of hardened leather, stayed his hand.

He shuddered, shook his head, turned away from them. Even in war, he had rarely known such a rage. He put hands to his face and pulled down, felt the taut stretch of his own skin. Then he was master of himself once more.

"Alright. Yes." He nodded to them.

Eithne's face was stern. "No doubt he deserves every stroke, Your Grace. But mercy now, and bid him speak."

"Aye. Aye, you're right." He took another steadying breath. He lifted the lord's broken face. "What would you say now?"

The man could naught but whisper. "Cael," he hissed. "Cael the Viper." Feoras spit teeth on the ground. "He'll dog your every step, he said. Dog you til he gets her." Feoras sneered at Eithne. "And then the things he'll do to you, you Fiatach bitch." He grinned drunkenly through bloody teeth. "Wish I could live to see it."

Eowain smacked him. "You will not speak to her. You will not look at her, as you value your life."

He spit blood. "What life? You bastard son of a poxy whore. You'll not let me live."

"How many? How many men does Cael have?"

"More than a hundred. Hard men. Harder than you." He jerked his chin. "And a hard-on for her."

"Where? Where is their camp?"

He hissed at Eowain. "Everywhere." He looked all about. "He's Kârn of the Wood, he is."

"Why? Why would you do this?"

"To keep her damned bastards off our throne." He snarled like a beast at bay. "Do you know how many sons I've lost, suppressing the north? Do you? Five. FIVE! Never trust a Fiatach. Never trust a Gwynn." He spit blood at her.

Eithne's hand went to her face, came away with blood and bile on her fingers. Her eyes narrowed.

In a flash, her dagger with the dark yellow schorl on the hilt was at the lord's throat. Her voice hissed. "Call me what you will. But insult my clan once more, sir, and I'll gut you from nave to chops. In that, my lord, you can most surely trust."

CHAPTER SEVEN

LORD FEORAS WENT silent as a stone thereafter, no matter how threatened. At last, Eowain had the traitor bound and slung indignantly over a mule.

At the thorp of Monóc Hill, Eowain halted their progress for the day. A settlement of some fifty souls, the goodman Cothaid had a hostel there for travelers coming and going through Ivea. It was the last friendly stop they'd make for the next several days.

A shoemaker there did a brisk business with wayfarers. Eowain engaged her to inspect his company's boots and make repairs. Nothing ruined a soldier's morale as quickly as bad boots on a long march.

A bread-maker there specialized in muslin, the hard biscuit of barley, rye, and bean flour that lasted years if kept dry. He expected the company to number more than a hundred and thirty before they left Monóc. He wanted them to be as self-sufficient as possible. To hunt and trade for food on the road would cause delays, without any guarantee they'd find enough to feed the whole company. It was still early in the spring. The Damara bean-crop would have been harvested already, but grains would be young and green. Any farm-produce at all would be hard to come by after Ivea's hard winter. Eowain loaded the company with more biscuit.

The local ostler had a look at their mounts, both the war-steeds and the draft animals. Legs were examined, shoes re-fitted, and a few mounts traded out for better steeds from the ostler's own selection. Eowain wasn't leaving anything to chance if he could help it.

Including Eithne's safety. Good silver put Cothad and his family out of their home and secured the place for the Ladies Rathtyen, Alva, and Eithne, and their two maids. Her warriors and his guarded the thatch-and-daub roundhouse.

Eowain turned Feoras over to the custody of Cothad's constable, to be sent back to Dúnsciath and interred in the tower cellars.

By sunset, Lorcán arrived with the foot-soldiers of the King's Guard. Lorcán had left his best lieutenant to secure Gluín Hill and harass the retreating Cailech-men. The remaining skeleton-crew of the Shield Company would garrison Droma in their absence.

It was well past the dark hour of completion before Eowain finally rested his head. It was well before sunrise when Medyr shook him gently awake. "It's time, Your Grace."

Eowain rubbed the grit from his eyes and pinched the bridge of his nose for a long, long moment. "Aye." He levered himself up from his field cot. A splash of cold water from a basin shocked him awake. Rivulets dribbled through his beard.

"Right." He shook the cobwebs from his mind. "Medyr?"

"Your Grace?" His minister handed him a cloth.

Eowain rubbed away the wash-water. "Do you believe Lord Feoras worked alone with Cael the Viper?"

"I think he's a treacherous bastard and not to be trusted, but no, not for a moment, Your Grace." Medyr shrugged. "Getting him to admit that your cousin encouraged him is another matter. If he fears his master more than he fears you, he'll keep quiet and pray for deliverance. And if his master has some hold over him greater than death, he may be willing to die for his silence."

Wonderful. Eowain took a deep breath and sighed. They went out to rouse the men.

Medyr led the company in the prayerful songs that welcomed the sun-god Grían back from darkness. Then they broke camp just after First Hour and set out again.

They passed the last Droma settlement on the High-King's Road, the hamlet at the hill of Fearnógrinn, just before Third Hour. As they came down the far side of the hill, a broad clearing opened around the High King's Road.

Two spiked timber hedgehogs faced each other over a narrow spit of no-man's land. Ten men in the green, white, and gold tartans of Eowain's Shield Company paced the near side of the blockade with spears, swords, and shields.

Another ten in the gold and azure tartans of the Chremthainn king's own company of warriors paced the far side, similarly accoutered.

Lorcán met with the men at the blockade. It was common practice to assess and collect tolls and tariffs from travelers there. After a few words with the lieutenants on each side, Lorcán returned.

"Two gold trimmids, six silver glynnids, and three bronze drychids for the whole company."

Eowain's brows rose. "That's more expensive than I expected."

Lorcán scowled. "That's what I said. He says his king just raised the rates."

Medyr rubbed his forehead. "Of course he did, knowing we approached, and with a large company."

Tnúthgal snorted. "That's outrageous, we're not common peddlers. Why discuss this? Just march through. They haven't enough men to stop us."

Lorcán glared at him, but replied instead to Eowain. "That'd be an inter-tribal incident, Your Grace. Dafyd would have a right to call us invaders. He only has a single company of the Rogue-Crushers, but it would still be a hard fight. And his cousin would certainly bring their whole battalion down on us. It's a long way from here to the Vale, and all through Rogue-Crusher country."

Tnúthgal shrugged. "If you want to look weak in front of the Chremthainn and let them extort more than their due, Your Grace, that's certainly your prerogative."

He certainly didn't want to look weak, but he was leading a wedding party, not a war-band.

"Pay it." Eowain eyed his cousin. "I suspect we'll have trouble enough on the road, we don't need to buy more by being stingy."

Tnúthgal smiled thinly.

They passed through the checkpoint, with the Rogue-Crusher lieutenant and one of his sergeants counting their company to be sure the proper toll was paid. Eowain left his brother to conclude the transaction.

"It's extortion," muttered Medyr.

"I'll certainly have something to say about it." Eowain had planned to meet with King Dafyd of Ivea anyway. As one of the three kings of the Fiatach tribes, and Droma's only Fiatach neighbor, it would be wise to keep peace with the man.

AS THEY MARCHED through the no-man's land from Droma into Ivea, Eithne imagined the land became more familiar. The people of those lands were related to her own. The mountains loomed closer. Even the air seemed native and ordinary.

Yet for all its homeliness, unease knotted her belly. She was glad of the change of clothes and the jack of stern leather she wore, grateful for the sword at her hip.

But the threat of more banditry, the loathsome regard in which Lord Feoras held her, the insult she'd suffered from the Lady Gluintír, those things worked at her mind. She worried at her lip with her teeth.

"What troubles you, Lady?" The ban-drymyn Alva rode beside her, dark and weathered, and put a hand upon her knee.

Eithne looked about. Eowain and his men rode somewhat ahead with her father. Aside from her own three horsemen, there were none near enough to overhear. "It's just—." She wasn't sure what to say. "Do his people truly hate me so?"

Alva patted her leg. "Not all of them, I wager. But there has long been blood between the Donnghaile and the Gwynn."

"Not with our branch of the Gwynn."

"Our people are far away in the mountains. But it was not so long ago that the Fiatach rose in rebellion against Murdach. The chief of the Donnghaile is also the Lord-Marshall of all the tribes of the East. It was Eowain's father that led the force that suppressed the Gwynn." She shrugged beneath her woolen cloak. "Feoras is certainly not the only father who sent sons to that war." She nodded meaningfully in the direction of Lord Tnúthgal. "Nor the only son who sent a father, I think."

"But that was nigh on twenty years ago. I was barely more than a babe."

She nodded. "Indeed. A great deal of time in which to sharpen a knife. And whatever gave you the notion this was about you, lass?"

She chewed over that, but it did little to ease the fear in her belly. If she married Eowain, would she always fear the knife in the dark, the poison in the cup? Would there be others like Feoras and the Lady Gluintír, with nothing but insults and contempt for her?

By the Sixth Hour of midday, they crested a hill and saw the large village of Midachath ahead. It lay hunched beside the river Gasirad. Smoke rose from the holes in the thatched roofs of modest round-houses. The house of their king hulked over the village, surrounded by a palisade of timbers.

In the fields below, many of the people were drably dressed, while others wore clothes patched and patched again, but always in contrasting colors, so that the patchwork was visible even from a distance. It became a kind of design, leggings and tunics in red and blue, orange and rose. The vivid colors stood out against the dark earth.

She watched a new field being plowed, the black iron blade hauled by two oxen. The ard-plough itself turned the Abred of the furrow neatly on both sides. Behind the plowman, a peasant sowed seed with rhythmic sweeps of his arm. The sack of seed hung from his shoulder. A short distance behind the sower, birds fluttered down to the furrow to eat the seed.

But not for long. In a nearby field, she saw the harrower: a man riding a horse that dragged a wooden T-frame weighted down by a large rock. The harrower closed the furrows and protected the seed.

Most of the fields were already planted, their furrows closed over. The spring planting of barley, peas, oats and beans — the Damaran crops — was nearly finished. Everything moved in the same gentle, steady rhythm: the hand threw the seed, the ard-plough turned the furrow, the harrow scraped the ground. And there was almost no sound in the still noon hour, save the hum of insects and the twitter of birds.

She saw the clear demarcation between the small areas of Mannish habitation—the village and fields—and the surrounding forest, a dense, vast green carpet that stretched away in all directions. In that landscape, the forest predominated. She had the sense of encompassing wilderness, in which Men were interlopers.

And only minor interlopers at that.

The woods around her felt cool. She relaxed to the chatter of birds and the sound of her horse's hooves plodding along on the path. Once she thought she heard something else too. She slowed a bit to listen.

Yes, there it was: a fainter sound, like the rumble of distant thunder. The sky was gray, but surely not threatening.

Then she realized what the rumbling sound was.

Horses.

Riding at full gallop toward her.

Charging up the hill toward them were six horsemen in full armor: steel helmets, chain mail and cloth surcoats of mixed liveries. The horses were draped in black cloth studded with silver. The effect was ominous. The lead rider, wearing a helmet with a black plume, pointed ahead and screamed, "Get her!"

She knew that man with the black plume. "Cael," she whispered. "Cael the Viper."

Two of her foot-men, Blathyen and Goreu stopped beside the path and just stood there, apparently in shock at what they saw galloping toward them. The black rider leaned over in the saddle and swung his broadsword in an arc at Goreu as he rode past.

Eithne saw Goreu's headless torso, spurting blood, as it toppled to the ground. Blathyen, splattered with blood, swore loudly as he ran into the woods. More riders galloped up the hill. They were all shouting, "Get her! Get her!" One rider wheeled on his horse, drawing his bow.

The arrow struck Blathyen's left shoulder as he ran, the steel point punched through the other side, the impact knocked him to his knees. Cursing, Blathyen staggered to his feet again.

An arrow struck him full in the chest. Blathyen looked surprised, coughed, and fell back, sprawled in a seated position against a tree. He made a feeble effort to pull the arrow out of his chest. The next arrow passed through his throat.

On the High King's Road, horses reared and whinnied, their riders wheeled in circles, shouted and pointed. The mixed tartans mingled among the black, red, and gold of her own guards. Swords and spears flashed and clanged. All along their line of march, men howled and leaped from the brush.

Eithne drew her sword and reined her horse around. Her three horsemen closed ranks around her and the ban-drymyn. She saw the young merchant, broadsword in hand. He slashed and parried at their attackers. *"Flôkan zhee!* Pelan!"

There too was the young acolyte. He clubbed one man with the knob of his blackthorn stick, then leaped in to parry a stroke intended for the merchant's unguarded left.

Beside her, Lady Alva shouted in the Old Tongue: *"Bánwærc! Blædderwærc! Bréostwærc! Cláwung-gást, myndgath!"*

The acolyte turned and stared round-eyed at Alva.

Eithne felt a shiver in her bones, her breast, her groin. A handful of their attackers clutched at themselves, shrieked in agony, and fell writhing to the ground.

The riders then had looks of fear on their faces. The black-plumed rider shouted something to the others, and as a group, they whipped their horses and raced down the hill, out of sight.

As the black rider turned to go, his horse stumbled over Goreu's body. Cursing, the rider wheeled and reared his horse repeatedly, stomping the body again and again. Blood flew in the air. The horse's forelegs turned dark red. At last, the black rider turned and, with a final curse, galloped up the hill to rejoin the others.

From the van of their company, she heard more thunder. Eowain and his five riders raked across the line of assault, cutting men aside. He reared his gelding before her and spared a grim look in her direction.

Only once before had she seen him arrayed for battle thus. Broad-shouldered as the bear, with the river-salmon emblem of his clan etched into his stiff leather epaulets, its curvilinear design chased with silver

filigree. His green, gold, and white tartan cape fluttered behind him. His
sword gleamed in the waning light of day.

Eowain and his men brought their steeds about, and added another
line of defense between her and the ambush.

But I can fight! The surprise was gone, and fury burned through her.
She was no straw-doll. She spurred at her horse, but Alva seized the bridle
and held her steed with surprising strength. The animal stamped its feet
and sidled.

"Ætstende!" Alva's command was firm. "Stay here!"

Despite herself, Eithne reined the horse back.

Eowain and his men, with a shout, charged after the riders. Her throat
clutched with fear for him.

All along the line, their attackers fell back and scattered into the wood.
The men of Droma and Dolgallu jeered their courage.

Eithne gritted her teeth, angry to be held back from the fray. Her
heart pounded in her breast. Fear and excitement struggled within her. *If
this is how it will be, let them bring their worst. I will not be cowed by these brigands like some
homely goodwife.*

Yet despite her rage, she sat impotent upon her horse, held by the
power of the ban-drymyn's word.

Before long, Eowain returned, blood splattered across his tunic and
his cheek-guards. He reined his horse in and regarded her with knitted
brows. "Lady? You are well?"

Beside her, Eithne heard the ban-drymyn whisper, *"Álæte."*

Eithne felt as if a great tension had been released. Scowling at the
ban-drymyn, she nudged her horse forward. "Aye, Your Grace. They did
not get within a spear's thrust."

Lorcán returned with the rest of Eowain's men. "We rode down
a few, but the rest are scattered." Around her, Eithne sensed her
men breathe easier. They moved their horses away, gave her and the
ban-drymyn more room. But they did not sheath their weapons, nor
relax their vigilance.

✝

TNÚTHGAL LEANED BACK on the cushions and took a long draught of *ôl*. The bitterness rankled at his nose. *The men of Ivea brew piss,* he grumbled to himself. He preferred honest Droma spirits. He watched his young cousin debase himself before the Ivean king.

The roundhouse of King Dafyd was large, the wooden timbers black with years of soot. The logs in the fire-pit roared high and crisped the flesh of a mountain ram.

The succulent smell made Tnúthgal's stomach growl with anticipation. He'd had nothing but biscuit soaked in water all day. Not unusual fare for a soldier in the field, but it had been three years since his last campaign. Three years since his cousin Findtan's ill-advised rebellion against Murdach of Aileach.

And what did that gain us? Tnúthgal knew it was very little, if anything. Eowain's father had wounded King Murdach and forced his abdication and exile in favor of the usurper, Domnall of Itha. But Murdach was an ambitious man, and not one to accept exile with complacency. Last year, he'd come back into power with a vengeance, put Domnall where he belonged, and settled his past grievance against Droma.

Of course, Findtan was dead by then, and beyond the reach of vengeance. His fool son Lorcán had taken his place, with the support of Findtan's sister and the Lord-Drymyn, and Murdach had limited his revenge to a hefty tribute that had impoverished the men of Droma.

Tnúthgal's stomach growled again. He hadn't realized how accustomed he'd become to three good meals a day, served hot. He grit his back teeth and picked from a plate of cold ham by his side. The smothering of herbs did little to disguise the rank taste. The ham was old, and smoking hadn't done it much good.

Eowain and Lorcán jested with the Ivean king. Tnúthgal thought it unseemly, the way they curried his favor in hope of peace. *How can there be peace between our peoples, after all the centuries of blood?* Tnúthgal wiped his mouth with the back of his arm.

The Lady Eithne looked at him over the fire with her unsettling green eyes. She had the look of hardship and famine about her, for all her pretenses to health and strength. She was as pale as snow, with rose-red lips and copper hair burnished by the firelight. Her long, lean face reminded him of a mountain wolf in winter, hollow and remorseless. The look of a thing that had starved once too often.

He sneered at her and looked away. *I'll not be cowed by a mere woman.* He took another long draught of his *ól* and silently cursed at the incompetence of Cael the Viper. The bandit chief had failed to seize that damnable woman yet again.

Fool. Tnúthgal wasn't sure whether he cursed the bandit-chief or himself.

Tnúthgal rose to his feet and stepped between and over the Fiatach-men about him. He pushed two men out of his way. They glared at him. The old hatreds were sharp.

Tnúthgal squared his shoulders, looked down his nose at them. Muttering, they slunk away.

Smugly satisfied, Tnúthgal went on to the board and poured more *ól* for himself from a pewter flagon there.

He'd lived to regret his decision to ally with Cael. Cael's failure through the winter to discredit Lorcán and defeat Eowain in the field had allowed Eowain to ride popular acclaim to the throne. While the bandit had since had some success harassing trade, terrorizing farmers, and abducting children, it wasn't nearly enough.

He glanced back at Eithne. If Eowain was permitted to marry that woman, he'd settle the old feud with Ivearda and secure a measure of watchful peace with the Cailech. He'd give the people hope for an heir and a dynasty of Eowain's own.

More laughter from across the fire rankled his thoughts. *And if he makes peace with Ivea into the bargain?* He drank again. Eowain would be that much more difficult to pry loose from the throne. Tnúthgal would have lost his best chance to secure the succession for himself and his own sons.

He stroked his beard. Eowain was no fool. Tnúthgal was watched, he knew. If not by Lorcán or the Lord-Drymyn, then by any of a dozen other men loyal to his cousin.

How can I coordinate Cael's efforts if I can't get messages to the damned man? He had less than a score of his own men with him. No doubt they too were watched.

Caerrhythrs, his chamberlain, stepped up to him, begged pardon. There was some matter with the horses. Tnúthgal waved him away to deal with it however he saw fit.

Then he turned to watch the man as he left.

And what of Caerrhythrs? Could his chamberlain sneak away to deliver a message to Cael?

Tnúthgal frowned. *Could Caerrhythrs even find the bandit?* He had no skill at woodcraft that Tnúthgal knew. *And if Caerrhythrs is intercepted? Would his tongue remain loyal?*

No. Tnúthgal had been fortunate in choosing Lord Feoras for his plan. The man's stubbornness and loyalty to Tnúthgal was beyond question. They'd both served in the north in their younger days, and lost kin to the Fiatach. They both believed in the old ways. He knew he could count on Feoras to keep silent.

But Caerrhythrs? He was loyal, Tnúthgal knew, but how far would loyalty carry anyone through torture? Eowain's rage at Feoras had been blind and furious. Tnúthgal doubted Caerrhythrs could bear up under such bearish brutality.

Tnúthgal made his way back to his place and sat once more. He sipped at his *ôl*.

So if there's no way to get a message to Cael, I'll have to take matters into my own hands, create my own opportunities. Abducting Eithne was the best of all possible outcomes, for her ransom would fetch a pretty glynnid and make Eowain look weak into the bargain. But a knife between her ribs would do the job just as well.

Eithne smiled disarmingly and laughed with King Dafyd. She made merry and played the role of help-meet and peacemaker, as befitted a virtuous lady and a queen.

It's a shame, really, he thought. With those breasts and hips, no doubt she would bear strong sons. Tnúthgal adjusted his seat to relieve the pressure of his breeches. *A shame indeed, really.* He entertained thoughts of her, bent before him and all unwilling. He would wipe that impertinence off her face, sure and Annwn if he wouldn't.

CHAPTER EIGHT

EITHNE STEPPED DOWN from her horse. The mossy turf beneath her feet was springy.

The company had marched north from Midachath with the blessing of King Dafyd just an hour after sunrise and the morning orisons. The High King's Road rose along the riverside through the Gasirad valley, higher and higher into the foothills.

By midmorning, the countryside had changed noticeably. Leafy green trees gradually mixed with then gave way to gnarled pines. Her breath began to mist before her. But though the sun struggled through ominous clouds above them and no breeze stirred the damp air, neither rain nor snow disturbed their day.

They'd passed through the small village of Attabaile shortly before the Sixth Hour of prayer. Eowain took advantage of local craftsmen to trade for freshly smoked and salted meats, fresh breads, maintenance on their horses' shoes, and repairs to some of the mens' boots.

He'd also spent a small fortune on furs to combat the fresh chill in the air. She pulled her new ermine cloak tight about her shoulders. Her maids similarly appreciated their own more common hare capes. Breda rubbed the fur against her arm as she came to Eithne with a flask of small beer. "He's a very thoughtful lord, my lady."

"Is he?" She thought so too. It had been kind of him to consider her maids' comfort.

Breda nodded as Eithne took the flask and sipped from it. "Oh, aye, my lady." She stole a glance across their camp.

Eowain ordered some men to rest and others to watch. It was then the Ninth Hour for prayers, midafternoon and a good opportunity to rest the men and horses once more, while the drymyn made ready for the company's prayerful obligations.

Breda raised an eyebrow at the figure Eowain cut moving among the men. "I wonder how far his thoughtfulness extends in... other matters?"

Eithne pursed her lips around a mouthful of beer and looked at him herself. "Hrmmm." The broad shoulders, the strong arms. His bearded face, soft but scratchy on her cheek. The angle of his cheekbones. The smell of leather and sweat when she was near to him. His uneven and drooping lips, the bottom full and rich, chapped and bitten in the spring weather. He'd dropped a kiss upon her twice. On her cheek, a spot of heat near the corner of her mouth, where a kiss might hide in her smile—if she dared allow herself that dangerous, inviting smile. Those wide, rough hands on her...

Heat rose in her face. She swallowed and handed back the skin. "Er, yes." She pulled up her fur-lined hood, mindful of her discretion. "There is—I suppose—that to consider."

The maid took back the skin with a nod of the head. "Yes, my lady." She gave Eithne a wink and a wry smile.

Eithne couldn't resist and returned the smile. "Yes, well." She composed herself. "So long as we're resting, I should make water. You'll inform Lieutenant Piran?"

Breda curtsied, and within a few moments, Eithne's three horsemen and two maids made their way off into the trees for a discrete place away from any lecherous soldiers' sight.

Her father had chosen his men well. She'd already traveled many days and nights with them, and she knew their honor well. They took up positions at a discrete distance.

She and her maidens tidied up. Eithne stretched the saddle-soreness from her back and shoulders, twisted from side to side and felt as much as heard bones crackle through her spine. The day's journey had been a long one, but pleasant enough, with the chirp of birds and whir of insects to accompany them. She took a long breath of air, listened once more for those pleasing forest noises.

And cocked her head to one side. *Where is the bird-song?*

She made a sharp gesture to her maids, stretching their own muscles and giggling quietly together. They went quiet.

She hadn't imagined it. The birds had gone quiet.

In a terse whisper, she told them, "Now. Slowly. Back to the company."

Their eyes widened. They looked about, but did as they were bid. Eithne looked for her men. They'd taken up position at the points of a triangle, with their backs to her, spears and shields held ready in their hands.

She whistled, low and urgent, to Piran, the horseman at the northeast point of the triangle. His helmed head swiveled toward her. Before she made any gesture, the baying of dogs erupted from the veil of pines.

"Run!" Eithne's command spurred her maids into motion.

Piran jerked around and brought up his shield. A huge, beastly pack of hounds bounded from the trees.

"Go!" His shout echoed as the first hound crashed into his shield and drove him from his feet. Before he could throw it off, another beast had his arm in its jaws.

Eithne reached for her blade and cursed. It was hanging from the pommel of her horse. She pulled loose the dagger decorated with the dark yellow schorl on the hilt and backed away.

The guard at the southeastern point of her triangle hurdled rocks and brush in his haste. "Run, my lady! Back to the company!"

Three more hounds ran him down. One seized his leg and he fell. The other two beasts came after her.

Her third guard seized her arm and pulled her around. "Now!" He pushed her toward the company and placed himself between her and the oncoming danger.

Little use I am with a belt knife. She cursed her carelessness and ran. *At least I'm not in damned skirts.*

She hurdled to the top of a rock in her path, caught purchase with booted feet, and leaped toward the camp. It was no more than fifty yards, she could make that distance in just a few seconds.

Ahead, her maids screamed for help. None of them had any better weapon than she, but Eithne'd made sure they, too, were dressed and shod sensibly, in leather jacks, breeks, and boots.

Then Breda's hare-cape caught on a branch and jerked her half-around.

From out of the pines to Eithne's right, three more hounds bounded. Breda shrieked and threw up her hands.

The lead dog struck Breda full in the chest. Foam spewed as it shook its head. Together, they tumbled into the duff of fallen leaves, bark, needles, twigs, and fallen branches.

Ahead, the ground rose toward the road. Cunneen scrambled up the slope into the waiting arms of Adarc the acolyte. Five more men, with swords, maces, and shields, bounded down the slope toward her. Another three, and the merchant Corentin, scrambled through the forest-wrack toward Breda.

Eithne ran as hard as she could. Blood and panic thundered in her ears. *Don't look back.* She could hear the expectant snarls of the hounds behind her, could see the slaver on the jaws that rushed her from the right.

Cold realization went through her mind. *I'm not going to make it.*

Above her, at the crest of the slope, Alva Damar appeared. Her arms rose and she howled to the sky.

The hounds skidded to a halt, growled and faced up-slope.

Eithne didn't stop to wonder why. She broke left, away from the beasts. Her men shouted at her to keep on. They slid across the fallen leaves to bring shields up between her and the dogs.

Archers appeared then at the crest, and Eowain himself charged down the hill with spear and sword. Arrows hummed through the branches.

Eithne ran, as hard as her legs would carry her.

Eowain stood over the hard-panting beast. Its flanks were feathered with arrows, yet still it lived. He raised his father's spear and put it through the beast's heart.

Eithne was glad for that mercy. No animal should have to suffer in death, even one that had so recently been intent on her life. Three of the beasts had turned and fled when a horn blasted recall through the branches.

Eowain's warriors went through the glade and put down the others. Two of her guards were sore wounded, but would live. *Thank Gods for small blessings.* She stopped beside Eowain and looked down on the body as he pulled the spear loose.

It was a massive beast, easily eight or nine stone in weight, heavier than many a young boy. It wore a thin coat of studded leather, and a spiked collar around its neck.

Eowain spoke her own thoughts. "These aren't feral curs." He scanned the forest for some clue to their masters.

Beside the hound lay Breda. Her eyes were wide and staring, her face a rictus of horror, her bloody throat torn open.

Eithne felt her jaw tighten as she looked away into the looming wood all about her. Her jaw clenched so hard, her back teeth hurt. "Wherever you are," she whispered, "by the Gods, I'll have the eyes from your head, Cael. I swear it."

Eowain looked at the maid at their feet, then at Eithne. Their eyes locked. His face was grim as he nodded. "You have my oath upon it."

She remembered one of the letters he'd written to her. *I have no gift for clever declarations. Only blunt oaths, which I never use till urged, and never break for urging.*

"My oath upon it," he said again. And she nodded to him, for she could see he meant it.

EOWAIN'S COMPANY MADE the village of Doba just as the sun set. The people were grim and sullen. They eyed the men of Droma with suspicion. The local chieftain welcomed them sourly, but offered what little he had in hospitality to the worthies of their company.

Eowain was glad enough he and his company were not spurned. His men settled on the pasture set aside for large companies. Eowain, Eithne, her father, his brother, and Tnúthgal dined on a spare meal with the chieftain.

Eithne had been rigid and silent since the assault of the war-dogs. The death of her maid weighed heavy on her, he could see that, but Eowain knew not how to comfort her. Men died in the field, from accident and injury, disease and misadventure. Sometimes, even in battle.

It was expected even. And a man could look forward to rebirth in Tirn Aill, the Other Land, a shynn-land of feasting and endless summer harvests, and a short happy life there with kith and kin, before returning to Abred once more to continue their progress toward the final peace of Ceugant. This was known.

He had known this since he began training with weapons at eight. He had known it when his father presented him his first spear and sword.

But he had only *learned* it on the battlefield. He'd lost count of how much death he'd seen. It was never easy, to watch a Man die.

So he understood how Eithne must have felt, to see her maid murdered by dogs. He just didn't know what, or how, to tell her. It was too personal a grief on which to intrude.

The chieftain spoke of recent days on the trail ahead that skirted the mountains from Doba to Maraydanayd. Banditry. Thorps looted and burnt. Granaries and local small merchants robbed.

Eowain was hardly surprised. Cael's men certainly wouldn't pass up chances for easy loot.

In the morning, after the sunrise orisons and the First Hour's prayers, Eowain ordered his company forward. They turned off the High-King's Road there, onto a trail that trended east by southeast. The way was less well-maintained, rutted with holes and rocks. The hills were difficult for his aunt's house-wagon. With each bump and jolt, her shrieks of dismay could be heard up and down the line.

Eowain's chest was tight, his jaw sore from gritting his molars over every delay and hindrance.

Medyr offered him a smoldering clay pipe of linden leaf. "You look like you need it, Your Grace."

He certainly wanted it, but not the mind-mazing effects that came with it. "Thanks, no. I should stay clear-headed." The pleasant, burnt mulch smell would have to be enough.

The company followed the winding trail up and down hills and around trees, through the Third Hour of morning, and then past the Sixth Hour of midday. As Ninth Hour approached, Eowain expected to find a fork in the trail.

Ahead, one of Eowain's outriders raised a fist and called for a halt. Lorcán, at his other side, also raised his fist, and Eowain heard the word, "Halt!" repeated through their column.

"Now what's the trouble?" Eowain looked to his brother.

Lorcán watched the outriders carefully, brow furrowed. "Better to be safe than sorry, little brother." One of the men made a gesture, requesting guidance. Eowain and Lorcán spurred their mounts forward.

Ahead of the outriders, the trail sloped downhill, then wound through a low place between scattered copses of trees. On the other side, another small hill rose. From his vantage point, Eowain could see a gang of men and horses gathered on that opposite hill, some five or six hundred yards distant. Their hill overlooked the fork in the trail he'd anticipated.

"Men of Ivea?" Eowain squinted to get a better look at them.

Lorcán grimaced and shook his head. "They're not flying Ivean colors. They're not flying any colors at all. The few tartans I can see are a patchwork of Cailech and Narada, but most aren't wearing any tartans at all."

"Bandits?" Eowain was confused. "Why would they arrange themselves for battle? And why so few? If it's Cael the Viper, he must surely know the size of our company. They can't have more than a score of men over there."

Lorcán tallied. "Twenty-two, actually. Ten a-horse, the rest a-foot." He tugged at his beard.

Realization dawned on Eowain. "They don't know which branch of the trail we intend to take." He pointed ahead and to the right. "That way lies Maraydanayd." It was the last Ivean village on the trail before they passed into the borderlands between Cailech, Celtair, and Ivearda. To stop at Maraydanayd meant breaking their day's journey early, but sleeping more securely.

Then he pointed to the left. "That way bypasses it." To take the bypass would mean camping in the wild, a prospect Eowain didn't relish, but it would cast doubt on the eventual location of their night's camp.

Lorcán nodded. "And it could be a diversion. Perhaps they have more men in hiding?" He gestured and two groups of footmen from Eowain's guard broke off and melted into the trees to either side of the trail.

Eowain considered the field ahead, with its scattered pine trees. "Or they mean to pick us apart, wear down our morale." He pointed to several places where the trees grew thick. "If I'm him, I have dead-falls or archers hidden there, and there. Maybe there. And over there."

Lorcán tugged at his beard again. "The trees will break up any cavalry charge."

"Unless we send cavalry there. See that corridor through the trees."

"Aye." Lorcan pointed with the two fingers of his left hand. "He's had time to prepare the field. He may have dug leg-breaks along that way, to cripple horses and break our charge."

Eowain nodded. "Like at the thorp of Maladarach."

He remembered that day in the winter too well, when he'd tried to surprise a suspected camp of Cael's men. The surprise had been on him. Snipers and hidden traps had picked his advance apart and slowed his men down, while the bandits withdrew without ever engaging hand-to-hand.

Lorcán looked at the position of the sun. "While we puzzle out this riddle, the sun proceeds a-pace. We have maybe five more hours of daylight."

They left their outriders to watch the bandits, then rode back to the company. Eithne and her father, Medyr, Alva, and Tnúthgal awaited them at the fore of the column.

"What is it?" Eithne had her sword bare, lying across her pommel.

"A blockade of Cael's men." Eowain made a trifling gesture. "Not many of them, that we can see. It's what I can't see that concerns me." He looked to her father. "You'll take your men and support my own in a cordon around my aunt's wagon. Your daughter and the Lady Alva will be safe in the wagon."

"No." Eithne's voice was firm, her green eyes sharp. "I'll not hide from this villain. I swore I'd have the eyes from him, for Breda's sake."

"Eithne, be—"

"No, Father. I'll not 'be reasonable.' I'll not allow others to bear the

risk. I'll not cower like some scullery-wench while they bleed for me."
There was a catch in her voice, and she swallowed hardly. "They killed
Breda." Her eyes narrowed and stared, as if at something a thousand
yards distant.

Eowain had seen that look in many a man. Men who'd seen comrades
cut down in battle. Men who'd seen much in the way of horror and cruelty.

"They killed Breda," she went on. "They'll hang. Every damned one
of them."

Eowain started to protest, but there was steel in her voice. "Do not
take my father's part in this quarrel, Your Grace. You may find yourself in
want of a bride at the end of it."

He stiffened. Lorcán beside him looked down and away.

She pointed over the hill. "Don't you both see? Cael seeks to divide
us." She shook her head. "If I'm to be consort to the King of Droma, then
I stand with the men of Droma. I stand with you, Eowain." She put a fist to
her hip. "And if not, then Annwn take you all, and damn your schemes."

Red anger rose in his gorge. "See here—"

"See what, Your Grace?" Her tone was insolent. Her green eyes
flashed at him.

Eowain felt his heart grow cold. "You would hold our wedding
hostage?"

She held her head high and jutted her chin out and up, exposing her
neck. Her breast-bone rose, her chest and shoulders widened. "I would
not put anyone else to a hazard I would not face myself." She crossed her
arms and clenched her fists.

Her father glanced at him, then he too looked down and away. Medyr
put a hand to his mouth and pulled at his cheeks.

Eowain struggled with the feelings that swept over him. Anger. Frustration.
He put one hand on the pommel of his saddle and gripped his wrist with the
other hand. She defied him in front of his men. And he felt— surprised. His
eyebrows rose. Then his chin. *She's no wilting flower, this one.* He nodded slowly,
looked down and to the right. *How would I feel if Lorcán had been murdered by dogs?*

He tilted his head and considered her again.

"Your Grace!" Eowain's scouts returned with their report.

Heavy forest and rugged hills to either side of the trail, but no sign of more bandits.

He looked to Lorcán. "Do we put Tnúthgal's men at the vanguard?"

Lorcán tugged at his beard. "If he's truly in league with Cael, can we trust that his men will actually clear any traps, or draw out any hidden bandits?"

Eowain saw his point. "Let the point-man pass and draw the rest of the column into the kill-zone."

Lorcán shrugged. "That is the first rule of ambush. If we know anything about Cael, it's that he's skilled at ambush."

"But do we really want Tnúthgal at our rear?"

His brother nodded to Eithne's father. "We could put Lord Ciaran's men—and Eithne—behind him? She wants to be in the fight, but there's no reason she can't be at the back of the fight."

Eowain considered that. All of Tnúthgal's men were a-foot, according to the best infantry traditions of their people. Tnúthgal's only concession to the new cavalry tactics that Eowain's father had introduced was that he himself rode a-horse on long journeys, rather than in a chariot. Without his chariot, Tnúthgal would be fighting a-foot.

So the three horsemen and fifteen foot-soldiers of the Gwynn would hem Tnúthgal's troops between the two lines? He nodded to himself.

"Well? What will it be, Your Grace?" Insolence crept into Eithne's tone.

I will regret this later, no doubt. Eowain took Lord Ciaran and Eithne aside. "I admire that you want to fight with us, my lady, but if Cael's men seize you from the field, or Gods forbid something worse happens, then all is lost. With you at our rear, you will be safer, and act as a knife at Tnúthgal's back, if needful. He will perhaps think twice about treachery."

"I do not like this idea of keeping me at arm's length from enemies that are surely mine as much as yours." Eithne glanced at Tnúthgal, organizing his own men. "But I see your point. I like him at my back less than I like Cael at my front."

"Good. We must hurry. Sunset is drawing near."

By Ninth Hour, their order of battle was arranged. Eowain left a score of guards around the mules and Rathtyen's wagon and brought up the rest of his men. Fourteen footmen with shields, spears, and swords, tramped to the advance in loose formation and tested the ground for traps as they went.

Behind them went the sixteen men of his personal guard, elite warriors all with ring-mail coats, shields, and swords. Another ten footmen with bows and axes would follow, also in loose formation, to support them.

Tnúthgal's sixteen men, with spears, slings, swords, and daggers, would follow behind, then wrap around the enemy's flanks if they stood to fight, or skirmish with undiscovered ambushers.

At least, that's what I hope they're prepared to do, thought Eowain.

He dismounted his eight cavalry scouts, armed with bows and swords, and ordered them to advance on foot along the corridor among the trees. They would test for horse-traps. Once they'd cleared or marked the way, Lorcán, holding the heavier horse in reserve, could decide whether to send cavalry through to flank the bandits.

Lord Ciaran, Eithne, and their eighteen warriors would follow Tnúthgal's men, to keep them honest. Medyr and Alva remained with Lorcán and the reserves on the hill, to say whatever prayers seemed appropriate.

"But the Gods," Medyr reminded him, "They are forgetful."

Eowain himself would lead his men against Cael. If Gods or fortune favored him, there'd be an end to this once and for all.

With that in mind, Eowain invited Tnúthgal to join him at the point of their vanguard.

His lines thus drawn, Eowain nodded to the banner-man beside him. Up went the green and gold banner with the white river salmon of the Donnghaile clan. The banner-man waved it side to side in the still air, signal to friend and foe-man alike that the advance had begun. Sergeants cried out to their squads to look lively, and Eowain took the first step, with his cousin beside him.

They marched down-hill into the scattered trees. Eowain remembered something his father had once told him: *You and your cousins against the world. You and your brother against your cousins.*

His brother, who commanded the cavalry reserve behind him. His brother, who'd been forced to abdicate a throne he'd held so dear. The throne to which Eowain himself had succeeded. *How far can I really trust my brother?*

Uncertainty gnawed at his gut as they came down off the hill into the trees.

CHAPTER NINE

TNÚTHGAL RAISED HIS shield and hefted his spear.

Within moments of descending the hill, the bolts flew. Ten yards to his left, his cousin shouted imprecations against Cael's cowardice. Tnúthgal had to admit, such craven tactics rubbed him the wrong way as well. Warriors should meet one another in open battle, man to man. This bandit's tactics rankled his honor.

His cousin did as well. Tnúthgal knew Eowain suspected him of treachery, despite the care he'd taken. Eowain had put him deliberately into harm's way on the front line. By keeping him on Eowain's right, he'd made himself Tnuthgal's own shield-man, defending Tnúthgal's left flank. If Eowain himself had treachery in mind, it would be easy enough to make good on it.

The bandit arrows came in threes and sixes from the thick copses of trees, and then there was a hare-scramble as the archers and crossbowmen fell back on new positions.

Eowain's men made a harrowing advance through snares and dead-falls. Men screamed as they stepped into shallow, barbed pits. Spiked logs swung from trees and impaled the unwary.

All this over a woman. Tnúthgal grimaced as a spiked branch lashed out over his head. He'd been thinking often of her since the night at King Dafyd's hall. Of what he'd do with her if he made a hostage of her. She'd make a good wife, he'd come to realize. His chief wife had already given him heirs. She was pregnant already with their next. But she hadn't brought property or cattle or trade rights with her. She'd cost his father a pretty glynnid for a bride-price, in fact.

Yet behind him then was Eithne, with cattle and fur-trade, and the key to a stalemate with the Gwynn. A stalemate in which the Cailech could still be quelled for a time. And with the income due from her estate, he could fund a war-effort against the Gruin-men, before they dared cross the river into Droma.

And there was that red hair. And that insolent look. Those hateful and shynn-like green eyes. He'd enjoy breaking her to the marriage bed as a second wife.

Then it was arrows again in threes and sixes. Men screamed as arms, legs, shoulders and shields were feathered. Their own archers in the rear unleashed volleys into the trees, but the odds of striking a target were short. The bandits used the thickest copses for their hunting blinds, and picked at the men of Droma as if they were hares in a meadow. The bandits fell back again.

Tnúthgal picked his way through another copse of pines. He tested every step with his spear, scanned with his eyes for trip-wires.

Down the line, branches adorned with daggers snapped loose from their moorings and slashed a man's arm to ribbons.

Another man cried out. As a bent sapling stood abruptly straight, he was dragged through the underbrush and hoisted up into the air. Thrashing in plain sight, he was an easy target for a handful of bandit's bolts, and died before any could cut him down.

As they came out of the trees again, they were met with more arrows. Several thudded against Tnúthgal's shield, their points splintering through to his side. He cursed all his Gods. *Damn it, Cael! I paid for those arrows!* He appreciated the sport of being caught in a fart of his own engineering not at all. *Aim to my left, damn you!*

Beside him, Eowain trotted ahead over the open ground. He took bolts of his own, but to no avail against his cunning shield-work. Tnúthgal thought of the days, long ago, when he and Eowain's father had still been friendly. He'd taught shield-play to the young boy and his brother. *I did my kinsman's duty too well.*

Then again, the hare-scramble ahead of them as the archers fell back from their blinds. Tnúthgal glanced right and left. Their line had staggered as some men met trees while others still had open ground. "Hold the line!" The old soldier in him scolded the men to discipline, despite his hope that Cael had some better plan than this to put Eowain in his grave.

The snicker of a wire snapped loose. Tnúthgal crouched behind his shield as knife-adorned pine branches slashed over his head. He slashed them loose with the blade of his spear and forced his way through the thick bracken, alert for more traps.

There was a blast of horns somewhere ahead. "Cavalry." The thought was sour on his tongue. He crashed through the pine branches and dropped down as arrows came out of the trees some twenty yards ahead.

He'd lost sight of the line of men on his right, screened as they were by trees. To his left and ahead of him was Eowain, then three more men and another screening line of trees. Ahead, more pines crossed their path. He was alone in a box with Eowain and just those other three men. With his hated cousin's right flank exposed. And Cael's cavalry coming.

From the trees ahead, branches and leaves snapped away. Cael himself with a flying squad of horsemen broke into view. They shouted, spurred horses, and lowered spears.

Eowain crouched and set his spear to meet the onslaught.

Tnúthgal rose. With all his strength, he threw his spear at his cousin's exposed back.

FROM A COPSE of trees to his left, the lead rider, with his black-plumed helmet, raised his shield, pointed with his spear and screamed. Five more horsemen in steel helmets, chain mail shirts, and tatterdemalion surcoats charged toward him.

Still more riders galloped from the trees.

Eowain drove the bronze-capped butt end of his spear into the soft, pine-coated soil. "Set spears!" He dropped down on it with his knee, levered the point up to receive the charge, and raised his shield.

The cavalry charge thundered down on him. The black-plumed rider swerved at the last moment. His horse whinnied in protest.

Like a hammer, something thudded into Eowain's back. It drove the wind from him. He lurched forward. The second horse in the charge reared up, impaled on the blade of his father's spear. That shock drove him back. Another blade shuddered his left arm as third rider tried to overreach his shield.

Steeds thundered past and kicked up clods of mud. His personal guard howled from the trees behind him, straight into the bandit's mounts.

Eowain staggered backward to his feet, away from the hooves of the screaming horse. The spear of Eowain's father, sturdy ash, had held firm. Eowain yanked it free of horse's chest, turned it around in his grasp and surveyed the situation.

The horse's rider had broken his spear on Eowain's shield and been unseated in the tumult.

The horsemen with crossbows desperately reloaded their weapons. Two of Eowain's men on the left were down, one with a bolt in his leg, another with his head smashed under horses' hooves. Two more of the bandit riders were down. The cavalry charge had carried the bandits rearing into the teeth of Eowain's second line of hard-bitten guard. He could hear them cry, "To the King!" as they slashed at the bandit riders. Eowain's third line, the archers, took advantage of the short range and the rider's elevation over the heads of their fellows. A volley of arrows buzzed from the trees like a hive of hornets.

The riders, in a swelter of confusion, reared and wheeled their horses, slashed about them with hastily-drawn swords. The black-plumed rider knew his bloody work well and laid about him with his sword, then reared his horse to strike with hooves, and spurred the beast loose from the mêlèe.

On the ground beside him lay Tnúthgal's spear, the blade coated in blood. Tnúthgal was nowhere to be seen.

Eowain hefted his shield and winced. His left shoulder felt as if he'd been struck by a mallet. He looked again at Tnúthgal's spear. *My blood,* he realized. *The bastard tried to spear me in the back.*

The rider he'd brought down staggered to his feet, drew his sword. Eowain ran the man through the gut and snarled his rage into his wide, round eyes.

A shout arose. More bandits came out of the wood on foot and shook spears and swords at the men of Droma.

The black-plumed rider retreated to his own men as Eowain's guard fought past the bandit's horsemen. Scar-faced Gaeth and barrel-chested Mahon, with three more of Eowain's men, formed a battle square around him.

Eowain's archers came out of the trees in a sudden hurry, shouting. Several had their bloodied swords in their hands, as if they fought a withdrawal.

The cold realization of treachery dawned on him. *Tnúthgal's men.* Eowain had arranged them behind his archers. "To me!" His shout rallied the archers. Men in Tnúthgal's livery, the river salmon surmounted by an upturned crescent, came out of the trees.

And there was Tnúthgal, in their lead.

He found Eowain on the field, cursed, and charged toward him with a handful of men.

Across the small clearing, the bandits too howled and charged.

"Defend the King!"

"Nay! Tnúthgal is mine!" Eowain exchanged spear for sword and sprang from his surrounding men like an outraged bear from its den.

Tnúthgal roared, spittle flew from his mouth. They crashed together. He parried aside Eowain's blow with his shield. His blade laid Eowain's right arm open.

Stupid. Eowain cursed himself. His cousin was no stranger to war. *Think, damn it.*

They parried, thrust, feinted, and slashed. Eowain's sword rang from his cousin's helmet. The point of his cousin's sword stabbed against his jack of steel-ringed leather, then cut down and slashed at his right leg. Eowain sliced his cousin across the forearm.

"You never should have crowned yourself." Tnúthgal bounced on the balls of his feet, feinted, and grinned as Eowain flinched. "You and your brother, you die here. Today."

Eowain turned as if to attack, then turned again. Tnúthgal stepped away from the thrust, then swung. Eowain parried it away with the flat of his blade and punched with his shield. His cousin knocked the punch away and came in for a thrust.

Eowain stepped aside, then leaped and stabbed. The point of his blade found its mark in Tnúthgal's shoulder.

On they went, thrust and parry, blade screeching from blade, shields clashing. Tnúthgal landed a swing against his back. Eowain sliced his cousin's thigh, then rang the bell of his helmet again.

Eowain saw his own men had the better of the bandit's and his cousin's men, despite being out-numbered. From north and south, more of Eowain's and Tnúthgal's men were coming through the trees to join the fray. Confusion reigned when they found their fellow-men had turned blades and spears on each other.

With a rush, Tnúthgal's slingers and spearmen broke from the trees. Her father and their horsemen, with her footmen behind, followed her with a roar. And Eithne, spear red with blood, chestnut steed lathered and frothing, drove Tnúthgal's men into the glade.

He caught a glimpse of red hair, and felt his blood chill at the ban-shynn keen of her battle cry—then conjured his veins to a heat he'd never known before.

Tnúthgal and his men sought to keep him from his land and his tribesmen. They strove to keep her from him.

With renewed vigor, he swung once more at Tnúthgal. *I'll make these bastards pay.*

Men and horses pressed between Eowain and his cousin. Eowain lost sight of his cousin and found himself carried across the field and threatened by bandits. He parried, snapped the spear of one in half, and laid open the throat of the other with his blade.

Then a horn blew. Some of the bandits sought to make an orderly withdrawal. Others turned and fled. Their abandoned fellows were soon overwhelmed or chased off.

In the confusion, Tnúthgal's men either surrendered or fled as well. Eowain was left with command of the field. His cousin was gone.

Eowain put his hands on his knees. His breath came in harsh gasps, this thighs burned with exertion. Gingerly, he probed at his left shoulder. Broken rings and split leather met his touch. His fingers came back bloodied. *Thank the Gods for my cousin's poor aim.* The wound hurt like hell, but the armor had done its business well enough and he still had a shoulder at all.

Eowain reorganized the men. Many had been injured, aside from himself. A few had been killed. He'd always intended to stay the night at Maraydanayd, but with wounded to tend, it seemed then the best choice in any event.

"I told you I could fight." Eithne lifted her chin and leaned her head backward toward her shoulder blades. Her cool green eyes rolled and looked askance at the field around her. The corner of her mouth tightened on one side, dimpled, and pulled toward her ear.

Eowain looked about at the field. The bodies of Tnúthgal's men spoke eloquently for her prowess. Nearby, scar-faced Gaeth and barrel-chested Mahon raised their eyebrows at him.

"Yes," admitted Eowain. He put his fists on his hips and nodded to her. "You certainly can."

AFTER THE SKIRMISH, Eowain and his company marched ahead to Maraydanayd. The beautiful forest slept peacefully about them, as if unconcerned about the violent affairs of men. Leafy green trees with silver and white trunks stood in grandeur as far as Eowain could see. The bright red, blue, and yellow of abundant woodland flowers punctuated the forest's carpet of ferns and deep green bushes. A stark contrast to the bloody business of the afternoon.

The fight had cost them about an hour's delay, but Eowain and his company arrived with some daylight to spare, ahead of the hour of evening prayers. Maraydanayd was a small place of barely a hundred residents who scratched their existence from the rugged foothills. Several faces mirrored the grace and delicacy of the woodlands through which they'd come, but most were drawn with the worry and care of daily life. Beyond their village, a mountain of grey stone rose up from their meadow grasses.

Eowain met with the village chieftain, a rough-handed older man with a wife of exceptional youth and a young son. He'd received word from the Bán-Drúmór herself, and from their king at Midachath, to treat Eowain with all due hospitality. With great relief, Eowain and his party shared the evening meal with the chieftain.

But the chief worried that Eowain's company would bring Cailech raids down on them. Maraydanayd was close to their savage borders, and there were rumors of a hosting of warriors coming north.

That news worried Eowain. There was a long, lonely stretch of the trail ahead that ran perilously close to the boundary stones of the Cailech. But what robber-lord of the Cailech would risk war with both the Gwynn and the Donnghaile?

The next day dawned brisk and frosty.

Eowain shook his head as he looked up at the morning sky. Clouds, grey and low, had gathered overnight. Medyr and Alva Damar puttered over their *coelbreni*, but Eowain didn't need them to tell him rains were coming. "Damn it."

He stood on the plank-wood porch outside the headman's home. A mountain breeze carried scents of wild mountain avens and black medicks.

Lorcán rubbed the stumps of his missing fingers as if they pained him. "What can we do?"

Eowain looked to the Lord-Drymyn. "Is there nothing?"

Medyr glanced to Alva, but she shook her head. "It's another eighteen and some miles to the Vale," he said. "Even if the Gods were so inclined, which is always unlikely, that is too vast a distance. Such a great change in the way of things would have... consequences." He didn't elaborate, but his face was grave.

Alva nodded her knotty-haired head. "Even together and with the aid of the Lord-Drymyn's acolyte, we should not dare ask the Gods for such a beneficence."

Eowain growled at them. "It's only because of your Order that we're making this damned journey. I would've been just as pleased to have the wedding in Droma, but you tell us the Gods want us at the Vale, and They can't even see fit to give us fair weather for the damn journey?"

Sheepish, Medyr shrugged. "The Gods, they are forgetful, Your Grace."

"By the Gods, I'm sick of hearing that!" He dismissed them. Lorcán put a hand on his shoulder, then went as well, to see to the day's preparations.

"You should have more care for the Gods' servants." Eowain turned toward the soft voice. It was Eithne, dressed already for the road in armor and breeks, with the black, red, and gold of the Gwynn tartan over her shoulder. Her small left hand rested on the hilt of the sword on her hip.

Eowain raised his arm and rotated his left shoulder. It ached, and he felt the tightly woven bandages resist his stretch. "If the Gods had more care for us, I might." He put his face in his hands and pulled, as if he could remove his worries. "I know," he admitted at last. "We finally have proof of Tnúthgal's treachery, and he disappears. We face many more miles of rough country ahead, and it threatens to rain. We defeat Cael's bandits in a skirmish, and the chieftain here tells us the Cailech are restless on his borders." He shrugged and sighed. "If it's not one thing, it's another. I'm just frustrated."

"Blood's been spilled. Tnúthgal stabbed you in the back. Breda is dead." She put a gentle hand upon his arm. "We're all frustrated. Tired. Angry. We've been a week in the saddle already, and you even more than that, with that business at Gluin Hill. But I can't believe the Gods would put these obstacles in our path if our marriage is truly Their will."

"Then—if not the Gods—who? What terrible spirit have we offended? I'd gladly appease it, if only I knew." He rolled his shoulder back and winced.

She shook her head, a worried look on her fair face. "I don't know, my lord. Perhaps none. As the drymyn said—"

He put a hand up. "Don't say it. I've had enough of the Gods' forgetfulness already."

A hurt look passed across her face. He regretted his tone. "I'm sorry. I know you're just trying to help."

"I understand."

He tugged at his beard. He had something more to say, something about the sense of foreboding that haunted his chest and belly. But he wasn't sure he wanted to hear her answer.

She furrowed her brow at him. "What is it?"

He didn't want to seem weak, or uncertain. He wanted to be strong and confident, and not disappoint her. Yet still, the unanswered question lingered between them. Would she accept him for her husband? Would they truly be wed, after all this, or would she find some fault in him? *Gods know, there are enough to find.*

He shook his head. "It's nothing." He dismissed the thought with a wave of his hand. "Just..." He sighed. "Just thinking about my aunt's damn wagon. Rain will make muck of our trail."

She seemed disappointed. "Oh," she said, in a small voice. "Well, I'm sure you'll find a way."

"I suppose." The silence between them grew long. Then awkward. "I should attend to the company," he said at last.

"Yes, of course. I will have my father make our men ready. We'll need every hour today."

Eowain took his leave with a perfunctory bow, and went to order the march. In the best of weather, he'd expected to make fifteen or sixteen miles with the broad daylight ahead of them. It was enough almost to reach the Vale before sunset, and close enough to march on into the early evening and arrive that very night.

But with rain? They would still be some ten or more miles from the Vale by sunset. He'd have to camp the company for the night in uncertain lands, near to the Cailech border and far from the Celtair stronghold.

Eowain tried to count his blessings. *If there's any justice, Tnúthgal died of his wounds and Cael has abandoned the chase.*

The chances weren't entirely unfavorable. He'd given his cousin two solid clouts to the head in the skirmish. Even if his cousin's helmet had blunted the blows, men had been known to die from less.

Eowain looked at the threatening sky. No matter how favorable the chances, he feared they were all against him nonetheless.

After the morning orisons and the prayers of First Hour, the company lumbered to its feet and struck out across the countryside, just as icy rain began to fall.

By Third Hour, the day had warmed somewhat and Eowain no longer feared slick ice on the rugged hills. Instead, the trail beneath them turned to mud as the trickle became a torrent.

Their progress soon became tedious. The thick mire sucked at the hooves and boots of his company, freighting each step. Every few minutes, his aunt's wagon had to be shoved and levered through muck.

Eithne rode beside him. They each had their hoods up, so that it seemed they each traveled alone, rather than in company.

By the Gods, I will seem thrice the fool if we slog all the way to the Vale only to find she will not marry. He wanted to put the question to her again, the question he'd asked so many times already: *Do you love me?* He remembered the first, awkward missive he'd written to her. *Tell me,* he'd written, *And let's clap hands and have a bargain.* She hadn't appreciated such a blunt proposal, but he'd have appreciated a blunt answer. Instead, she'd been coy.

They all want proof, Lorcán had told him once. *Proof of what?* That they hadn't opened their knees for naught.

What manner of man did she take him for, if that was her concern? Had he not sworn to honor her? He did not like to think himself a man to make such oaths lightly.

"Hoy!" Ahead, one of his outriders raised a fist to signal a halt. Eowain looked to Eithne, who returned a wan smile from beneath her rain-soaked hood. He tried to return the smile, then spurred his mount forward.

"Travelers on the trail," reported the lead rider, nodding ahead.

Six men, five mules, four heavily-laden carts, and a brightly-painted house wagon struggled uphill through the mire, headed in Eowain's own direction. The way was not wide enough for his company to pass unless they put off into the trees.

"Shall we shirk them from the trail, Your Grace?"

Eowain took a deep breath, held it a long, calming moment. "No," he replied. "They're better than halfway up the hill. Let them finish the climb." He sent word back to the company to put scouts out and to bring up a squad of men, then rode up to meet the travelers himself. His riders followed with caution.

It was only then as he approached that he realized they were tinkers.

The Travellers slipped and slid in the mud as Eowain approached. Four of them were armed and armored, hands on their sword-hilts. The other two seemed like poor merchants. "Hoy there, m'lord, peace of the road?" Their spokesman, middle-aged and portly, clearly feared they were robbers. He looked familiar to Eowain.

"Aye," replied Eowain. "Peace of the road." He held up his empty right hand, as did his men.

"Sorry for the trouble, m'lord. We'll clear the way just as soon as we can, sir." He looked up at the skies. "We'd hoped to make the Vale before the rains came."

"We're neither of us so fortunate today." Eowain stayed on his horse and gave them a wary eye, then looked to the forest by either side of the road. Not a bad place for an ambush. "I am Eowain, King of Droma. We're also on our way to the Vale."

"Kerron, sir, Kerron Vanis." He gestured to the other men. "My son and his cousins." The men tried to make obeisance, but the footing was treacherous and the result clumsy. "Oh, aye, we'd 'eard ye might be abroad, Your Grace. On yer way to the Cétshamain festival, are ye? As are we, as are we." He slapped at one of the stubborn, two-wheeled mule carts. "There'll be good trading, if only we can get there. But just give us a bit of time and we'll have ourselves out of yer way, Your Grace."

"No, you've come this far, don't make way until the top. But I'll bring up men to help, if that's alright?"

The tinker and his young, spare partner eyed him warily. Eowain saw them come to the resigned conclusion that if robbing them was his intention, they really had little choice in the matter. "Aye, Your Grace, we'd appreciate that mightily, I'll tell ye."

Eowain heard a loud bird's cry from the forest. A heron's cry. Not a bird likely to be found in those rough forested hills. *All's clear,* that cry told him. No ambusher skulked in the trees. He waved acknowledgment and invited the portly merchant to join him for a mid-morning break with their company. A squad of his men slogged up the hill and went to their work.

Eowain spotted a pair of roe-buck, half-hidden among the trees. He wished them well and threw a rock to spook them away from his hungry company.

Eowain's company milled around at the bottom of the hill and waited for the tinkers' carts to be moved. Eowain offered the tinker a seat on a log and a wooden cup of small beer. "Oh, thank you, Your Grace, thank you, that's very kind of you, sir."

Eowain seated himself beside the tinker. "So, Master Kerron, what news of the road?"

The tinker swigged at his cup and shook his head. "Little enough of good, I'm afraid. We was at Rath Celtair two days ago. The way down from the mountains was treacherous, I'll tell ye."

"Any trouble on this trail?"

"None what we've met so far, Your Grace, but we camped with a hunting band last night. They said there'd been banditry all up the trail, maybe as far as Castas even. Not many are wishing to make the trip to the Vale this Cétshamain, roads being what they are."

Eowain raised an eyebrow at him. "Yet you expect good trading?"

He shrugged. "We hear good things, traders from Narada and Ivearda what will be there."

Eowain found that encouraging. If Iveardan traders did not fear to make the journey, it could mean that King Ardgar, Eithne's cousin, had sent men to secure the trails. And the Naradans of the mountains were a stern people. They would not send traders into the lowlands without a heavy guard. "But the Fiatach king at Celtair? He's not making the journey?"

The tinker eyed Eowain's company before he replied. "Not so as I've 'eard, Your Grace."

"But he's sent patrols to secure this trail, surely."

Kerron swallowed hard. "No. Not as I've 'eard, Your Grace."

"Please, Master Tinker, what have you heard?"

He took a drink from his cup. His eyes darted around Eowain's company. "Only, Your Grace, and begging yer pardon, sir—"

"Yes?"

"Uhm, only that the way would be dangerous, Your Grace. On account of Toryn the Stout of the Cailech, sir..."

"What about Toryn the Stout?"

He swigged what remained of his small beer. "Only, sir, and I'm sorry to say it, sir, but that 'e's sworn that yer company will never reach the Vale, sir. And that, uhm, any who travel with ye are dead men, sir."

"This trail doesn't pass through Cailech lands. King Eochy of Celtair would let Cailech men raid across his borders?"

"As I, uhm, as I 'eard it, sir, he wouldn't 'let' them exactly, not so much as he wouldn't stop them, y'see."

"Yes." Eowain stroked at his beard. "Yes. I see."

WITH AN ANGRY snap, Tnúthgal broke aside the branches that barred his way. He muttered curses at the rain under his breath as it seeped through his cloak and trickled down his collar.

Five men followed him. They were all that remained from the debacle at the crossroad, the rest of the cowards having fled. *They'll see. I'll make Droma great again. We'll close our borders, drive out all the Foreigners and the migrants who drive down wages and steal jobs. I'll make the Gruin-men think twice about crossing the Gasirad. And the Lord-Drymyn will get in line, or I'll make him get in line.* He and his men had spent a cold night in the wild, and a wet day tracking. Tnúthgal's mood was foul and angry.

"My lord?"

He turned back. One of the men pointed to the south, where a thin plume of white smoke was visible through the murk of the rain. Tnúthgal looked back at the vague track they'd been following. *Hmm, yes.* He nodded to the men and three of them took the lead as they moved off toward the smoke. The other two brought up his rear.

It wasn't far, and they didn't even have pickets out. Tnúthgal and his men strode in unchallenged.

The camp was a shambles. Filthy men shivered in the rain. One feeble cook-fire struggled against the rain. Wet pine wood sizzled and popped, with more smoke than heat. Nearly a score of emaciated women and children, bound with iron collars to trees and logs, dug at roots, grass, and into wood-bark to find food. Other women were being used for a variety of vile perversions.

The appearance of six healthy, heavily-armed men in their camp brought several to their feet, weapons drawn.

"Easy, mates," came a smarmy voice. Out from under the only sizable, well-patched canvas, Cael the Viper slithered. "That there is our benefactor. We wouldn't want to see him meet any unfortunate accidents." Cael dropped an elaborate and mocking bow. "Your Lordship, you honor us."

Tnúthgal made an impolite reply. "Fetch us food, you thief."

Cael adopted a look of hurt. "You wound me, my lord."

"I wish." Tnúthgal pushed past him. "Food. Now. And make sure my men are well-attended."

Cael's voice changed from mocking to dangerous. "You seem to misjudge who commands whom here, sir."

Tnúthgal turned and put his blade to Cael's throat. "Have I?" He didn't bother to look at the bandits who gathered about them. His men took up positions around him and Cael, weapons drawn and ready. "Each of my men is worth three of yours. I'm worth nine. Do you really wish to try my patience?"

Cael considered him for a moment, then put his hands in the air. "As you like it, my lord." He snapped fingers. "Food for our guests."

Tnúthgal turned away and continued into Cael's tent. Cael rubbed at the bloody spot on his throat and followed. "Don't speak to me that way in front of my men."

"My men," corrected Tnúthgal. "You've just been demoted." He looked about his ramshackle new command. "I'll want to see your maps and inventory." He made himself as comfortable as he could on a cushioned pile of furs. A girl slunk into the tent with a plate of food. He took it from her. "Stay," he commanded, snapping fingers. She sank to her knees. He looked up at Cael. "Maps and inventory." He snapped again. "Go."

"These are my men—" Cael's voice held a hint of threat.

Tnúthgal cut him off. "They were your men. You've done damn-all but waste time and money with them. That changes now." He took some of the fatty, rare-cooked meat in his fingers. Venison, he noted. He chewed at a piece of gristle. He could see Cael trying to figure the odds in his head. "Or do we have a problem, Cael?"

The bandit chief seemed to come to some conclusion. "Maps we have. Inventory, we ain't. We got no one what can cipher."

Tnúthgal sighed. "Fine. Bring the maps. Then get out."

Cael fumbled around the tent and dropped a handful of vellum and parchment in front of him. "Maps." Then he left the tent.

Tnúthgal looked at the girl. Maybe she was even old enough to be a woman. However old, she'd clearly been used, and not gently. Filthy rags hung from her trembling frame in tatters.

He sucked and chewed at another string of meat. She kept her face down to the ground. He flicked idly through the papers with a greasy finger. *Eowain likely will get to about there by tonight.* He rubbed a finger at a spot on one map. *And we're about here.* He considered that with a night's rest and a quick march, he could get ahead of Eowain, but where? He turned over two more pages. *Hmmm. That's looks promising.*

Cael returned with two men. Tnúthgal knew the first, a broad, squat man with a shocking thatch of red hair and a knotted beard. Toryn the Stout of Cailech. He limped, favored his lower left abdomen.

Gored by the cattle he'd presumed to steal at Gluin Hill, Tnúthgal guessed.

"My camp seems to be a hive of villainy tonight." Cael regarded Tnúthgal sourly. "You know each other, I presume?"

"We do," he admitted.

Toryn nodded. "I have my own grievance now against Eowain."

"Aye. A matter of thirty cows, I'm told." He nodded to the bloody linens wrapped around the man's stomach. "You're fit to fight?"

Toryn grunted. "Fit enough." He showed the exit wound on the other side. "Went clean through."

A lucky man. "Billet your men wherever you may. I'll have no dissension in the ranks. Understood?"

Toryn nodded, put a fist to his breast, and left.

The other man was a wild-eyed fellow. He fidgeted around the tent, picking at things and putting them down. His hair was stringy and brown. He was thin enough to make only a mean feast for crows. Around his neck, a weasel was curled. Its head was up. Its beady, black eyes observed everything. Its whiskers twitched.

Cael nodded. "This is Kúlkak. He claims to be a sorcerer. It's by his divination we've been able to track Eowain's progress."

A chill went across Tnúthgal's damp, clammy skin. "Sorcery?" He stood and drew his dagger. "What nonsense is that?"

Cael's voice was low, almost reverential. "It's true. He speaks to the Gods."

Kúlkak's voice was reedy and girlish. "Not the Gods! No, not them." His eyes roamed without focus around the tent. There was something unhallowed about those eyes. Yellow-rimmed and oily, in the dim light of the tent, they seemed almost... reptilian.

"The spirits. Spirits of wind and air, fire and water. Spirits of land and æther." He poked a finger at Tnúthgal's chest. "We know you, mighty lord. Know you well."

Tnúthgal batted the bony finger aside and kept his dagger between them. He spat on the ground and held up three fingers to ward against evil. "What is it you think you know?"

"You are wolf-king kin? Yes? Yes? When sixth time the Dragon flies, yes? Fly, Dragon, fly!"

"Wolf-king kin? What in Annwn are you talking about?" Tnúthgal leaned away from the spittle that flew from the man's lips. "What is this, Cael? Have you adopted a mad-man?"

"I tell you, he's a sorcerer."

The man, Kúlkak, began to mutter and turn in a circle. *"She-ga inim na Me!"*

Tnúthgal felt fear grip his throat. "What's he doing?"

"Ku-shag-kesh na Zag-du, Ku-shag-kesh na Abul!"

Cael's eyes went round. "Conjurin' demons!"

"Du-ig-shu-úr-du Mur-Ig!"

Tnúthgal shook his dagger at the man. "Stop it!" The girl at his feet scuttled away on hands and knees.

"She-ga inim na Lagar na Me!"

There was a sniff of something, like the air of a thunderstorm. The parchments and vellum rose up, as if caught in a whirlwind, and circled around in a widening gyre.

Tnúthgal's stomach clenched with terror. "Stop it! Stop it!" The girl on her knees screamed and darted under the edge of the canvas and away.

The maps dropped and the knife twisted from Tnúthgal's hand, turned twice in the air, then dropped and buried itself to the hilt in the ground.

"Kàm!" Kúlkak's exclamation was girlish and shrill. Abruptly, the smell of thunder was gone.

"I will help you." Gone was the wild look of a caged beast. Kúlkak's eyes were clear to him then, slitted like those of a lizard, and blinked at him impassively. "Ere Wolf-Moon light does wane, Curséd Wolf-King must be slain."

Tnúthgal swallowed hard. "What in Annwn does that mean?"

"I do not know," said Kúlkak. "But I will help you."

CHAPTER TEN

THEY MADE ABOUT eleven miles through the rain that day. As they settled into camp, Kerron the tinker and his crew ambled in behind them and begged to join them, for safety's sake.

"We're all dead men, I thought you said." Eowain was disappointed at their progress. Medyr and Alva predicted the weather would clear on the morrow, but that would do little for the condition of the trail, and they still had at least seven more miles to the Vale.

Kerron looked around as the camp materialized around them. Squads dug ditches, others bundled sticks into hedges. Tents a-rose, men coaxed small, cheery cook-fires to life. "I don't know much of such matters, Your Grace, but seems to me Toryn the Stout bites off more than he can chew."

"If he were my only concern, I'd say you were right." Eowain slapped him on the shoulder. "You and your men are welcome to share our fires. Find Sergeant Cathasach, he'll see that you're settled and your men assigned to stand a watch."

Darkness settled, and the rain slackened at last. Eowain sat with his staff on a log around a fire. Men had gone off into the wood a-hunting and returned with a hare and an elk. Not enough to feed the whole company, of course, but Eowain ordered the meat shared around as far as it would go. If they had to sleep in a cold, wet camp, at least every man would do so with a hot morsel in his stomach.

One of the men strummed at a lyre. A handful began to hum. Another began to sing, a slow and mournful tune.

Let's call me rebel...
Let's call me friend...
Together we stand in the end...
From north and from south...
all over the land...
my brothers, my comrades, my friends...
The gentle song of a flute joined the lyre.
So raise your cup to the boys
no longer here...

The flute-song rose in circles and came back to the tune.

So raise your cups and always be proud...
Stand for the fallen...
Stand here and now...
Without fear...

The tempo picked up. More flutes whistled through the night. Hands drummed whatever they touched. The singer repeated the refrain, but the tone had changed, from mournful to defiant.

As the refrain came to an end, all the men joined in.

HERE WE GO! HERE WE GO!
For the stories we've been told!
For the history forgotten,
For the land our father's rode!

HERE WE GO! HERE WE GO!
For the ones we left behind!
Let us honor their traditions!
Let us keep their dreams alive!

The others went silent as the first singer raised his hands.

Here we go-oooo-ooo-ooo-ooo...

Three others joined in harmony.

Here we go-oooo-ooo-ooo-ooo...

Then again, all the men:

HERE WE GO!

"Should they be singing?" Eithne looked about at the dark woods.

Lorcán chuckled. "I don't think we could stop them if we tried."

Eowain smiled and shrugged to her. "Cael surely knows where we are. Toryn the Stout, too, if he's out there." He waved his cup to the troops. "And they know it." He shrugged. "So they sing. Let our enemies suffer in darkness, silence, and damp." He stood and raised his mug amid cheers.

"SO RAISE YOUR CUP!" he shouted, and all the men joined him and together they all sang on.

To the boys no longer here!
So raise your cups and always be proud!
Stand for the fallen!
Stand here and now
without fear!

Eithne leaned in at Medyr's elbow. "A spear to the back, and surely worn to the bone. Yet he dances? Your lord is a vigorous man."

Medyr stroked the goatee he wore under his half-shaved head. "He certainly can be, my lady."

"In times like these, does that make him a good man?"

The drymyn shrugged. "In times like these, who can afford to be a good man, my lady? I shouldn't hope for so much from a king, I think." He took his pipe of linden leaf and puffed it to smoldering life. "No, in times like these, I would settle for a just man."

Eithne watched as the men arose to impromptu dances and jigs.

She had to admit, the music infected her. She tapped her foot, drummed fingers on the log under her backside. There was never so much music in her village. It was thought best there not to attract attention from the Ancestors in the grim mountain forests.

But these men dared the night. They challenged the darkness and whatever lay beyond the firelight. She laughed as Eowain turned his legs to a jig.

HERE WE GO! HERE WE GO!
For the stories we've been told!
For the history forgotten,
For the land our father's rode!

Eowain smiled at her, then turned his eyes again to the darkness as he went through the dancing steps. *The Cailech are out there now too,* he thought. The rain would have them hunkered down as well. He thought of maps he'd seen of this land. They were incomplete, but good enough to know that the Cailech were likely camped south of him.

And what of Cael the Viper and his bandits? Had Eowain's break-through at the crossroads been enough? Had the dogs given up their quarry?

HERE WE GO! HERE WE GO!
For the one's we left behind!
Let us honor their traditions!
Let us keep their dreams alive!

And what of treacherous cousin Tnúthgal? Eowain danced back through the jig and bowed out of the dance. He took back his cup from Medyr and sat on the log by his minister.

Eowain nodded to Lorcán, who clenched his three-fingered fist on the hilt of his sword. "What do you think, brother?"

Lorcán scowled. "I'd be happier in Dúnsciath."

"The hearth." Eowain nodded.

"The mighty rack of Father's elk flickering in the shadows." Lorcán wiped small beer from his lips and leaned forward. "The bandits have to be southwest. There's no way they could have made better time than we did, not through the wild." His lip curled into a snarl. "We gave them a fight, we did. They won't be happy, after such a slap, and then a day and night in the rain and the cold."

Eithne's father, Lord Ciaran, leaned into the fire as well. "Your men have suffered in this. I'm sorry."

Eowain put him to rest. "It's not on your account. It's on theirs." He pointed to Alva and Medyr. Their faces remained impassive, but their eyes were bright and watching.

"We did not pronounce this oracle." Medyr put his palms up to the heavens and shrugged.

Alva nodded. "Nor is this what was agreed when we left to come to Droma. We would have made the straightway here and not risked the lady or yourself like this." She shrugged. "The Gods, they are forgetful."

Medyr rolled shoulders. "Sometimes, they leave out details. Sometimes things best left forgotten. It is for those more learned than ourselves to judge such things."

Eowain's mouth went sour at the thought. "But for what? Why would the Gods give any more care for this marriage than any one before it?"

Medyr shook his head. "I've not been privy to such matters in the Order, Your Grace. Forgive me."

Alva brooded by the fire. She would not be compelled to speak.

Eowain stood and put a finger to her. "She knows more than she's telling of this."

The voices around their fire went quiet. Alva's eyes glared at him, black and glittering in the firelight. "Stand back, boy."

Medyr put out a restraining hand. "Your Grace. Eowain. Do not."

Eowain took back the angry finger and seated himself again. "I'm sorry, my lady. It's just that this is grim business, and I don't like being played for a fool in it." He waved at both the drymyn. "They know more about this than they're telling."

"Only more than you would understand, lad." Alva snarled at him. "Do not think to lay your hands upon me in anger, or I will see you blasted where you stand. I speak for the Ancestors of Ydrys. Who do you speak for?" She waved at the camp, where a complicated triple-time jig had the men's skin glistening with sweat in the firelight. "A pack of prancing jack-a-napes."

"Those jack-a-napes are the only thing standing between you and Cael's bandits, old lady. And now the hornet's nest of Toryn the Stout is kicked up too." Eowain and Lorcán met eyes. "It seems he took exception to getting trampled by his own stolen cattle. The bards will be singing satires of it. He wants to restore his honor."

The tinker Kerron bowed as Eowain raised his cup to praise of his intelligence, then turned back to Alva. "So, now, Matron, I must ask you. How far will they go? Will they dare the holy Vale of Thaynú itself? These are brigands, thieves, and desperate men."

Lorcán nodded slowly. "And we don't know where Tnúthgal is, or what survived of his men."

Eowain scratched at his beard. "Oh yes. There's that." His tone oozed with irony.

Lord Ciaran rubbed his hands to the fire. "So what would you have us do? My men and I are at your command."

Eithne drummed a fist on her log. "We carry on and fight, Father. We fight for every step, if we must."

Ciaran shook his head. Eowain's look calculated her, as if she stood weighed in some balance. "None of them could have made better time today than we did. If Lorcán and I are right, we've turned a corner on the journey. For once, we are between them and the Vale. But not for much longer. The weather promises to be fair today, but it won't last. The spring rains have begun, that will flood our lowlands a week hence."

He nodded to Lady Rathtyen's house-wagon. "We can't move at any speed with that. The trails will be sodden. They will catch up to us, it's only a matter of time. The question is where? Would Tnúthgal and Cael the Viper and Toryn the Stout bring war to the Vale? I wouldn't put it past them."

Medyr looked pointedly at Alva. "Nor would I. If I may at least say that much?"

She gave him a dark and dangerous look. "Say what you like. It will make no difference."

Medyr scowled at her, but Eowain raised his hand. "Fine. Keep your oaths. She's right. We have to assume they will bring war to the Vale." He turned to look at Eithne. "And the Vale is the safest place within fifty miles for the drymyn, and Aunt Rathtyen. And for you."

He proposed to send her away to safety. "I will not." She put a fist to her chest. "It is over me that this damned squabble arose. I'll not let other men fight for my virtue before I'll fight myself for it."

Lorcán grunted at her. "Then defend Rathtyen's." He waved to her house-wagon. "It's her policies for trade that have brought us to this way in the road. Tnúthgal's upriver wharves were eclipsed when we grew the market at Dúnsciath. And he's not wrong about the hard years of harvests we've had. Little of the reward from her trader's schemes has been seen back in the people's hands." He shook his head. "Gods, I'm sorry, brother. I left the kingdom in dire straits for you."

Eowain shook his head and raised his cup as the chorus came around again.

HERE WE GO! HERE WE GO!

Eowain took a drink.

Eithne looked at each of them, and to her father. She could see it in their faces. *The indignity!*

Eowain saw the defiance building in her green eyes. "It's not a debate, Eithne. You and your father will go forward with Rathtyen and a troop of my own men. The rest of us will defend your rear and give you time to reach the Vale. If we can, we'll break these bastards. But whatever we do, we'll hold them, and fight backward toward the Vale and safety. You'll bring word of the danger and have their forces waiting to receive and reinforce us if needs be."

"But that's what they want, don't you see? They only need to kill one of us, if their aim's only to scuttle the wedding."

Medyr agreed. "And they only need to kill you, Your Grace, to put Tnúthgal on the throne at home."

Lorcán nodded. "I'll do it. You go on, Eowain. Go with Eithne."

Eowain shook his head. "Never. I didn't ask for the kingship, but I aim to put any further doubt about it to rest." He flexed his wounded shoulder. "He speared me in the back. Like a coward. And ran from my justice, like a villain. I'll have that stain on our great-grandfather's name wiped clean. None should speak of the sons of the Donnghaile so." He pointed to Eithne. "But you, my lady. You will go. There will be time enough for you to prove your courage. Now I need to see your wisdom. I need you to do this thing, so it's going to get done."

She could see he meant it. It did not sit well with her. "What of my own Ancestors and their honor? Should the Gwynn be thought of as cowards and villains too?"

"Should the Gwynn be known for fools? My lady, it is the safest way for us all. Many more will die otherwise, and some..." He nodded to her, to Rathtyen's wagon, to Alva, "In more terrible ways than others." He shook his head. "No, my lady, you and your company will go, as quick as you may. Lord Lorcán and Medyr will remain with me, leading the rear-guard. The mouth of the Vale is narrow, where the waters of Gaelen fall. The Vale can muster its defense there. We will fall back on that position in good order, or not at all."

THE NEXT MORNING dawned frosty. Rainwater had frozen to slush overnight. Eowain shook ice from his canvas as he rose from his tent. Eithne's team was already mounted up. He found Eithne's steed and took its bridle. "My lady."

"I shouldn't be speaking to you."

"It's the safest thing for you."

"To Annwn with that!"

"And I won't be arguing it with you." He felt heat rise to his face. "I would have your answer, my lady. Have you decided, after all this, that we'll be wed?"

She turned up her nose at him. "When you have so little trust in me? I can fight as well as any one of your men. I needn't be bundled away lest I break."

Anger burned in him. "And when you have so little trust in me, not to see wisdom."

"What wisdom?" She looked at her horsemen and her men-of-foot. "A score of the finest Men of Ivearda stand ready to fight, and you turn them away. Who is foolish here?"

He lowered his voice. "Damn you, woman. Would you throw their lives away? And your own?"

"Why not, when you choose to throw your own away? Are their lives—or mine—worth anymore than yours? You're the King of Droma, you idiot."

He clenched his leather-bound fists. "I'll not be called a fool and an idiot."

"You will be when you act like one."

He jerked on the bridle of her horse. "No, I will not be. Not by any man alive, and certainly not by you!" The horse nickered and sidled.

"Or else what?" Her sneer cut him to the bone as surely as any sword. "You've had months to capture and kill Cael the Viper. Months to flush out your cousin's treachery. Months to set your house in order for a new bride. Yet this is the best you can do? Snarl like an old bear at a woman?"

There was no sunlight in that grey dawn, but she seemed radiant to his eyes nevertheless, proud and upright in her saddle. He remembered then the first time he'd seen her. She and her father had come secretly into Droma, to meet with him on the matter of marriage. Cael and his brigands had seized her, carried her away to their stronghold at the center of a wintry marsh. He'd worried enough for her safety then, not even knowing her. But then he'd fought his way into the bandit camp, found her in Cael's own pavilion. A petite, fair-skinned, red-headed waif of a girl, bound and gagged on her knees.

His throat choked at the memory. The responsibility and guilt he'd felt. The fear she must have known.

He shook his head at her, suddenly weary of the fight. "I—." He choked and stumbled, in search of words. As if he'd chewed on old iron nails, or swallowed bad asparagus. "It's—fear, my lady. Fear for your safety. I don't want to see you killed."

The hard look upon her face turned to surprise. She furrowed her brows, tilted her head to the side to consider him. Then she softened.

Her small hand reached out to his hold upon her bridle. "Nor I you." She sniffed, then stiffened. "Fine. I'll go. Keep yourself well."

With that, her company struggled through the slush with Rathtyen's wagons and their supply-mules. She took a score of her own men, as well as Eowain's eight horse-scouts and ten skirmishers in light gear, with hunting bows and axes.

As they slogged out of sight, Eowain turned to his own men. He had the sixteen men of his bodyguard, fifteen horsemen, and his brother, Lorcán. There were also thirty men on foot with shields, swords and spears, as well as a squad of archers.

He looked over the terrain with his brother. It was lightly wooded pine-land, rising up through their position and to either side of the trail. They'd camped on a high-point between the rising sides of the hills. "We'll put the archers here on the high ground, at the center of our line."

Lorcán nodded. "That will let you bring them to bear anywhere along the line."

"Just so. We'll hold the horsemen in reserve, for fast reaction to any breakthrough attempts."

Lorcán pointed across the frontage to either side of the road. "Your bodyguard to hold the center. They're the most reliable in terms of courage."

"With a troop of sword and spear to either flank. Yes, I see it."

Lorcán looked up the road at the rising land. "The question is, to where are we falling back?" He scratched at his head.

Eowain pointed through the folds and gaps of the pine-covered hills. "There's a ridge, about a third of a mile up, beyond those hills. That's as much as we give them today."

Medyr and his young acolyte stepped up to them. "How may we serve, Your Grace?"

Eowain nodded to his soldiers. "Give them courage, Lord-Drymyn. The Gods grant them courage." The acolyte's eyes were wide and fearful. Yet also, resolute. "Don't be scared, boy."

He shook his head. "Sure and I won't, Your Grace." Then he knuckled his forehead and bowed.

Medyr nodded to him. "Go and prepare our orisons for the morning." As the boy went away, Medyr leaned toward Eowain. "What are our chances, Your Grace?"

Eowain rubbed at the back of his neck. "Best guess? They have about eighty men out there. Maybe more. We have about sixty. We're fighting backward, uphill, and through the mud. We'll succeed at holding them, I think, but it's a meat-grinder waiting to happen."

"I see." Medyr nodded quietly. "Very good, my lord. I'll go lead the men in prayer."

Eowain took the Lord-Drymyn's sleeve as he turned. "Medyr." His old mentor looked back at him. "If ever the Gods needed to be mindful, since they set us on this way...?"

"I will endeavor to gain their attention, my lord." With a resolute jerk of his head, he followed on after the acolyte.

A cold wind riffled down out of the mountains and blew needles and grit before it. Lorcán moved off to order the men, and for a moment, Eowain was alone. He pulled up the bear-skin cape against the cold.

Squads bustled to their positions. Archers hustled up the hill, kit jingling. Spears bristled this way and that across the trail.

Medyr and his acolyte picked their way through the mud. They blessed each man with a token of Echraide, goddess of their homeland, as they passed. Each man knuckled his forehead in thanks and went on.

He took a deep breath. It would be a hard fight.

Lorcán came up beside him. "What are we trying to accomplish here, brother?"

"Buying time. To get Eithne and Rathtyen safely to the Vale."

He nodded and observed the preparations as men moved to their tasks. "But why?"

"Why get the women, one of whom is my bride, to safety?"

Lorcán looked down and away. "Forgive me, brother, but—." He shifted from one foot to another "Is she your bride? It seems to me she's yet to promise her suit one way or the other."

Eowain felt his jaw tighten. "It's true. She hasn't formally accepted my pledge."

"So why are we doing this?" He shrugged. "I mean... Well... I didn't want to say anything before, you see. It would be a good match, I know, and for all the right reasons, don't get me wrong..."

Eowain knew his brother was hedging about something. "But...?"

"Well, that's just it. There are many fine women in Droma. And there's the daughter of the Khaibe chieftain. Surely that would settle some problems we have on one border. Why are we so intent on gaining this woman's favor? She's a Gwynn, after all. And a Fiatach. What if this is some plot between the Fiatach and the Order to undermine Droma? To weaken the East Kingdom's line against Gruiniath? To strengthen the Order's position against reform?" He put up his hands as Eowain made to reply. "I know. It'll put to bed an old feud, and will give the Cailech something to consider before they try another incursion over our borders. That's what Rathtyen and Medyr have been saying for weeks." He shook his head. "But it's prolonged this trouble with Tnúthgal—made it worse even—and now we're faced not just with Tnúthgal, and Cael, but a vengeful band of Cailech as well. The promise of this wedding hasn't blunted their spears, why should the actual wedding do so?"

Eowain tried to make reply, but found he had no good answer. "The drymyn's predictions." His words felt lame on his own tongue.

"Medyr I trust as well as any man," said Lorcán. He clenched his three-fingered hand. "Yet, when I was king, I never forgot he served his Order first, and the Gods second. Matters of state are a distant third in his priorities." He drummed a fist on the pommel of his saddle. "And we don't know this Alva woman at all."

"The Ban-Drúmór Corchen herself pronounced this *thayn*. Only the Mór-Dára of their Order and the Gods themselves speak with more gravity. Am I supposed to ignore their advice?"

Lorcán looked at him gravely. "Many kings do. Else the reformations of their last Mór-Dára would be a fact across the whole land, and not a piecemeal affair of squabbles between shrines and sanctuaries."

"I'm not king of a Fifth of Iathrann, Lorcán. I can only do my best to tend our own little garden."

"But how is this 'tending our garden?' We're miles away from home. Dissent brews among our chief-holders. We're in hostile country, threatened by treachery and enemy tribesmen. For what? Why should we trust in this girl and this marriage to resolve anything?"

"Where else should we put our trust, brother?" He shook his head. "Of our allies, only the Hagan are trustworthy, and they have other troubles." Eowain put out a hand. "So in whom should we put our faith, if not the Gods?"

Downhill from where they sat astride their horses, Medyr and his acolyte led the men in prayers to greet the dawn. The incomprehensible words of his chant drifted back over the babble of the men, and he moved hands through the air in intricate patterns, with beads in one hand and a cube of cast iron in the other.

Eowain remembered how haggard his Lord-Drymyn had appeared after the conjury at Ruakhavsa. Skin as sallow as a fish-belly, shoulders stooped. He'd seemed far older than his three-dozen years. He remembered what Medyr had told him, that the Gods exact a terrible price for such magicks. He'd been too preoccupied at Ruakhavsa to appreciate what the Lord-Drymyn had suffered for his sake. And he was sure he didn't want to know the dark details of such sacrifices. How could he distrust a man who would wager his health and sanity on only the scant evidence of faith?

But could Eowain afford to believe so blindly? Could he trust that Eithne truly was the right woman to wife? He wanted to believe so. He felt... What? A longing ache in his chest that he couldn't explain, except by her absence. A warmth and comfort in her presence. A deepening affection that grew the longer he knew her. But was this love? And was it enough? Would she be able to soothe the concerns of the people? Would their marriage really bring him the legitimacy his kingship needed? And what if she denied him, after all of this? Then how great a fool would he seem?

He and Lorcán lapsed into silence, and Eowain wrestled with his doubts as the morning drew on. Medyr completed the orisons to greet the dawn, and led the men in prayers and sacrifices, asked the Gods for courage and blessings. Then he and his acolyte fussed with Eowain himself. They chanted prayers in their ancient drymyn's tongue, cleansed him with incense and smoke. They called upon the Gods to be mindful and grant him their special blessings in the conflict yet to come, and the foresight to guide the battle wisely.

The morning drew on. Restlessness passed like a ripple on still water through the men as they faced down-trail into the trees and hills.

Eowain sat astride his white gelding atop the hill where they'd camped. The horse wore a medium-weight coat of scaled leather on its shoulders, girth, and flanks, with war-bridle to match. The bulk of his foot-archers were arrayed on their knees before him. Their mission was to harass the enemy's rear and contain break-out attempts, and to fall back from any serious engagement.

Behind him, his fifteen horse-men stomped and steamed in the morning light. They wore leather jacks overlaid with rings of steels, and stern leather greaves. On their saddles, they carried straight, steel, unadorned, serviceman's broadswords.

Each hefted a round, oak-plank shield on their left arm, decorated with the white, curved lines of the river salmon of Droma. Couched in their elbows, they each carried a wicked-looking, ash and steel spear. They'd been made with boars and bears in mind by the best weapon-smith Droma could afford.

He would hold the horsemen in reserve, to contain breakouts, support breakthroughs, and hold the right flank of pine-strewn hills from being out-maneuvered.

Along their left, a brook splashed through a narrow gulley some ten feet deep on each side. Not difficult to ford, but easy to defend, so he'd set a handful of skirmishers with bow, spear, and shield there to discourage a flanking assault.

But unease began to run through the footmen on the line across the trail. Eowain himself wondered, *Where are they?* He bridled his impatient horse and squinted downhill, over his line and into the dark trees.

From the center of the line, where Eowain's own guard of stout footmen brandished swords in the gathering daylight, there arose the

chanting of Medyr and his acolyte. Every good Droma-man knew that
prayer, The Cry of the Deer. The chanting rose from among the men,
and they drummed the shafts of spears and the blades of swords against the
iron-shod rims of wooden shields.

I arise today
Through the strength of the love of the Shining Ones,
In the obedience of Abred-spirits,
In the service of guardian-spirits,
In the hope of rebirth to perfect my being,
I arise today, through
The strength of the perfect liberty of Gwynfyd,
The light of the sun,
The radiance of the moon,
The splendor of fire,
The speed of lightning,
The swiftness of wind,
The depth of the sea,
The stability of the Abred,
The firmness of rock.
In the name of Holy Peredur of Ard-Cátha, REMEMBER!

Eowain himself took up the chant, under the spring sunshine, in the
defense of a righteous cause. His breast swelled with the burgeoning love of
Manred all about him. He drummed the scarred, ashen shaft of the spear of
Fintan, his father, against his shield. He displayed the curved, knotted lines
of the white river salmon and the proud white, gold, and green tartans of
his kin and shouted the lines in a deep resonate bass. The horsemen behind
him followed suit. The archers kept watchful eyes and stayed silent.

Suddenly, there were horns from the silent forests ahead. Anticipation rippled out from the center of his front-line, through the flanks
and back up the hill.

Medyr raised the knob of his polished blackthorn staff to the suddenly
dim skies. He shouted loud enough for all upon the hill before him to hear:

I summon today
All these powers between me and these evils,
Against every cruel and merciless power
That may oppose my body and spirit,
Against incantations of false prophets,
Against black laws of heathenism,
Against false laws of heretics,
Against craft of idolatry,
Against spells of witches and smiths and sorcerers,
Against every knowledge that corrupts man's body and soul.

But then there came out of the dark forested trees a galloping steed that rode up the bend in the trail toward the center lines.

Or he thought it a steed. Eowain squinted. It had a black head and body for certain, and a gray mane and tail that whipped in the cold breeze that came down from the mountains.

Yet its hooves made no sound as the smoke-colored, insubstantial hooves struck hard upon the packed stone trail.

"Sorcery!" hissed Eowain.

Upon its back rode the black-plumed rider, Cael, the viperous bandit that had eluded Eowain for so long and caused so much death and destruction in Droma. He bore a long sword of gleaming steel high in his right hand, ready for the fray, and wore the crest of some dead southern Foreigner upon a stolen shield.

Beneath his seat, Eowain's white gelding stamped and shimmied to the right, away from the apparition. He felt a wave of apprehension pass over him and across the men behind him. There were fearful shouts from the right flank, where dark shadows concealed what more terrors, Eowain dared not imagine.

CAEL RODE HIS fearsome steed of smoke and shadows back and forth across the line. His archers harassed Eowain's front lines from cover. Cries of pain and panic filled the air.

Then the brigands came up out of the wood.

Medyr and his acolyte rallied the men at the fore with their chants. The bandits surged up the hill at them, spears and swords thrusting. With their iron-shod blackthorn sticks raised like swords, Medyr and his acolyte met the villains not as drymyn, but as men of Droma.

From the hill, Eowain saw Cael slip out from between the closing lines. "Hoy, the right!" He pointed. Cael's horsemen had materialized from the trees and formed up for a charge on Eowain's weak right flank. Lorcán and the horse-lieutenant shouted orders. Eowain's meager wing of cavalry spurred their mounts. Eowain on his dappled grey leaped to the van. He bore down on Cael with the spear of Findtan raised to strike.

Cael answered Eowain's volleying challenge with sword held high and shield to the ready. The steed of smoke and shadows beneath him thundered, preternaturally silent, up the hill. Its milk-white eyes rolled.

Eowain's horse reared and shied from the phantasmal steed. He fought for control of the beast. Cael howled through this black-plumed helmet, his sword swung at Eowain's head. Eowain's horse whinnied and bucked.

Damn it! Eowain fell back on its rump and let Cael's sword swing over him, then parried the return slash with his spear as Cael rode by. It was a hard blow and shuddered through his arm all the way to his shoulder. His horse blew hard, kicked, then reared again.

Annwn with this! Eowain swung loose from the saddle and let go the horse before it got him killed. Free of his command, the horse plunged away from Cael's phantom beast as fast as it could go even before Eowain's feet struck the ground.

The horses of Droma snorted, fought their riders, and broke formation as Cael passed straight through them without the least impediment. Two men went down under his hacking broadsword. Four more were thrown from fearful mounts and trampled under plunging hooves.

Then the two cavalry wings crashed together all around Eowain. The brigands had the better of that meeting. Confusion reigned among the Horse of Droma. Riders struggled with spooked mounts. Loose horses reared at anything in their path. And Cael's ragtag bandits put spears through many a man.

Eowain knocked aside blades with his shield, took down two men with his father's spear. The barnyard smell of leather, horse-sweat, and dung rose in his nostrils. Everywhere was a welter of horse-flesh, and men towered over him in their saddles. Hot blood drenched him as he cut a rider's leg off.

Then he was shouldered aside by one plunging beast, battered by the hooves of another. His mailed chest blunted a spear-strike that drove the wind from him. A sword-blow rang from his helmet. Dazed, Eowain fought and shoved himself free from the mob.

He shook his head. Up the slope, the black-plumed Cael twirled his sword, then leveled its point at Eowain. His phantasmal steed stamped its hooves eagerly.

Eowain flexed his neck to right and left, felt vertebrae crackle. "All right." He hefted his shield and his father's spear. "Come on then, you bastard."

Cael's steed rose up and stamped both feet twice, then plunged down upon him. Eowain raised his shield and took the full weight of Cael's hammer-like blow upon it. He went down on one knee as Cael rode past.

Wherever the sorcerous beast rode, horses—both the bandits' and the Droma-men's—shied, shimmied, and shunned it. Cael reined it about and charged again on Eowain.

That nightmare has got to die. Eowain didn't normally care to target a man's steed. Good horseflesh was too valuable, and it was a cowardly way to fight, bringing down a man's horse. But this was no natural creature.

As Cael rode him down again, he swung the begrimed blade of his spear low. The animal didn't even flinch. The sharpened edge of the spear struck at its forelegs.

The shudder of the blow went up Eowain's arm painfully as if he'd struck an anvil with all his strength. Cael's sword rang off his helmet. Eowain spun and went down again on a knee.

He shook his head. Cael wheeled the beast around once more. The animal capered on its legs as if Eowain hadn't struck it at all. *Like its hide is made of steel.* He shook his head again.

Eowain could almost see Cael's grin through his visored helm. The bandit chief spurred the beast again. It leaped sprightly to its bloody work.

He set the butt of the spear in the churned mud of the field, twisted his hands around its ashen shaft, and dropped on it with his knee to lend it his weight.

The black chest and legs of the beast filled his vision. Cael aimed to trample him down into the mud and be done with him.

Annwn if he will. Eowain raised the blade of the spear and roared like a bear. "DROMA!"

Like a catapult stone, the full, freighted weight of the beast crashed into him.

The spear of Findtan held firm. Cael and the beast cartwheeled up over Eowain's head, then crashed down on him as they—all three—tumbled down the hill.

Eowain found himself flat on his belly. He'd lost his shield somewhere in the mud. He looked up into the milk-white eyes of the sorcerous steed. There was no natural fear there. No pain. Yet the spear of Findtan was plunged half its length through the beast's chest. It blew twice from its flared nostrils. Then its black, lathered hide melted away into the ground and disappeared. The spear of his father lay on the field coated in nothing more than oily black ichor.

Sore and shaken, Eowain pushed himself up and rested a moment on his knees.

Cael was not far away. He sat up slowly, pulled his black-plumed helmet loose and tossed it away. He shook his head and looked about to find Eowain.

His long, oily hair fell to his shoulders. His face was narrow and flat. Blood spurted from a nose surely broken, and grime covered his cheeks. He wiped at his mouth and looked at the blood on the back of his glove, then spit several teeth loose. "Well, Yer Grace?"

Eowain knew what he meant. "Aye." He nodded to the bandit-chief, levered himself up to his feet, and drew his sword. "Let's have done."

Cael nodded in return, found his sword in the mud near to hand, and rose to his feet. "I'll have that pretty little bride of yours, you know." With blade raised, he went on. "I'll split her *gee* wide open, I will."

They fought all through the day and into the twilight. At last, as sunset approached, weary of their sparring, Eowain and Cael each knelt in the mud, facing each other and breathing hard.

"Yer... a hard man... ta kill..., Yer Grace." Cael clutched his injured left hand close to his chest.

But Eowain had to admit it: the bandit was no slouch with a sword. Quick and agile, he'd picked and slashed at Eowain and worn him down through the long day. Only Eowain's bear-like strength and obduracy had kept him on his own feet.

Eowain's men had fallen back all around them, save for a handful of his personal guard. These held off Cael's bandits, who had less honor about their single combat.

Eowain lifted one knee and planted his foot on the ground. He intended to rise and continue.

Cael raised a hand. "Stay, Yer Grace." He nodded to the sun. "The light is gone. A night's truce? To meet again on the morrow?"

It was a gentleman's agreement. *Perhaps Cael wasn't always a bandit?* Eowain wondered where he'd come from, how he'd come to his present state.

But he was blowing hard, and his back and shoulders ached. He didn't really care enough to ask. "Aye," he agreed. "Upon the morrow then."

Eowain left the bandits in possession of the field.

EITHNE PICKED UP a white stone and considered the fickle board. They were well into the second phase of the game, and Alva Damar pressed on the King Stone at the center. Eithne struggled to hold off the ban-drymyn's assault.

They were in a night's camp at the very border of the Vale of Thaynú. A few small cook-fires were all they permitted themselves as the last hours of the night lingered toward the dawn.

"But what is love, then, Alva, if one can't expect one's wishes to be respected? There was no need for Eowain to send me away as if I were

made of some rare Narician glass. You and my father know just as well that
the fray holds no terror for me."

Eithne placed the white stone, blocked Alva's advance, and stole away
one of her black stones.

"I don't think His Grace doubts your heart, my lady. That is simply
not the manner of wife he needs right now. One of the duties of a wife and
queen is to manage your lordship's kingdom and properties when he is
away on his overlord's business. If the rumors are true and the Gruin-men
attempt an incursion this summer, he may be away for weeks at a time
on campaign. It will fall to you to stand his ground at home and secure
the integrity of his kingdom. Then you will find combat enough, as you
wrangle with the fractious cattle-lords for the full-share of their taxes and
the full measure of their war-like young men."

There was a call from their perimeter, a challenge from one of their
guards. There was a murmured reply. A moment later, a boy was led into
the camp. "He comes from Eowain," announced his escort.

Eithne waved him close to the fire. The lad was out of breath and
sweating. Eithne summoned a cup for him. "What news?"

The messenger, short of breath, accepted the cup and took a long
drink before he made reply.

Eowain put down a black stone. Across the fallen log they used as a
bench, Medyr, wan and haggard in the firelight, raised a white stone
and considered the board between them.

Eowain was satisfied that he'd secured at least two possible paths to
the edge against Medyr. With his latest move, he'd unhinged the Lord-
Drymyn's defense and threatened the King Stone at the center.

The sun had set some hours earlier. The night around their campfire
was full of shadows and darkness. Ól came around and Eowain poured
himself a cup, passed the skin to Lorcán's three-fingered grasp.

It had been a long day. Eowain ached in places he hadn't known
he had.

A quiet murmur of talk floated around the camp. The men were weary. Eowain sat up, stretched his aching lower back. With that move came pain to his bruised and battered chest and shoulders.

Medyr placed the white stone and called Eowain's attention back to the game. His Lord-Drymyn had acquitted himself well on the field, with nothing but his blackthorn stick. Eowain rebuked himself for ever doubting the man's loyalty. "Are you well?"

Medyr nodded wearily. "When They are not forgetful, They demand a steep price." He put two fingers to his nose and squeezed at the bridge.

"Are you still sure this is the right thing to do?" Eowain nodded to his brother. "Lorcán has his doubts."

"Are you sure yourself, Your Grace?"

Eowain shook his head and considered the board that Medyr had left him. "I won't lie. She hasn't accepted the pledge of my troth. It makes me wonder. She's a Fiatach, and a Gwynn. Could this be some ploy to weaken Droma? Have the Fiatach made cause with the Cailech or the Gruin-men? Is this whole action meant only to bleed us?" He took a black stone and placed it aggressively, threatening the King's Stone at the center. "Old Time, he is a-flying. She should not be so coy in times like these."

Having heard that Eowain was alive and healthful in camp, Eithne dismissed the messenger to find food and drink as he might. Across the fickle board, Alva took up a black stone and found advantage, pressing a line toward Eithne's King-Stone at the center of her board.

Eithne's maid Cunneen sighed and gazed up at the thin sliver of waning moon that still hung in the sky. "He's so brave."

Eithne wrinkled her nose at the game-board. "Not so brave."

"Oh, but he is, my lady." She put her cheek in her hand. "And so noble, standing to the hazard to protect your virtue."

"I can care for my own virtue." Eithne took up a white piece and blocked Alva's line toward the King Stone.

"Oh, I'm sure your husband would care quite well for your virtue." Alva placed a black stone seemingly without thought, captured Eithne's white piece and exposed her King-Stone once more. "You must make a decision, you know?"

Eithne scowled at the state of the game, and looked to the east. Dawn had begun to chase away darkness. Damara, bright Watch-Maiden of the Night, gleamed at her from the bruise-purple sky. "What if he's not the right man for me? How am I to know? If only I were older..."

Alva harrumphed. "For a marriage, that age is best when youth and blood are warmest. Don't be coy. Use your time, and while you may, get married."

She looked to the east and the brightening dawn. "The lamp of heaven, it's getting higher. We should make ready to go. The safety of the Vale can't be much further." She placed a white stone on the board, smiled, and took one of Alva's. "The morning is yet dry, but I fear we'll have rain."

Medyr placed a white stone and took one of Eowain's blacks.

How like life the game of fickle is, considered Eowain. He picked up a new black stone and placed it on the board. There was no obvious advantage in the move. Medyr furrowed his brows and considered his position.

Despite the sorcerous steed of Cael's, Eowain's men had held the center, only falling back when they felt the enthusiasm of the bandit's falter. Medyr and his acolyte had played no small part in the success of that action. They'd fought with skill, brained many an incautious brigand, and heartened the lads all the while. The very roots of the forest seemed to tangle the bandits' advance, and allowed Eowain's men time to fall back in good order, using the archers for cover.

But what would the morrow bring? He'd often said that luck could save a man, if only his courage held. *But there's sorcery involved now.* Was there some dark witch lurking in the wood, or had Cael somehow conjured that steed of smoke and shadow himself? Could Eowain uphold his courage against such dark magicks?

And what of Eithne if he failed? He'd sent her away, but she might be camped somewhere in the night behind him, close to harm's reach and not yet safe. He'd wanted her close to him all through their journey, to better protect her. *But I have to protect her from a distance now.* Despite himself, he feared for her.

Medyr placed a black stone upon the board. "Challenge, Your Grace."

As the sunrise approached, the thin sliver of the waning moon hung low in the Fish, a constellation of stars low in the western sky. Their camp was packed, and Eithne stepped up into her saddle. The trees in the twilight seemed dark, without the yellow-green blush of coming spring.

Alva too considered the sky. Wind was bringing rain clouds from the northwest mountains. "Tomorrow night will bring the darkness of the Witches' Moon. Cétshamain approaches swiftly."

"Why is this so important?" Eithne heard the shrill tone in her own voice. She'd slept poorly, worried for Eowain and his men, and played at fickle the rest of the night. Alva's last gambit had put a black stone on the board and compromised the King-Stone that Eithne defended.

Alva pointed into the east. "Because the Dragon is coming."

"The dragon? What dragon?"

She looked from star to star in the firmament, as if calculating some strange geometry. "Maelgenn's Dragon." She put her switch to the flanks of her pony. "We must hurry."

"We're all rushing to the Vale as if I've made my decision. I've not." She shook her head. "This arrangement has brought me nothing but danger. Kidnapped by Cael, rescued by Eowain, now betrayed and chased all through Ivea by Eowain's own cousin. Why would I want to risk my life by laying down with such a man?"

Alva shrugged. "Don't be stupid and selfish, girl. Would you really go through all this, yet not marry him? If for no other reason, it would save lives, and honor those spent for your sake."

"I didn't ask for any of this, you know. I had my doubts, even before Corchen put us on this road to the Vale."

"Then why put us all through this?" Alva's voice was stern, irritated. She too had slept little in the night.

"I'd hoped Eowain and I would have more— more time. To know one another. To be sure."

"There's nothing sure in this world, lass. Least of all love. And will ye or nil ye, the Dragon is coming. If you choose not to take Eowain to husband, then the course of *thayn* will run... not straight."

"But what if I don't love him? We've barely been together in all this time. When we are together, there's always some threat just around the corner. How can I be sure that he loves me?" She worried at her lower lip. Surely, Eowain would be facing another assault from the brigands as the sun rose yet higher.

"Love is being together." Alva fixed her with an eye. "Even when you are far distant."

CHAPTER ELEVEN

EOWAIN'S COMPANY SLOGGED backwards uphill in the rain through another whole day and night. The bandits continued to pick at them with archers, but the stream in its gully on their left and Eowain's work with his cavalry on the right prevented any breakthroughs. The steed of smoke and shadow had not been seen again, and neither Cael nor Tnúthgal had appeared on the field.

Dawn could barely be perceived beneath the overcast skies. Rain continued its light, steady thrum on the canvas of his tent. A servant brought in three wooden cups of hot birch tea. Eowain took one for himself, and waved for Lorcán and Medyr to sit by the fire with theirs. He ushered out the servant, taking a look at the dreary landscape before pulling the flap closed. "Unless I'm wrong, Eithne's company should be safe in the Vale by now, or will be before the day is out."

Lorcán nodded agreement.

Medyr seemed unfocused. Pale and haggard, he slouched and stared into the fire. A tight linen bandage showed a rust-red splotch of blood on his upper arm. He'd been praying and fighting in the front rank with the men again, and taken a gash from a blade for his trouble. "What's that?" He looked up from the flames, then nodded agreement. "Oh, aye," he murmured. "Even if the rain slowed them down yesterday, they'll surely make the Vale today." His gaze drifted back to the flames and he slouched once more into silence.

Eowain gestured to the flap of the tent. "It looks like we'll have another day of rain. Cael and Tnúthgal must know by now that they're only hope for scuttling the marriage is to break through and face whatever defense the Vale can muster to get at Eithne, or to kill me. And I'm certainly near-to-hand."

Lorcán's face was grim. He took a sip from his tea. "You should go on to the Vale. Let Medyr and I hold the line here."

Eowain gestured with his cup. "No. If anyone's going on to the Vale, it's Medyr."

Medyr looked up from the fire. "Me? But why, Your Grace?"

"You're worn out, Medyr. We can all see it. If you stay here, you certainly can't be fighting on the line anymore. A weary mind makes mistakes, and a mistake will get you killed." Eowain pointed to the bandage.

"But, Your Grace—."

"I'm not really asking you, Medyr. What kind of king would I be if I let my drymyn get himself killed?"

"But the sorcery, Your Grace?"

Lorcán shrugged. "We saw no sign of sorcery all yesterday, nor any day before that. Perhaps they have no more?"

Eowain chewed at his lip. He didn't relish the thought of facing black magick without Medyr. But neither was he willing to see what further price the Gods would demand of his drymyn. If he could send Medyr to safety, he'd feel better about what must surely come. "No matter. We'll face whatever they bring against us and continue our withdrawal, holding them back from the Vale as long as we can. If there's more you can do, Medyr, then use it to prepare the Vale's defense to receive us. We'll likely arrive with wolves on our heels."

Medyr tried to rise in protest. He put a hand to his back, winced, and sat back down heavily. "Fine." He accepted Eowain's decision all unwillingly. "I'll take my acolyte with me?"

Eowain agreed. "And that merchant's apprentice. He's a brave lad, but this isn't his fight. We need no trouble with his father back home. Take his pet Foreigner too. And the scout, Corvac. Just to be safe." He paused a long moment. "And tell Eithne…" Tell her what? A welter of confusion arose in him. They'd come so far, through so much already. What was left for him to say? "Tell her I wish I had loved her better."

Lorcán raised eyebrows at him.

Medyr shook his head. "No. Tell her yourself, Your Grace. Love is an act of courage, after all. An act of faith. And you certainly do not lack for courage. Nor, I suspect, for love."

Eowain grunted at the Lord-Drymyn. "Hmph. Time will tell."

Before taking his leave, Medyr insisted on heaping blessings on him once more. He purified Eowain with smoke, and wrapped a tiny strip of white cloth around his arm, held in place by sticky tree sap on its ends. Then he handed Eowain a whitish-metal coin. Eowain turned it over in his palm as Medyr chanted. It bore the likeness of a horse's head in profile upon the one side, and a woman's likeness on the reverse.

As Medyr finished his chants, Eowain held up the coin. "What's this?"

"*Findruinne*, Your Grace. What the ancients called 'white bronze,' though there's no bronze in it. An alloy of white gold and silver."

Eowain didn't know much about metallurgy, but he thought he knew that much: "You can't alloy gold and silver."

A wan smile touched Medyr's lips. "No, you can't, Your Grace. Not without magick." He nodded to the coin. "It will act as a focus for Echraide's special blessing on you. Perhaps it will encourage her to be less forgetful of you. You are the Goddess's husband, after all." He patted Eowain on the shoulder and left to gather his acolyte and the merchant.

Lorcán snorted. "I found the Goddess to be a damned negligent wife." He clenched the three fingers of his left hand.

Eowain considered the coin. The goddess of Droma had done little enough for his brother's kingship, it was true. But safe was better than sorry, he supposed. Eowain put the coin into the purse on his belt.

Medyr's acolyte and the merchant's apprentice approached. The merchant seemed displeased. "I should not go, Your Grace. It would be zhe first honor to stay and fight wiz you against zhese savages."

"These," corrected the acolyte. The merchant scowled at him.

"Your bravery is admirable," said Eowain. "But your father will want you back alive. This is not your fight."

"But sure and it is *my* fight, begging Your Grace's pardon." The acolyte straightened his shoulders and lifted his chin. "I'm a man of Droma, sure as any here."

Eowain shook his head. "You're a man of the Drymyn Order. You and Medyr shouldn't be fighting at all. Your Order is usually quite stern about its neutrality."

"Sure and this isn't politics, my lord. We're fighting bandits and raiders." Adarc set his jaw and crossed his arms.

"*Ja*, Your Grace." The merchant crossed his arms as well. "And the bandits, they are the hazard to the trade, and so it is my fight too, *ja?*"

Eowain looked at the two of them, obstinate in their protest. He glanced at the merchant's Foreigner in his steel-ringed jack as he stepped up behind his charge. The Foreigner seemed hard-bitten, no stranger to war. Eowain had noted his work over the last several days. *I know his name... From the meeting in my hall. When Eithne told me what the hag from Gluintír had done.* Corentin was the merchant, Corvac the scout. What was the mercenary's name? "Yokel."

The mercenary looked at him strangely and grunted. "Do not speak *zhee* Gallavach."

The merchant slapped the mercenary on his broad chest. "You don't have to speak, Jôkull. Just stand there and look menacing. It's what you're good at."

The scout, Corvac, hovered nearby as well, and scuffed the ground with the toe of his boot.

Eowain pursed his lips. "Are you all resolved on this then?"

The Foreigner simply raised eyebrows at him and shrugged. Corvac nodded, but said, "I'm at your command, Your Grace."

"*Ja*. We are *ráidjana*, as you say. Resolved."

Eowain conceded. "We'll be honored to have you fight beside us."

"Well," said Medyr. "It looks like we're ready then." He'd come up behind Eowain. He hemmed, and his head and neck moved forward with a twisting motion as he looked down. His eyes closed, and his lips went thin and pulled back at the corners. "Eowain—."

A horn sounded from downslope. The bandits were coming. "No time." Eowain jerked a thumb at the merchant and the acolyte. "Go on, you lot. Find a place on the line." Eowain clapped Medyr's shoulders in his hands. "Go, Medyr. Gods be with you."

"And with you, Your Grace." Medyr's voice was husky. He sketched a holy sign in the air between them.

Eowain nodded, then slapped Medyr once more on the shoulder before he turned down the hill, drew his sword and called for his horse.

If we can just hold them one more day, just make it back to the Vale before sunset... The knot of fear in Eowain's belly ached, as it always did before battle. He glowered at the raining, gray sky. *If we can just get a little luck.*

Eithne's face came to mind. Knowing green eyes. Fair skin, high cheeks. Rose red lips. Luck will only save a man so long as his courage holds. He remembered the Lord-Drymyn's words. *Love is courage.*

EOWAIN HOISTED HIMSELF up into the saddle and looked down the slope of the trail to the line of his men. He'd chosen the best field he could for their camp overnight, but a handful of forested hills limited his sight distance. Bandit archers sniped at his skirmishers across the brook on the left flank. Heavy forest on the far side frustrated his men's efforts to return volleys.

The men along the front were restless. No assault was yet forthcoming, but there, too, snipers picked with arrows at the line, and rattled the men's confidence despite Medyr's blessings. They huddled behind their shields, or cursed and cried out when a shaft found a rare opening. His archers at the center returned volleys over the line with judicious discrimination. Arrows had become a valuable commodity through the last two days, and no man was willing to take a shot without a certain target.

Eowain breathed easier when he considered the right flank. The hills and trees would make a cavalry charge difficult at best, and a full day of rain had left the ground sodden. Valuable mounts would be lost to accidents in the mud before they ever reached the handful of spear-armed skirmishers he'd ordered to hold that corner.

Over the anxious murmur of the men, there came to his ear a new sound: chanting. But not the familiar chanting of the drymyn. This was a rough tongue, agglutinated, and in all ways strange.

Líl na Izzi, Sagèntar!
Gibil, Líl na Izzi, Sagèntar!
Girra, Líl na Izzi, Sagèntar!

On and on the chanting went, and the men on the front line grew silent. The sniping from the wood ceased. Men peered fearfully past their shields.

What new villainy is this?

Beside him, Lorcán licked at his lips and rubbed at his throat, clenched his half-handed fist. "Should we pull the men back?"

"I don't know. Pull back from what? It's just nonsense so far."

Lorcán scowled. "We've seen what their nonsense can do."

From the wood, fire light suddenly erupted in the shadows, as if several torches had been kindled at once. Eowain felt fear seize his belly. "FIRE!"

From the trees, flaming arrows shot forth into the company's center. Most struck at the round wooden shields his men carried. With a pop, those shields burst into flames. Men screamed in fright and threw them away.

Elsewhere in the center, the arm of a man's leather jack ignited. His neighbors broke formation and shoved to get clear of him as he flailed the flaming arm. Shouts of "Hold the line!" arose from the sergeants.

Another swarm of arrows broke from the trees. These carried no fire, but found three men in the front line who'd thrown away their protection, and killed just the same.

Smoke from the wet, burning shields billowed up from the ground. The man on fire was tackled to the ground by his companions and rolled through the wet mud. Men echoed, "Hold the line! Hold the line!" and the center rippled.

A deep-throated shout arose from the trees, and the bandits boiled forth, swords swinging.

The men of Droma at the center, Eowain's own bodyguard, experienced men of war, brought shields and spears to bear with a grunt. Bandits battered against the hedge of spears with their shields. Men cried out, blood flew through the air, smoke obscured the mêlée.

To the left, an ominous shadow settled along the near bank of the brook. The rainclouds already obscured the sun, yet all down the course, darkness like a patch of midnight obscured the far bank. His skirmishers, caught in the unnatural darkening, were barely visible, dim shadows. They cried out with fright and surprise. A dozen of them fell back in disarray into more healthful light. Bolts sang through the darkness into the welter of their confusion.

"I'll take the left!" Lorcán spurred his steed down the hill, with five cavalrymen at his rear, spears leveled to meet any assault that might emerge from that unwholesome dark.

Eowain stood in his stirrups and squinted at the center line. With no wind to disperse the billowing smoke, it spread across the field.

On the flank, Lorcán rallied the skirmishers amid a hail of bolts.

Realization dawned on Eowain. *The assault on the center is a bluff!* Eowain raised a horn to his lips and blasted the center's withdrawal note. At the rear, men looked back and saw their flag-bearer's signal. With spears and shields set before them, they marched backward, slow and steady. As they moved, the men before them did the same, until the whole center was moving backward, out of the smoke.

A shout rose then from the left. Bandits, wild-eyed with terror, charged through the gloom. Eowain's skirmishers answered them with a volley of spears and arrows. Half a dozen bandits went down, but Eowain could see that neither Annwn nor high water would turn them twice across that gloom of terror. On they came, two dozen bandits against Eowain's scant dozen skirmishers.

"Hold the left!" Eowain's shout echoed from a dozen throats.

Then he emerged from the smoke—Cael the Viper—and wreaked havoc on Eowain's center. He drove men—near to panic already—back against the steady withdrawal.

Rage boiled up in Eowain's breast. *Now! For Eithne! For Droma! End this!*

He blasted the horn and spurred his steed. Hooves thundered down the trail. He leveled his spear as footmen panicked and pushed to clear the charge. Eowain's vision narrowed. Pale, bearded faces—mouths wide with both horror and cheers—passed through his sight as he rode. The spear of Findtan found one such mouth and ripped the skull behind it open, pulled it loose from its shoulders and hurled it, spraying blood, over the fray.

A bandit with a shattered spine lay face-down on the ground. His fingers clawed spasmodically at the ground. Half a dozen others swarmed around Eowain, swords and axes lifted. They'd cast away their bows, useless at such deadly close quarters.

With a leap, Eowain bounded from the saddle, broadsword in hand. He sheared two bandits half-asunder as he came to ground, then stood astride them and bellowed like an enraged bear.

Cael hurled an axe at Eowain and rushed after it with lifted knife. Eowain ducked the axe, then caught the wrist that drove the knife at his throat. He and Cael went to ground together, rolling over and over.

Cael was like a wild beast, his muscles like streel strings. Eowain strove to hold the bandit-chief's wrist and bring his own broadsword into play, but so vehement was the struggle that each attempt to strike was blocked. Cael wrenched furiously to free his knife hand, clutched at Eowain's sword arm, and drove his knees at Eowain's groin.

Then Cael shifted the knife to his free hand. In that instant, Eowain, struggling to one knee, drove the bandit-chief back with a desperate swing of his blade.

Cael sneered at him, and Eowain got a good look at the knife for the first time. It was an odd choice for the battlefield, with its short reach. But its blade did not gleam or shimmer. A dark, viscous slime seemed to coat it.

Sharp pain lanced through his arm of a sudden. Cael had sliced him above the elbow with the knife, not deep enough to bleed, but already the cut looked red, swollen, and angry. *The snake's fang is poisoned,* realized Eowain.

A handful of bandits came to their master's aid. Eowain beat down the thrust of a short sword, avoided the stroke of an axe with a sidewise spring that brought him within arm's length of a squat brigand stooping for a bow. As he straightened with it, Eowain's red sword flailed down and clove him from shoulder to breastbone, where the blade stuck. Cael and the remaining bandit rushed in, one from each side.

A cry of "Pelan!" resounded across the field, and a well-hurled axe reduced Eowain's attackers by one. Abandoning his sword, Eowain wheeled and met Cael with his bare hands. The wiry bandit, a head shorter than Eowain, leaped in with his axe, and at the same time stabbed murderously with his envenomed knife. But the blade snapped on Eowain's mailed chest, and the axe was checked in mid-air as Eowain's fingers locked like iron on the descending arm. A bone snapped. Cael winced and faltered. In the next instant he was off his feet, lifted high above Eowain's head. He writhed in the air for an instant—kicked—thrashed.

Then Eowain dashed him headlong to the ground with such force that he rebounded, and came to lay still on his back. His awkward posture spoke of a broken spine.

Eowain fell heavily on Cael the Viper's biceps. He felt those muscles rupture under his knees. Then he leaned in close to Cael. "For every widow and orphan. For every kidnapped child. And for an oath I made to Eithne." His hoarse whisper was terrible even in his own ears.

Then he dug his thumbs into Cael's eyes.

"RALLY HERE! RALLY here!" Tnúthgal's shout was taken up by all the men near him, and heard through the wood. Cael's bandits and the Cailech men under Toryn the Stout heard the cry and gathered into a ragged camp as sunlight waned.

A rough pavilion of canvas was pitched at the center of the clearing. Beneath it, a plank of wood over a saw-horse stood for a table. Tnúthgal pounded on it, his fists clenched in well-worn black-leather gloves that gleamed with use. He gnashed his teeth at the lame-witted lieutenants he'd inherited from Cael's rabble. "How could you not take their left?"

Toryn the Stout, red hair wild and tangled, clutched at an injury to his left shoulder, bandaged and filthy with blood and mud. "Even half-handed, Lorcán is no mean warrior. He rallied their skirmishers and broke us with their cavalry charge." Dark circles had gathered under Toryn's haunted eyes. "That thrice-damned gloom of black sorcery didn't help matters." His gaze flickered sidelong to Kúlkak, the pallid, dirty, bone-thin sorcerer.

Tnúthgal turned his gaze on Kúlkak as well. "And what in Annwn was that—that unhealthful air? What vile goblins of darkness did you conjure?"

The hollowness in Kúlkak's wyrd, yellow-rimmed pupils met his gaze. There was no humanity in that look at all, just empty madness. "Five times the Dragon has come before. Now the Dragon comes again, in fulfillment of Maelgenn's Prophecy."

Tnúthgal pounded the table again. "No! Speak plain, sorcerer."

Kúlkak's stare grew long, then he blinked, slowly and languidly. "We must not allow Maelgenn's Prophecy to be fulfilled." His voice trembled with a mad glee.

"Does anyone understand what this mad-man is talking about?" Tnúthgal fingered three of Cael's men, sergeants that had survived the day and rallied their retreat. They'd been in the field with the sorcerer several weeks longer than Tnúthgal.

They stared back at him with ghastly eyes. The things they'd seen in those weeks. Tnúthgal shuddered to think of it. Cael the Viper had kidnapped children from the hinterlands of Droma, Ivea, and the Cailech, and inflamed tensions all through the region. And this sorcerer had done atrocities upon those children.

This wasn't supposed to happen. He gritted his teeth. "Fine. Cael is dead. What are we going to do now?" He pointed a finger at Toryn the Stout. "Can I depend on you and your men to see this through? Eowain can't possibly withstand another assault."

As haunted as he looked, Toryn set a stern grimace upon his own face. "He and I have a grievance over thirty head of cattle. I'll see honor satisfied."

Tnúthgal nodded. "And I'll see you satisfied for your thirty head of cattle. Once Eowain is dead on his shield."

Toryn shook his head. "No. I'll have the Lady Eithne."

"Like Annwn you will." Tnúthgal wasn't about to let Toryn challenge his authority and deprive him of his trophy.

"Annwn has everything to do with it." Toryn glanced at the sorcerer again. "It's rumored she's freighted with portents and fortunate *thayn*. Your cousin's Lord-Drymyn is up there, and the whole Drymyn Order gathered behind him, on the strength of this woman's *thayn*. If she's important enough to draw Bán-Drúmor Corchen from the Vale for the first time in an odd-dozen years, then control of this woman will give her master leverage against the Order's interference. I'll have her, and the power that comes with her."

Tnúthgal felt his own lip curl with a snarl. "I am Tnúthgal Fork-Beard son of Ferudach, of the Clan of Donnghal of Droma. The portents favor an heir of Donnghal, not your ill-begotten clan." He thought about that red hair, that fair skin, those pale, rose lips and those hungry, defiant eyes. Eithne's beauty had infatuated him. And the heirs he would sire on her would be strong boys with good family alliances, destined to be great men in the Northeast. "She'll be mine. That's not a question. If you doubt it, you will die here and now." Tnúthgal drew himself up and put his hand on the hilt of the sword on his belt.

Toryn's gaze measured his commitment, then looked away. "Forty head of cattle."

"Thirty-five."

"Thirty-eight."

"Thirty-five."

Toryn shrugged. "Thirty-five head, then. Fine. Take the girl."

Kúlkak licked his lips, tasted at the air, sniffed. "Ah. The time is right." His wyrd gaze abstracted. "Will not the dread Master also be there? Lord of all fevers and plagues, grinning Dark Angel of the Four Wings, horned, with rotting genitalia, from which he howls in pain through sharpened teeth over the lands of the cities sacred to the ULLAKHPHA even in the height of the Sun as in the height of the Moon; even with whirling sand and wind, as with empty stillness, and it is the able sorcerer indeed who can remove the Master once he has laid hold of a man, for the Master lays hold unto death."

He rose and rushed from the tent, called out to two boys in his thrall. They gathered up a child from among their kidnapped slaves and dragged him through the camp. Kúlkak ordered a fire built up and urged men with drums to steady rhythm.

Tnúthgal and Toryn watched together as the shadows gathered in the firelight and the twilight dwindled. Clouds obscured the sunset. Toryn nodded. "Whatever we do, we must kill that sorcerer when all is done."

"Agreed. What do you know of him?"

"A madman wandering the trails of Cailech since autumn. Misery and ill-fortune travel in his wake. There are rumors of the dark mistresses he claims to serve. Evil witches in the southern woodlands, toward Aileach." Toryn pulled at his beard. "But I've never seen anything like what I saw today. We can't let him live."

"We won't. But we've seen what he can do, and he shares our goals. He lives until this is over." Tnúthgal secured his helmet to his head and watched as Kúlkak's bonfire grew and the child, no more than three, wailed and cried.

Revulsion shivered through Tnúthgal. He twisted and stretched his neck and shoulders. *Without the sorcerer, I'm not even sure we can do this now.* Tnúthgal drew his sword from his sheath. "Tell the men to get ready."

IA

IA

IA

IO

IO

IO

I AM the God of Gods

I AM the Lord of Darkness, and Master of Magicians

I AM the Power and the Knowledge

I AM before all things.

As Kúlkak chanted, he drew a sharpened bone dagger, took the wretched slave-child by the hair, and slit the child's throat all in an instant. Then he shoved the blood-spewing child into the flames. The greedy fire roared and flared. The child flailed. Absently, Tnúthgal wondered if the child would bleed out first, or burn.

I AM before all things.
Before ME was made Nothing that was made.

Kúlkak drew forth a square of linen cloth, stained red. He wiped the knife upon it until it was sodden with blood.

I AM BEFORE all gods.
I AM before all days.
I AM before all men and legends of men.
I AM the ANCIENT ONE.

Kúlkak released the red linen cloth. The heat of the flames became like a furnace, drawing wind, and the red linen cloth fluttered into the flames and sizzled.

NO MAN may seek my resting place.
I receive the Sun at night and the Moon by day.
I AM the receiver of the sacrifice of the Wanderers.
The Mountains of the West cover me.
The Mountains of Magick cover me.

To Tnúthgal, it seemed like Kúlkak's wyrd, yellow-rimmed eyes flashed with a hint of sickly green. The sorcerer's hoarse whisper scraped through the air like a sand-devil over arid rocks.

I AM THE ANCIENT OF DAYS.

All around him, Tnúthgal felt the uneasy attention of the darkening mountain forests. From the duff of the soil emerged every crawling thing, every spider and centipede, and every kind of verminous rodent from the earth, the trees, and the air. Like a blanket, they swarmed over the ground, and moved together uphill. Toward Eowain's camp.

Kúlkak howled in agony, fell to his knees, and gripped his head between his fists.

"Now?" Toryn held his spear and shield at the ready.

Tnúthgal shook his head. "Not yet." If the sorcerer really had summoned that swarm of vermin and could do so again? *I'll see them eating my cousin alive, once he's paid for his insolence.*

The sorcerer cocked his head and locked eyes with Tnúthgal. The yellow-rimmed, lizard-like eyes were devoid of any merely Mannish understanding. "When Sixth Time the Dragon flies..." Kúlkak licked his lip. His eyelids fluttered, his brows knotted. "Why can't I ever remember the rest...?" He rapped his head with one fist as his face twisted with pain. "Do you feel it?" His ophidian stare locked onto Tnúthgal's eyes in a moment of lucid recognition. "Do you feel it? The acute sense of dislocation? The wrongness of where we are?"

"What're you talking about?"

"I belong somewhere else. Don't you feel you belong somewhere else?" He seemed confused.

Tnúthgal spit on the ground. "Where else, sorcerer?"

Kulak furrowed his brow. "I really can't say. Can't say where it might be." He squinted at Tnúthgal. "Is that strange?"

Tnúthgal grunted. "Hmph. Decidedly so." He put a hand under the sorcerer's arm and pulled him to his feet. "Go on, then." He nodded up the hill. "Show me what else you've got."

CHAPTER TWELVE

THE SKY WAS sea-grey, a sullen battalion of clouds from the Summer Sea, and the wind wet with the kisses of mournful waves. The sun set unseen as Eithne and her company turned the final bend of the pass and came in sight of the Vale of Thaynú.

From the pass, the land and pine forests sloped down steeply into wide, open meadowland. Sheep and cows grazed the pasture, and some land had been brought under cultivation. Eithne watched the tatterdemalion display of people at their labor and felt relief, as if there, at last, were civilized people.

The meadows were a riot of wild-flower colors, muted by the mist and rain. Amid the riotous colors sprouted a village. Or rather, what the village had become. The village proper was a tiny collection of houses and a few shops, not unlike a hundred other hamlets of similar size in the Five Kingdoms. But for the few days leading up to Cétshamain, the village had swelled out into all the surrounding fields. Pavilions were pitched; market stalls sprang up. Carpenters built stands beneath awnings so the nobility could watch contests in comfort. Targets were erected for archery, a sand floor made for the swordsmanship contest, a circuit drawn for chariotry. Paddocks appeared, as did wattle pens for ducks and swine, sheep and kine. Butchers sharpened their knives, and ovens were built brick by brick. Banners flew, people pushed in and out of gates, servants set up lists for the games, and pavilions were sprouting all over the Vale of Thaynú and on the slopes of the hills like strange and beautiful flowers. People had come by wagons, mules, horses, and a-foot on pilgrimage to the high-spring festival of Cétshamain in the Vale.

Far across the wide meadow, along the tree-line, there moved a majestic, Great Horn Elk with a rack of antlers fully as magnificent as those in Eowain's hall.

Nearer to hand, a small herd of noble, shaggy aurochs roamed the meadow and feasted on the spring growth.

At the center of the valley, upslope from them, a tall, level-topped hill stood, upon which stood a crown of stones arranged in circles.

Beyond that hill, the mountains rose precipitously to snowy heights lost in clouds.

Eithne felt her heart lift at the sight of the place. Consecrated to the spirit of the Great Mother, the Goddess Thaynú, and source to a well of pure, lustral spring water, it was a shrine dedicated to bringing life lightly forth upon the face of the Abred.

Behind her, their raggle-taggle band of stragglers began to bunch as they came in sight of the stream-crossed mountain valley. Wounded men, tired men, and the great creaking hulk of Lady Rathtyen's wagon breathed a collective sigh.

What of Eowain? Not for the first time, the thought rose unbidden to her mind. She gnawed at her lip.

Her father snapped a finger, and a scout on a light horse galloped down into the Vale with the grave tidings of bandits behind them.

Alva Damar on her pony put a hand upon Eithne's leg. "We should be moving on, my lady."

Fear welled in her breast then and she put out her hand to the old matron. "Will Eowain survive the task I've set for him?" She suddenly couldn't bear the thought of him dying in some stupid effort to prove himself worthy of her love.

What is my love, after all, that it should be deemed worth any of this killing and murder that has pursued me? And by all the Gods, hasn't Eowain done enough to earn so trifling a thing by now?

She thought of Alva's words, that she should simply marry him, if only to save lives and honor those who'd died on this journey. Shouldn't she, after all, accept his troth in good faith, and agree to this arrangement, trusting him to be a good man to her?

Yet what if he dies? Straggling groups of wounded, falling back from the battle, told of dark horrors and hand-to-hand bloodletting with the bandits and savages.

Eowain might be dead already. She put her hand to her throat. *No,* she insisted to herself. *I will not pledge troth to him simply because he's a battle-hardy fool.* But how could she know what else he was? Yes, she'd played at fickle with him, and seen him care for his men for himself, heard the respect and honor with which he treated his fellow-king of Ivea. Even seen him jig among his warriors despite their cold, wet journey. But it seemed so little by which to measure his honor. How could she know her own feelings, when they'd spent so little time alone together? Was this love, this anxiety and fear that clutched at her heart, regardless of her doubts?

She remembered the taunting missives she'd sent him. She'd dared him to assault the fortress of her own self-doubt, and spurned him each time. Yet he defended that fortress by the same main force when Tnúthgal's plots endangered her.

She could not bear the idea that he might die thinking her coy for its own sake, without knowing this fear she felt then for him.

"Come, daughter." Her father rode up on her other side. Ahead, she could see the men of the Vale ranging through the land, coming to meet them at the pass. "We must hurry."

She turned back and looked down the hill, where dark smoke and fog marked the place where Eowain stood fighting.

EOWAIN LOOKED OVER his sleeping encampment as he sat on a log. The night gathered, and rain continued to fall. The few fires were smoky and irritating. No one could find anything to burn that wasn't sodden by the cold, relentless precipitation that soaked them to their bones. He clutched down his bear-skin cloak over his shoulders.

He was proud of himself, proud of his men. They'd held back both the bandits and the Cailech tribesmen. Lorcán had embarrassed Toryn the

Stout by tumbling his men back down into the stream gully and their own arcane gloom.

But he felt ill too. The mere scratch of Cael's blade had been enough to sicken him. The cut, though shallow, had grown black and swollen. Nausea roiled his guts. He felt pale and clammy to his own touch, and didn't know if it was the incessant cold and rain, or fever in his blood.

At least I finally have the eyes from Cael the Viper's head, as I swore to Eithne I would. He rolled the bloody eyeballs between his fingers, then turned to look through the flaps of his rough canvas tent. In the ancient days, it was said that Men had gained magickal powers in battle by throwing occult talismans at them, round balls known as *tathlum*, a slingstone made of cement.

Eowain had learned the ancient magick of making such a talisman from Medyr as one of the rites in becoming a young warrior. To make a *tathlum*, all one needed was a caustic bucket of noxious lime, a handful of prayers to invoke the spirits of Trógain Many-Skills and the Great Queen Mórrigú, and the hero's portion of the Mórrigú's acorn crop, the severed head of the chief man in one's calamities.

The ancient warriors used to make them from the brains of dead enemies hardened with lime.

> *A tathlum, heavy, fiery, firm,*
> *Which the Tuath Thaynann had with them,*
> *Was what broke fierce Balor's eye of old,*
> *In the battle of the great armies.*
> *"The blood of toads and furious bears,*
> *And the blood of the noble lion,*
> *The blood of vipers and of Osmuinn's trunks;—*
> *It was of these the tathlum was composed.*
> *"The sand of the swift Bælsasan sea,*
> *And the sand of the teeming Tâmaryan Sea;—*
> *All these, being first purified, were used*
> *In the composition of the tathlum.*
> *"Briun, the son of Bethar, no mean warrior,*
> *Who on the ocean's eastern border reigned;—*

It was he that fused, and smoothly formed,
It was he that fashioned the tathlum.
"To the hero Trógain was given
This concrete ball,—no soft missile;—
On the Plain of Towers amid shrieking wails,
From his hand he threw the tathlum.

The head was taken from one's victim, cracked open, and the brains rolled into the lime to make a concrete paste while the prayers were uttered. While the concrete was spun and mixed, the bones of the skull were cleaned and broken down into fragments. The bone was then mixed into the lime paste and rolled into a ball the size of a fist. A blessing was then said, calling for the battle-favor of Lord Trógain to reside there in the ball. The ball was then sprinkled with lustral water and left overnight to set.

The night air was damp with fog and rain. In such conditions, it was permitted to bake the *tathlum* to speed the hardening. In his tent, two men were turning a hardening ball of lime suspended on spears over his cook-fire.

Cael the Viper had finally paid for his crimes: murder, banditry, arson, rapine, kidnapping, burglary, robbery, assault, riot. Eowain had brought him to justice.

He looked back out into the camp. Night had fallen quickly after sunset. He'd ordered as many men to rest as he dared. With the back of the snake broken, he wanted the bandits to thrash and die like any honest serpent. That would be one less worry.

But Toryn the Stout had only been embarrassed, not defeated. And Tnúthgal was still unaccounted among the living and the dead upon the field. If Toryn and Tnúthgal could agree on differences, and their sorcerer was still abroad, and they could rally enough men between them, Eowain wasn't sure they would stand firm another day.

He'd fallen back four times already. The men were tired, and many of them wounded. Many more had been killed.

All this for love? Eowain wondered if Eithne was satisfied yet. Had he done enough yet to earn her love? He'd been up to his elbows in a man's brains that day. Hadn't he done enough to prove the trustworthiness of his pledge? To prove that he'd hazard any calamity with his own main force on her behalf? What more did she want?

Down in the camp, he heard a man cry out, "Damn rat!" He saw a shadow in the night rise and fall, heard a knife drop and a squeal.

Then another man cried out, and there was the meaty sound of a hand slapping a bare neck hard.

Eowain scratched at his beard. Under his arm.

Ouch. He slapped at a stinging knee absently through his leather greaves and breeks.

There were footsteps nearby, and a hushed challenge from his guard. A hushed reply, and a messenger came through, breathless. "Sir." The herald put a fist to his breast and knelt. "From Lady Eithne, with all speed. They are safe to the Vale. The Huntsmen of the Vale stand ready to receive and relieve you if you can fight a withdrawal over another half day. I have the word of their captain on this." He presented seals obtained from all those he'd served as proof of his word.

Eowain scratched at the back of his neck. "Well done. Check in with your sergeant." He dug a silver coin from a purse and tossed it to the messenger. "But get food and drink first."

The man caught the coin, knuckled his forelock, and went.

Eithne was safe. *At least that's done.* Her cousin, King Ardgar of Ivearda, would have arrived for the wedding with a small company, and the Huntsmen of the Vale were known to be stern and loyal defenders of the drymyn sisterhood's shrine. Between them and whatever Eowain could salvage from this fighting withdrawal, they would be able to stop the combined strength of Tnúthgal and Toryn the Stout.

But Eowain had to control another half-day's withdrawal through rough forested hills soaked with rain and still fall back with only minimal casualties. If he allowed himself to be overrun, the combined force of bandits and savage Cailech-men might still be able to break through to the Vale itself. He had to fall back with enough strength to make the victory decisive, or risk losing Eithne anyway.

And he had to stay alive—*Ouch!* He slapped at another sting on his inner leg. Scratched behind his ear. He'd lost the trail of this thought. *What was I ...?* Another man cried out in the camp, and there was another knife drawn and a squeal. Then another cry, from a different darkness in the night.

Then another.

Eowain slapped at another sting on his leg. Something crawled up inside his breeks. *Ow!* He stamped a foot. *And in my boot.* He stamped again, looking down at his foot.

Revulsion filled his throat. Torchlight glistened on the slimy hide and carapace of every crawling, biting, stinging thing that dwelt in the soil under the Abred as they erupted from beneath his place on the log.

He slapped at his neck, where a spider bit. He rubbed at his armpit, where lice conspired.

He slapped at his arm, where a centipede wriggled and reared and snapped its minuscule mandibles. His throat clenched with chthonic, primordial horror. He shook his vacant arm free from even the haunting memory of that moment.

On his legs, spiders and other vermin crawled, wriggled into nooks in his clothing, stung at him. He clawed at his crotch and rose. "By Annwn!" He slapped the assailants from his legs, his arms, clawed them from his neck.

All around, cries of surprise, pain, and fear arose. One of his guard stumbled past, clawing a swarm of millipedes from his face. A stray infantrymen slapped at a handful of rats that clawed stubbornly at his arms and head.

More sorcery! Eowain shouted for his brother, found him amid the growing welter. His brother stamped at a writhing nest of serpents. "Take the horsemen and the steeds. Flee north to the Huntsmen. It's said there is open meadow in the Vale, room enough for cavalry to maneuver. Go, and bring a charge back to support the Huntsmen. That will break them, if nothing else will."

Fear was gathered there in Lorcán's eyes. "Aye." His older brother put a hand on Eowain's shoulder, then raised his three-fingered fist to his breast.

Eowain felt his chest swell. "Aye. Go now." He slapped his brother's shoulder and turned to his guard. "Sergeant Cathasach!" They were all of them stabbing with knives and slapping with hands at rats and insects. "We have to walk the men out of here. They'll be coming."

The sergeant nodded, saluted, and shouted orders to assemble a line. Men broke off what they were doing, grabbed what they could, and ran to comply. There wasn't a Droma-man there who didn't know this was more sorcery. There wasn't a man there that didn't fear death in that moment.

Eowain didn't see a single man break. Every man went to his place. Scar-faced Gaeth and barrel-chested Mahon stood at his side, weapons ready. The acolyte slapped and scratched. The merchant and his Foreigner cried out with bites and stings. But the King of the Droma commanded. The King of the Droma stood with them.

Eowain beat a rhythm on the rim of his shield. He hammered it with the haft of his spear, given from the honored right hand of his father. He pounded it as he called men to form up for the King, to stand their ground, for the honor of the Goddess by whom the men of Droma swore.

Raise your spears
For the boys
No longer here!
Raise your spears and always be proud!
Stand for the fallen!
Stand here and now
Without fear!

Then all the men joined in.

HERE WE GO! HERE WE GO!
For the stories we've been told!
For the history forgotten,
For the land our father's rode!
HERE WE GO! HERE WE GO!
For the ones we left behind!

Let us honor their traditions!
Let us keep their dreams alive!

Out of the Abred came every rat, snake, and vermin. Out of the trees came every gnat and hornet. And out of the dark, rain-wet night came the howling, savage Cailech-Men and the fiercest and most hard-bitten bandits ever seen on a dark and rain-wet night.

Axes rose and fell, spears gleamed in firelight and smoke, swords parried and stabbed. Throats were slit and bellies laid open, and men paid their share to the Mórrigú's acorn crop of skulls.

From his tent, Eowain took up the *tathlum* of Cael the Viper, slimy and hardening, and set it in a sling of leather. He slung the *tathlum* above his head with all his strength, mocked the deeds of Cael the Viper, Villain of Droma, as his men sang and fought beside him. He cried out the song to Lord Trógain and summoned his battle-favor once more. He keened the dirge to Queen Mórrigú, and extolled the courage and honor of the dead Men of Droma.

Then he released the *tathlum* of Cael the Viper. The serpent's skull and brains, ground to a pulp of concrete, hurtled through the onslaught of Cailech-men in their rags and spears. By the powers of the Gods by whom the Men of Droma swore, it shrieked like a ban-shynn through the rain and fog to strike dead the first man it touched.

The *tathlum* of Cael the Viper shattered a jaw, interrupted a muttered invocation to a heathen Cailech god on a savage pagan tongue, and pierced the underside of a brain before it shattered the back of a skull and ricocheted on. It carried with it into the night the dying curse of Cael the Viper, Scourge of Droma, and the death shriek of his last victim.

Yet the Cailech-men came on. And there then, in the firelight, was red-haired, wild-eyed Toryn the Stout, defeated at the hill of Gluin by the very cattle he'd sought to steal. The dishonor of that defeat demanded Toryn's bloody and vengeful visage.

Eowain was just as glad to lay eyes on him. Good men had died scaling Gluin with him to win that victory. Toryn the Stout owed those men a blood-debt, and Eowain intended to collect.

•   •   •

MONSTERS DANCED IN bloody steps through a nightmare. Eowain slipped on bodies writhing in the mud, clawed at spiders and stinging, chitinous horrors, split open the skulls of all Cailech-men foolish enough to step to him. The killing took on a rhythm of chanted prayers that rose from the throat of every man. His spear stabbed, his shield parried, his steps staggered across an uncertain floor of mud and bodies like the prancing dance of a bear aroused to battle.

And onward came Toryn the Stout. He was young and strong, a raging bull, the pride of a generation of Cailech-men. For a blight on his vanity, his vengeful spirit burned. His broad sword flashed and stabbed, drove Eowain back, cracked against the haft of his father Findtan's spear, and shuddered through the wood of Eowain's shield.

Eowain cursed and scrambled for better footing. Toryn grinned and stabbed in at him. Eowain twisted and took the blow on his shield.

His heel landed upon a hissing beetle of notable girth, and burst its belly in an explosion of slime. Mud, slime, and blood, doing their grim work, gave loose beneath that heel. His ankle twisted, he heard a sharp, blunt crack, and blinding pain went through his eyes. His knee twisted, the sword of Toryn struck with all its force upon his shield, and down he went on the leg.

From the darkness, he heard the sorcerer's chant:

> *Líl na Izzi, Sagèntar!*
> *Gibil, Líl na Izzi, Sagèntar!*
> *Girra, Líl na Izzi, Sagèntar!*

Eowain saw bright flashes of firelight in the black forest down slope, like wisps of light traveling in blobs through the darkness.

Savages and bandits cut and slashed. Eowain's bodyguard fell back too far without him. He was enveloped. Toryn raised his sword and leaped upon him.

He battered away Toryn's blow with his shield. His knee and ankle, trapped awkwardly under him, winced like raven claws at his eyes.

The burning globules in his sight rose in a wave and went steady. Then there came the shout of Tnúthgal, his cousin and kinsman.

"Fire!"

Sparks flew through the darkness, spirits of calamity riding the bolts of Cael's surviving bandits. All around him, good Droma men cried out in shock and fear. Despite the rain, woolens burst into oily flame and the common sons of the goddess Echraide shrieked.

"No one left to save you, Eowain." Toryn steadied himself in the uphill mud. Eowain laid down his father's spear and drew forth his own plain sword of service-man's well-oiled steel. "Not your half-handed coward of a brother, not your lily-livered drymyn, not even your cousin. Just you and me. We'll see who the better man is. I'll see your father's spear shoved up your guts, and your brains for my own *tathlum!*"

Eowain braced himself. Sparks danced in his eyes. His head spun with vertigo and the shock of pain. He gritted his teeth. *Not broken. Sprained. My right ankle. Sprained.*

There wasn't a man of his guard in sight.

Toryn lowered his head, raised his shield and his sword, pawed at the ground for his footing.

This is gonna hurt, thought Eowain.

Yes. Eowain gritted his teeth. *Yes, it is.*

He twisted his knee for leverage, put torque into his hips, and thrust himself up. His sword stabbed, and pain lanced from his ankle to the sudden tears in his eyes. He cursed Echraide for doing to himself what needed to get done, and felt another snap.

From behind him, a song rose in a clear, strong Droma-tongue:

> *I arise today, through*
> *The strength of Ceugant,*
> *The light of the sun,*
> *The radiance of the moon,*
> *The splendor of fire,*
> *The speed of lightning,*
> *The swiftness of wind,*

The depth of the sea,
The stability of the earth,
The firmness of rock.

With a bear-like roar, Eowain, King of Droma, rose and stabbed Toryn the Stout, Bull of the Cailech, through the throat.

Beside him, the merchant slashed and parried with strange Aukrian manners, and cut down a Cailech-man. His Foreigner mercenary clattered like a junkyard in his rings of steel as he beat men with a stout, iron-knobbed truncheon and a hoarse shout in his motherless Foreign tongue.

The scout, Corporal Corvac of the King's Company of Droma, Shield of the East, cut and stabbed for all he was worth.

And there was the acolyte. Barely fourteen years of age, he battered and beat at bandit arms and heads with his blackthorn stick. Worse, he delivered a country church-master's perennial instruction on the merits of a stout stick of virtue to men of errant faith.

I arise today, through
The Gods' strength to pilot me,
The Gods' might to uphold me,
The Gods' wisdom to guide me,
The Gods' eye to look before me,
The Gods' ear to hear me,
The Gods' word to speak for me,
The Gods' hand to guard me,
The Gods' shield to protect me,
The Gods' host to save me
From snares of fiends,
From temptation of vices,
From everyone who shall wish me ill,
Afar and a-near.

CHAPTER THIRTEEN

The Gods' host to save me
From snares of fiends...

TNÚTHGAL HEARD THE lines of *the Cry of the Deer* through the smoke and fog.

Beside him, Kúlkak snickered and capered. "Almost. Almost." He shook visibly and his head twitched. He stooped and plucked at the mud.

"Drop of slug," he muttered, and pulled a small earthen crock from a bag. He dropped the slug into it and fetched a small earthen vial from another fold of his ragged woolens. He cracked the vial like an egg and spilled a thick, oily, greenish-black ichor into the crock.

He dropped the shards in as well and out came a wooden pestle. Kúlkak ground the ichor and the pottery shards and the plump, spitting slug together.

The lines of *the Cry of the Deer* sang eerily through the fog.

From everyone who shall wish me ill,
afar and near.

"Not likely. No, not likely," muttered Kúlkak. He shouted, full-throated and hoarse:

Lîl na Izzi, Sagèntar!
Gibil, Lîl na Izzi, Sagèntar!
Girra, Lîl na Izzi, Sagèntar!

Tnúthgal shivered with revulsion at the sound of that harsh, agglutinative tongue, and the mad swirl of firelight in rain that rippled around him.

But does the light grow dim? Tnúthgal cocked his head. The fires of Eowain's men burned strangely cold and dull. The smoke grew noxious and dank. From the Abred beneath their feet rose the stench of cold, chthonic dread.

With a motion, Kúlkak the sorcerer flinched, and the gloom rippled outward from him, as if a door in the night had been opened to a cold, implacable wind from some shynn-mountain winter.

It seemed then to Tnúthgal as if the night itself keened, and he was fear-struck as with a bolt to the guts.

What madness is all this? Fear stabbed at his eyes and clutched at his throat. *What more madness is this?*

But ahead, his wretched cousin roared his courageous bear-cry. Ahead of him in the mirk, he saw it: Toryn the Stout, impaled through the throat on the blade of Eowain the Bear.

His hedge-king cousin stood a moment and held Toryn aloft on the blade amid the gathering darkness. Then Eowain hobbled. His right leg buckled. Tnúthgal watched it. He *heard* it, even from a spear's throw distant. The sickening crunch of two bones cracking together as they ought not to.

The Foreigner mercenary caught his cousin under the arm, bore him up.

What more proof do I need? He'd always known no good would come of mingling with the Foreigners and their pagan ways. There and then, he had the proof of it. The Foreigner merchant killed for his cousin. The drymyn acolyte fought for his wretched claim.

Beneath Tnúthgal's foot, a Droma-man writhed, the green, gold, and white tartan of his surcoat barely recognizable through the mud and blood of his own guts. He might have been a man of Dúnsciath, or Tirimbaile, or even Avainnglynn. Tnúthgal didn't know him.

Kúlkak shook and trembled as if he were thunderstruck, then giggled like a girl.

Líl na Izzi, Sagèntar!
Gibil, Líl na Izzi, Sagèntar!
Girra, Líl na Izzi, Sagèntar!

Smoke and light and a terrible caustic stench of lime and mustard arose from his crock. Green and white slime frothed and gleamed and bubbled from the gourd. Kúlkak danced a short, mad, spinning dance and let loose the earthen crock.

Tnúthgal looked up at his cousin, held aloft by the foreign mercenary. The frothing crock of vitriol arced through the gloom, burned through the fog like a beacon. Tnúthgal put his sword point through the man beneath him, his own dying countryman. *This ends now.* He gave the blade a twist.

"EITHNE, IF THEY'VE overrun Eowain's forces, then it isn't safe to linger here." Her father put his hands on his hips, looking up at her on her chestnut horse.

"I'll retreat no farther." She pursed her lips at him. "No matter what you and that witch Alva want, there's only so far I'll run."

Dawn approached. Alva had joined the handful of drymyn priests and priestess that had come out with the Huntsmen from the Vale to meet them on the last ridge. They were singing the First Hour orisons.

The Huntsmen and her cousin's men of Ivearda had established a skirmish line over three dozen yards to either side of the trail, atop the bare, rocky crest of the pass. Barely an arrow's swift flight stood between them and the murk of smoke and dread that gathered in the pines below.

"But it's not safe here, cousin." King Ardgar of Ivearda sat astride the roan gelding on her other side. He wore scaled mail of hard lacquered leather, and the black, gold, and red tartans of their clan. His voice was gentle.

She didn't know him well—few from her small mountain village did. Rarely did their lowland cousins come to Dolgallu. Rarer yet did any of her mountain kin descend to the rough foothills over which Ardgar ruled. She wasn't sure why, but his branch of their clan seemed content to let her father guard and patrol the eastern mountains of his kingdom, while he managed the lowland affairs of the tribe. Yet he'd come from his hall to the Vale with nigh on fifty men of foot and nearly a score of horsemen, to stand witness at her wedding. As patriarch of their clan, it was a duty that he owed to her, though they'd met only twice before—and briefly—in her life.

"These villains have been out to kill me, cousin. That may not mean much to you, but I'll be in the van to relieve Eowain's retreat when he comes."

Ardgar shook his head. "But that's the trouble, isn't it? If we charge in down there, we're as like to meet an ambush of bandits and Cailech-men. So he has to keep coming, doesn't he?"

"Damn it, girl." Her father stamped his foot. "Craning your neck to stare at the horizon will not make his lordship appear any sooner." His father's lips were drawn tight, his expression sour.

She snapped at him. "I'm looking at the weather."

"Rain yesterday, rain the day before, and more rain today, I'd wager. And worse, by the look of it. Now come down to the village. Please, Eithne. You're going to catch your death out here."

Her elder cousin sniffed. "Listen to your father. The Donnghaile fool can drown, and with all this Droma-men too, for all I care. We can get you another husband, now that your father's let you out of the house."

"You'll *not* find me another—." She bit off her words.

"There!" A sharp-eyed archer pointed through the gloom and down from the height of the pass.

And there, where the trail emerged from the forest, was that something pale in the darkness? Aye, she thought. Her heart caught in her throat. *Aye, Movement through the rain. Between the trees and the rocky grasses.*

Medyr on his white pony emerged from the murk. Behind him, Eowain's brother Lorcán led what remained of the horsemen of Droma up out of the forest.

The Lord-Drymyn rode as if he had no care, puffing on his clay pipe. Yet as he drew abreast of the Huntsmen's line, Eithne saw the haunted, dark circles under his eyes.

Lorcán's grim visage told her much, even before he made his report to the Huntsmen's captain. "Every vermin of the Abred rose up against us. We knew it had to be more sorcery. That the bandits and Cailech-men would be coming."

She pushed closer, put her hand on Medyr's saddle. "Eowain?"

Medyr nodded, pointed the stem of his smoldering pipe at Lorcán. "The lad's got the right of it. He was there."

Mastering himself, Lorcán told the tale. "From the rain-swept dark, there rose a gloom. So help me, it was like the grave's own shroud..."

Eithne frowned. "But what of Eowain?" She stilled the tremor in her voice. She'd told the men—her father, her kingly cousin, the huntsman's captain himself—that she was fit for this. She dared not show herself a coward. "Where is your King?"

He shook his head. "He sent us away. To save the horses, and what men he could." He clenched his fists. "I abandoned my brother. Left him on the field of honor." He looked away. "Mother and Father, forgive me."

"You fought beside him?" Her heart sank.

She could see him fight for control. Then he saluted her, as a soldier does a queen. "I did, my lady. And never was there such a king as your own groom." His voice filled with contempt, but his tone high-court formal. "You have my word on it."

Pride swelled Eithne's breast. *There.* She put a hand to her throat. *And there? Is this love? Has he breached the tower of my doubt at last?*

"But what's become of him?"

Medyr turned his sad, hollow gaze to her. Despite his evident fatigue, his eyes gleamed. "Love is patience, my lady. Especially such a love as yours. For the dread Mórrigú in her selves are come, and all the Manred holds still and awaits their judgment. It will soon be told."

CHAPTER FOURTEEN

THE ACOLYTE, ADARC, continued to chant *the Cry of the Deer*. He met the next bandit to oppose him with a ferocious swipe of his blackthorn stick, cracked open the bandit's skull, and sprang over the falling body to grapple with another.

The merchant killed a brigand who came within reach before he could strike a blow. His long straight blade split the skull even as the brigand's own sword lifted for a stroke. More brigands, and Cailech-men too, came from the gloom. The merchant sidestepped a thrust even as he parried a slash. His sword darted past a blade that sought to parry, and he sheathed six inches of its point into a leather-guarded midriff.

Eowain shook his head. Cael's poison still crept through his body, sapped him of strength, and the stings, bites, and pricks of a thousand venomous vermin made his vision swim.

A song came to Eowain's mind, then, as he faced down the slope in the dark, propped up by the merchant's Foreigner mercenary. A song heard on many an evening of pipes, lyres, and fiddles around a crofter's fire for the night. He started to sing it himself then.

> *When will we be married, Eithne*
> *When will we be wed,*
> *When will we be bedded in the same bed*
> *I made a black bow*
> *for your bonny head…*

From the smoke and gloom, a spear's throw distant, emerged the sorcerer, yellowish eyes shining despite the murk. His face was drawn into a hideous rictus of a shrieking scream.

Beside him was Tnúthgal. Eowain's own cousin, his kinsman. A veteran of a fierce history and a slave to his own burning ambition, he'd betrayed Eowain with a spear through the back.

And what did Eowain have? A silly country ditty about getting married.

The sorcerer cavorted in a circle, swung his arms round and round, shrieked nonsense:

> *When drymyn blood is shed*
> *When the river-source is red*
> *When the flames of war are fanned*
> *When are found the Eye and Hand*

An earthen crock rose from the sorcerer's grasp, spun out through the gloom of the ancient mountain forest's dread spirit-sovereigns. From it, green slime frothed and bubbled as it came, scalded branch, stem, and leaf against which it spewed.

"You, at least, will be silent!" Eowain pushed away the Foreigner, found his father's spear, and threw with all his strength.

Eowain almost stumbled over, but the scout, Corvac, took up his left arm, raised his shield against the rain and the gloom.

The spear of Findtan flew its course.

The earthen crock shattered on Corvac's shield in a flash of sharp, pale, eldritch green and bright frothing white. Corvac screamed as caustic sludge overwhelmed his defense.

Scalding tendrils splashed over Eowain, set his armor, clothes, and skin to burning. The scorching scent of slime and burnt beard filled his nostrils. Corvac pushed him back and away from the eruption of corrosive vitriol.

The night skies, dark with cloud, opened a deluge upon the mountain trail.

TNÚTHGAL SAW HIS cousin push aside the Foreigner, find his spear, and let it fly. Everything seemd to move very slowly then. He watched as the spear passed the sorcerer's crock of frothing slime in mid-air. Saw the crock of slime burst against the shield of a Dro-ma-man, late-come to defend his king.

Beside him, the cavorting sorcerer suddenly grunted and went to the ground. Tnúthgal looked back over his shoulder. Tnúthgal recognized it as well any spear he knew. He'd long coveted the spear of Findtan, once-king of Droma. There was no finer length of ash-wood, no better blade of steel, in all of Droma. And there it was, quivering in the night rain. The sorcerer was impaled to the ground through the chest.

Tnúthgal sneered at the sorcerer's twitching corpse. *No great powers saved you.* It had been a clean throw. *Damned good throw for a man on a broken leg.*

He thought for a moment of his servant. Where the hell had Caer-rhythrs gone too in all this? He couldn't be sure. Dead or wounded, his servant was somewhere else behind Tnúthgal, on the trail of blood and ruin that Tnúthgal had traveled to that moment and that place.

He shrugged and looked back at Eowain. The sorcerer's crockery had shattered in a flash of yellow-green light, like the gleam in the sorcerer's eye at the gloaming of the day. Sizzling froth exploded from the fragments and drenched the scout's wooden shield, his head, his legs.

The lad screamed out, "On to Tirn Aill! For the Hedge King of Droma!" Then the caustic slime burned him to the ground.

Eowain staggered backward through the mud, into the arms of the foreign mercenary, splattered with burning globules that hissed in the rain.

He saw Eowain's ankle twist under him when he fell.

Tnúthgal shouted to his remaining men: "Kill the Foreigner!" He put his boot to the sorcerer's guts, wrenched the spear of Findtan loose. His hated cousin Eowain writhed on the ground not a spear's throw away. "I'm going to spit you on your father's own spear, you arrogant little whelp." Tnúthgal hefted the spear in his hand. Well-crafted of ash and steel by a master, a weapon to be admired. And he'd see his hated rival's son impaled on it. "As the Gods are righteous judges of my cause, I swear it!"

With all his strength, and the skill learned of long years in battle, he drew back Findtan's spear and let it fly.

THE COOL RAIN fell hard on him. He was laying on the ground, over the body of the Foreigner against whom Corvac had thrust him.

Eowain twisted. His cheek and chin burned, and it seemed fire oozed down his neck and shoulder. He twisted again and his ankle shrieked agony at him. Gritting teeth, Eowain rolled over. Down every fiber of his left side, caustic vitriol sizzled in the rain. He straightened his leg out. More pain lanced through him. *Is it broken, after all, my ankle?*

Down the hill, his cousin Tnúthgal shouted, urged on his bandits to finish them. His cousin wrenched a spear loose from the fallen sorcerer. The spear of Findtan. The weapon of his father, a man of good fame. His cousin balanced his father's spear in his hand, drew it back for a throw.

Is this how it ends, Eithne? He'd never considered that he might not succeed against his cousin. Never considered that he might not defeat the bandits. Never considered that he couldn't drive back the Cailech-men, or put a spear through Toryn the Stout. *Do you doubt me still, Eithne?* He'd always imagined that this ended with him facing her, on two strong legs, on a sunlit hill in the spring-time.

But that suddenly seemed unlikely to him. He knew this was about himself as much as it was about Eithne then. He knew that whatever fortunate *thayn* the drymyn's *coelbreni* foretold, it was true. For good or ill, he and Eithne had been freighted with some dread portent that he still could not understand.

He lifted himself up to his elbows. Eowain would have stood if he thought he could, but lighted globs in many colors flickered in his sight and threatened his equilibrium.

Tnúthgal drew back the spear of Findtan and let it fly. To Eowain, the spear seemed of a sudden to travel as if through a fibrous molasses of threads and colors, each thread vibrating with the melodic frequency of a harp string. He knew every curled line inscribed on the blade, the river salmon crest of the Donnghaile clan etched into the steel and iron, prayers for courage and victory burned into the curvilinear designs along the hard ashen shaft.

He even knew that iron shod heel it wore, blunt-spiked and weighted, stamped with the mark of the master weaponsmith who'd assembled it, and the mark of his father Findtan, once-King of Droma, who'd commissioned it. He knew that spear.

So he knew it would pull to the left.

CHAPTER FIFTEEN

THE FLIGHT OF Findtan's spear went past his propped up left shoulder like lightning and buried itself to the wide boar-guard in the hill beside him.

Tnúthgal gaped at the quivering spear, a hand-span to Eowain's left.

For a moment, Eowain thought he would weep. Perhaps the Gods were not so forgetful after all.

But, wondered Eowain, *what can I do with it? This is impossible. The kind of star-crossed love that the drymyn and the mystic* coelbreni *foretell, it is impossible. We are beset upon all sides by the sins of the unfaithful and the tricks of the wicked.*

The cooling rain dissolved the burning, viscous sludge from his cheek. *How can the love of which they dream and tell stories, how can that love survive in a land of brigandage and cattle-raiders?*

Eowain thought back on a missive he had sent to Eithne once, soon after their first meeting. *If I could get love by leaping into my saddle...* He chuckled a bit through the taste of blood in his teeth. *Well, I would surely rather do something so simple now, Eithne. I surely would.* He imagined her red hair, her narrow, pale, hungry face, her strong arms, her noble spirit. She seemed to shine before him in his mind's eye.

"Fine." Eowain heard his cousin's hiss and saw him draw a short-handled wooden axe of oak and black iron from his belt. "I would've made this easy on you, boy. But I see your father is as disappointed with you as I am." The rain pelted down, splattered on his cousin's helmet, drummed on the shirt of tight-knit chain-link mail on his shoulders, soaked into the green, gold, and white woolen tartan of the Donnghaile clan.

Eowain remembered something his father had once said:

Trust your cousins against the world.

Had he trusted Tnúthgal too much? Eowain had insisted on law and order, on loyalty and family before all else. And so allowed himself to be maneuvered into all this. Why shouldn't Tnúthgal have been king, after all? Wouldn't the vote of the people have carried it that way? Was one son of the Donnghaile clan not much like another for the sake of stars and oracles?

His cousin took a long, stalking step up the hill toward him, found footing in the rivulets of rain amid slick mountain valley moss, and took another.

Eowain knew he could grab the spear. Get up on his knees and offer one last fight. Or he could let go. So Tnúthgal would take Eithne to wife and sire sons to the benefit of whatever portentous *thayn* she bore. What did Eowain owe to the Gods anyway? He had another life awaiting him in Tirn Aill, the Other Land. He would be reunited with many of his fine, fallen comrades, all newly-arrived to that shynn-touched feast. Why should he not let pain and regret go?

Down the steep slope of ferns and rocks, behind Tnúthgal, beneath the gloomy pines and the unrelenting rain, the sorcerer sat up.

Eowain blinked twice at him. His eyes were white and blind in the firelight. His chest was caved in. His knotted hair hung around a great bloody gash where his heart should have been. Where the spear of Findtan had done its gruesome work.

Revulsion washed over Eowain once more. *There's no way in the Three Spheres of the Nine Worlds any man survives such a blow.* And yet the sorcerer suddenly bounced to his feet. There was a long, wicked dagger in his hand. It dripped with black, viscous oil.

Eowain saw the look on Tnúthgal's face change, from hatred to confusion. His cousin's brow knotted. His cousin turned his head.

The sorcerer lunged into Tnúthgal's unguarded back and stabbed like a frenzied wildcat with the dagger.

Then something else his father once said came back to Eowain:

But trust your brother against your cousins.

EOWAIN'S MEN STRAGGLED then up the trail, limping, lame, wounded. The scouts of the Huntsmen went down trail to relieve burdens and guide them in. Many shook with the venomous fever of stings, bites, and lacerations. More shook with fear. All bore tales of darkness and terror witnessed in the night, of snakes, scorpions, multilegged horrors, rats, bats, beetles, and other vermin.

"An' the woods're swarming with Cailech-men! There're 'undreds more, 'idin' in the wood! An' more comin', from the farther villages! Like wolves, they is!"

Eithne dismounted and joined a handful of drymyn priestesses who'd come from the shrine to tend the wounded. "What of your king? Where is Eowain?" Haunted eyes looked away from her.

"Mighty as a bear, 'e was," reported one man. "A man of iron," said another.

But, "No, my lady. I'm sorry, my lady." None knew what had become of Eowain in the darkness.

"Damn it." Eithne's patience was exhausted, her fear for Eowain's life too great. She seized her family's banner from their standard-bearer, stepped up into her saddle, and raised the banner over head. "Lorcán!" She rose in her stirrups and waved.

The horsemen of Droma had turned in the meadow behind the Huntsmen's line, formed up for a charge, and stood idle ever since. Horses stamped impatiently and blew gusts of mist in the chill dawn. Men fidgeted in the renewed downpour.

Across the field, Lorcán's raised his spear to her in salute. She knew he felt a blood-debt toward his brother, a deeper love than that of mere family for its own. Lorcán slapped his helmet into place and blasted the charge on his horn. The Huntsmen of the Vale, arrayed in skirmish lines with spears and bows, gave them lanes to hold their formation. The horses lunged and plunged through the mud and down the slope. It was a mad charge, a reckless chance with horse flesh. They knew not what else might still lay behind the dark pines of that accursed trail.

Eithne wrenched the reins of her steed around to join the charge, but

Lady Alva and her father caught her bridle. Alva whispered a word, and the horse went still beneath her.

Behind her, Medyr scuffed at a rock. He looked away, to the charging Horse of Droma.

"That is twice you've ensorcelled my horse, Mistress-Drymyn." Eithne drew her short steel blade from her belt. "Release me at once, both of you."

"It is too late, you risk too much." Her father's face was desperate.

Only cool, detached strength dwelt behind the leathery mask of Alva's aged face.

"But Eowain—."

Alva was blunt. "May be dead already. There is little hope he's survived his cousin." Alva nodded downslope after the charge. "This charge is noble and they'll surely break whatever strength remains to Tnúthgal, but I tell you now. There is almost no way Eowain survived." Her gaze grew troubled. "That was Kúlkak, the sorcerer, against whom he strove."

Eithne yanked back on the horse's reins. The beast stamped its hooves but remained where it was. "Damn you, ban-drymyn, release me! Who is that? Kúlkak the Sorcerer? I'll run him through. For Dolgallu. For Eowain."

"Stop it!" Alva's tone brooked no cross-word.

Eithne felt herself brought still with a shiver. She yearned to move, to thrash, to fight and kill and avenge. Yet her own traitorous body would not yield to her desires.

Alva tugged at Eithne's bridle. "Kúlkak the sorcerer is no man you want to trifle with, I will tell you that, you fool girl. Now sheathe that damned sword."

In spite of herself, Eithne put away her sword at her hip. "Release me," she snarled through gritted teeth. "Release me this instant."

Alva ignored her. Eithne wanted to shake her head, run her hands through her hair, grab onto something. *But Eowain needs help, he needs—.* She squashed the thought, struggled to move, willed herself to raise an arm, but her body would not respond.

"Medyr!" She appealed to the Lord-Drymyn of Droma. He'd been Eowain's tutor as a young man. *Surely he must feel something for his charge.* "Medyr! Tell her to release me! Eowain needs us!"

He turned eyes full of sadness toward her. "It is beyond my powers now, my lady. Beyond my authority." He opened his hands helplessly before him.

Her father's mouth opened as if to gasp, but he put a hand over it. "Is it true then?" He spoke to the drymyn priestess. "Has it begun already?"

Alva's expression grew grave. "There are rumors of witches gathered in the southern woods. Terrible hags that eat the souls of children right from their bodies, who slaughter their kills in the most gruesome manner, and leave dead bodies to hang in trees."

"You knew this?" Lord Ciaran pinched the bridge of his nose, then took a step closer to Eithne's leg in the stirrup. "You baited these witches with my daughter? Twice? Is this what all your schemes have been about?"

Alva shook her head. "I cannot say. Gaffer Ydrys only says so much. But He swears by His astrology, and you've seen the fruit of it here."

"But what of Mælgenn's Prophecy?"

Alva looked to left and right, thin-lipped, guarded. "We will not speak of that here."

Realization dawned on Eithne. "But—." Father knew something he hadn't told her. She felt her eyes grow wide, her breathing grow rapid and shallow, but she could not turn to him. Could not beat her fists against his chest and demand to know what—

"We will not speak of it." Alva's voice was firm once more.

Eithne's anger and frustration boiled over. She couldn't move, but she could still speak. "By Annwn, we certainly will speak of it, you witch! Have you not schemed all this together with your own evil cunning?" Eithne would have put the point of her sword to Alva's throat if she could have. Every fiber of her was a-tremble with that murderous intent, yet she could move not even a finger. "What is this of prophecy? How can Eowain be dead?"

Alva frowned at her, spat words in the Old Language. Then she went on in vulgar Gallavach. "We don't have time anymore, my lady. He's dead or as near to it as prophecy will allow. But the moment's drawing near. You must be prepared and in your place when it comes." With surprising strength, Alva pulled Eithne's horse around. With her father, the strange old wild-woman of the woods led her down the trail toward the shrine of the Vale of Thaynú, away from the Huntsmen's line. Away from Eowain's plight.

CHAPTER SIXTEEN

THE GROUND TREMBLED beneath Eowain's hand. Over him, a gelding leaped, spurred to glory by his own brother, the golden-haired son of Findtan, Lorcan Half-Hand.

Lorcán's spear went through Tnúthgal, impaled the sorcerer as well, and drove them both to the ground with a force that snapped the spear of Lorcán in half, killed his steed, and threw his brother from the saddle.

The rest of the Horse of the King's Company of the Shield thundered over him. Lingering gloom vanished, and the pelting rain slowed its relentless journey back to the distant sea. He heard the shrieks as remaining elements of Cailech-men and bandits were crushed under the war-horses of the grassy Gasirad hills of Droma. His kingdom.

These were his men. *And by the Gods, I'll die on my feet in front of them.* Eowain twisted himself around, leveraged himself up to his knees, then rose on his left foot. Pain burned through his leg and stabbed at his eyes. A detached voice, cold and military, the voice of his arms-master as a young man, spoke to him in his mind: *You are going into shock.*

Eowain gritted his teeth and swayed up-right on his one good leg. With a grunt, he wrenched the spear of Findtan loose from the soil. The steel sang against a rock as it came free and shimmered in the light of day and spring water that rose from the heart of the well at the Vale of Thaynú.

He turned the spear over and planted the butt of the spear in the mud. With pragmatic care, he hobbled, with his father's spear for a crutch, to the bodies of his cousin and the sorcerer.

Lorcán's spear had taken Tnúthgal through the right lung and the sorcerer behind him through the belly. The sorcerer grinned with blind, dead, lizard-like eyes. His mouth moved and worked around a dead tongue. The hiss of a death-rattle passed his lips.

Then the sorcerer went silent. The sorcerer went still.

Tnúthgal lay upon him, bound to the sorcerer by Lorcán's spear. He laughed and choked up blood into his own fork-braided beard. "Go on then. If one son of Findtan isn't enough to kill me. Go on then! Make it two." His teeth showed white and yellow like corn amid the streams of rain-slick blood in his mouth. "The mother's sons of saintly Findtan."

Every day as a king, he'd been required to render judgments. The right or wrong of a property dispute, the proper body-price for a farmer injured by another man's negligence.

But Eowain had waited long for that judgment, and pronounced it with the air, the rain, the earth, and the setting sun for his witnesses.

"Tnúthgal Fork-Beard son of Ruadan, of the Clan of the Donnghaile of Droma, I find you guilty of treason against the crown and people of Droma, and the honor of the Goddess Echraide, by whom our people swear. As King of Droma, I sentence you to death."

Eowain turned the spear of Findtan around, and put his father's spear through his treacherous cousin's heart, and the heart of the sorcerer beneath him. They keened their portentous death-shriek together.

EOWAIN RAISED THE blade of Findtan above him. Tnúthgal watched the rain-water drip from it like a roaring cascade.

Tnúthgal cursed himself silently. He should have known it would come to this. He'd asked Caerrhythrs once, "How would you beat Eowain?" With his usual dry professionalism, Caerrhthyrs had replied without pause: "At night. In his bed. While he slept." He'd sniffed a moment then, and added, "With a stick."

Tnúthgal choked on blood and phlegm, spit it up and felt it ooze through his beard and proud moustaches. *Won't you go to sleep now, Eowain? I'm sure I could find a stick somewhere.* He laughed at his own joke and choked up more blood. "Go on then," he said. "If one son of Findtan isn't enough to kill me. Go on then! Make it two. The mother's sons of saintly Findtan."

He'd been taught to look forward to this moment with joy all his life. The opportunity for the proud warrior to be reborn into the bright *shynn-brúgh* of the Other Land. To see his long departed kith and kin once more, and to live in merriment and war.

He heard his young cousin pronounce his kingly judgment. Tnúthgal imagined the bright, torch-lit feast-halls of never-ending bounty: acorns and boars, stags and steaks, quail and duck of the field. Tart-jellied berries and bitter *ól* and fiery *uisce* to parch his throat.

He saw Eowain turn the spear of Findtan around. He practically saw himself sitting at that feast.

He felt the spear pierce through his own heart. He heard screaming.

Musicians played a stirring tune for dancing, tankards clacked in friendship and threat, and all would fight again upon the morrow.

But there was a dark shadow in that hall. A shade that slipped and slithered through his vision. All through that one, long, endless, shynn-night feast in the darkness, tentacles of mad, writhing darkness gathered. They wrote it out, in the interstices of the Manred, in the spaces between the Limits, dark *coelbreni* runes that Tnúthgal had learned to read as a boy.

The answer has been there all along. Tnuthgal wanted to believe in the rebirth in Tirn Aill. He wanted to believe that his own love of country, and his jealous desire for Eithne too, that it was all justified. He wanted to believe that his choice in Toryn the Stout and Cael the Viper as conspirators had been necessary, to achieve a greater good.

But Tnúthgal realized then the depth of his treachery against Eowain. And against more than his cousin. His treachery against the fate decreed by the Gods themselves through their portents and agents. He realized his complicity in that dark, preternatural conspiracy among the shadows of the world, just beyond the fields we know.

Tnúthgal had betrayed not just his tribe, not just his clan, not just his own cousin, he had betrayed the very Gods themselves.

From that darkness that curled and coiled in the heroic, curvilinear designs of his forefathers, a voice whispered along the threads to

Tnúthgal's body. A voice that whispered from Tnúthgal's mouth as the spear of Findtan pierced his heart.

> *Shall be the land for spring a-grieving*
> *When Black Cromm comes a-rieving.*

He did not know what those words meant.

Another voice came to him, along the threads. *It does not matter that you do not know what it means. It only matters that it was uttered, with the stars and the Watchers of the Night so aligned.*

An image of star patterns in a night sky emerged from the curving lines of the words.

Tnúthgal still didn't understand. But he knew he wouldn't go on to Tirn Aill.

✝

THE BROAD, FORBIDDING hill was tall, flattened on top. Moss and stones and green grass covered its steep slopes. Upon its southern side, wide stone steps had been carved into the hill, to either side of a channel of worn, granite bricks. A river of water cascaded, pure and clear, down the channel. Upon the stones, half-hidden by pale lichens, were carved spirals and arcane *coelbreni* that the Gods and Shynn hadn't chosen to share with Men. A dark opening in the hill lay at the top of those steps.

Eithne was told to dismount, and she did, gritting her teeth. Alva told her to climb the stairs. Each was tall, she had to bend her leg almost double to take each one. But against her will, up she went. Sixty tall steps she counted. Sixty more steps from Eowain.

How can they all be so calm about this? Alva was at her right elbow, her father at her left. Their faces were grim, hooded against the rain that plummeted from the sky. They kept a firm grip on her arms, as if she might somehow break the ensorcellment on her limbs. Behind her, she knew that Medyr too climbed that hill. "Damn it, why? Why don't we help him?"

Alva shook her head.

"Father, please!"

"I can't, child. I—." His voice choked. "I just can't."

Behind her, Medyr was silent.

Atop the stairs, more than halfway to the summit, the high-priestess of the sisterhood, Corchen the Bandrúmór, awaited them in her robes of office. Her hood was up, against the chill of the mountain rain.

Medyr, the matron Alva, and her father bowed to the high-priestess.

Eithne had not been told to bend, and she chose not to. "I can't believe you orchestrated all this just to kill Eowain and flush your rivals out of hiding. How dare—?"

Corchen raised a bony finger.

Eithne went silent despite herself.

A yellow-bellied warbler alighted upon the old woman's finger, as if it were the most natural thing for a yellow-bellied warbler to do in the middle of a driving rainstorm. It chirped at her and ruffled water from its feathers.

Corchen cocked her head at the bird. "And this Neued of Avainnglyn is trustworthy?"

Medyr raised his eyebrows, then nodded. "I would vouch for her, aye."

Corchen smiled wryly at him. "Well then, we'll just overlook her fondness for the leaf of the linden. Since you vouch for her." Then she fixed Eithne with a glare. "Your hedge-king lives."

Eithne blinked at her, not understanding for a moment. She found her voice once more. "My hedge-king—? Eowain? He lives?"

Corchen demonstrated the yellow-bellied warbler on her finger with a bob. "So says Neued of Avainnglyn."

Eithne shook her head. "Who is that? I don't know who that is."

The High-Priestess gestured to Medyr. "A diviner of the Lord-Drymyn's acquaintance, I believe."

Medyr nodded. "True, you might not have met her, during your brief stay in Droma. She is the seer at the shrine of Avainnglyn, keeper of its lustral waters. Gifted with the imbas forasnai of old, the true light of foresight."

Eithne waited as if for more, but Medyr seemed to think that explained it. "And where is she, exactly, that she knows the fate of Eowain?"

Medyr coughed. "Oh. Well, she's in Avainnglyn, after all. I think?" He looked to Corchen.

"Oh." Eithne's fury rose again. "The one that's fifty miles from here through those savage foothills?" She put an edge to her voice. "How would she know?"

The yellow-bellied warbler chirped. Corchen answered. "She read it in the *coelbreni*. While she was smoking a bit too much of that linden-leaf, don't you think?"

Medyr shrugged. "Everyone has to get through their day somehow, High-Mother."

She sniffed at him. "This is what I'm given to work with." She despaired with a wave of her hands and set the warbler loose to fly away in the rain. "Lord Ciaran, perhaps you could instruct your men to bring His Grace the King Eowain to us in the shrine at his earliest convenience." She looked up at the cloudy skies above, as if reading something there. "Mind you, sir: Time presses."

Eithne's father snapped to attention like a soldier and saluted, then ran off down the steep stairs they'd just climbed.

She nodded to Alva and Medyr. "Thank you for your service. Please, find dry clothes and hot food within. I'll summon you when Eowain arrives." Corchen turned to enter the black hole in the hillside behind her. "Come, child. I am told you're still undecided about your fate. Let us discuss it over a cup of hot tea, why don't we?"

A thrill went through Eithne then. *Eowain is alive.* She savored those words on her tongue, yet dared not speak them aloud. *But wait—?*

Her limbs of a sudden were her own again. She stormed after the high-priestess. "How does some girl fifty miles away know what happened to Eowain? And how do you know what you know? And, and—?" She stopped and shouted at the high-priestess's backside. "And what in Annwn do you know, anyway?"

The shrine opened in the hillside, dark and mysterious, behind Corchen. Great granite blocks had been cut, and carved, set by hand, without mortar, to form the mouth of the shrine.

Between the bricks at the top of the stairs, the waters of the sacred well flowed out the center of three openings and down the steps in the channel cut into the rock. The channel was as wide as a carriage lane, and near as deep as a man was tall. The waters that ran there cascaded down the tinkling fall to the meadow below. The whole wide vale opened up to her sight from that vantage upon the height of the hill.

Four of the Huntsmen of the Vale stood upon the platform, two to either side of the opening. Each bore a sword and two spears and wore a vest of hardened leather. Their trews were tri-colored with stripes of red, green, and white. They wore no clan tartans, no tribal insignia. Their stony expressions betrayed nothing.

Between them the two dark passages to either side of the channel led into the heart of the hill.

Corchen turned from one of those passages. "I know you'll follow me."

Eithne sneered. "What makes you so sure?"

"Because you're not a damned fool, and you've stood in the rain long enough. Come inside, girl. The novitiates have water on for tea. Come get warm and dry. Your adventure's not over yet."

CHAPTER SEVENTEEN

EOWAIN FLOATED. BOBBED. As if he were on the river beneath his tower in the sunshine. He felt free of all care, as if a great weight had been lifted from him. Water, cool and fresh, washed over him. Hands moved across his body. His armor was gone.

Where has my armor gone?

He rose and fell with the rhythm of the water's current beneath him. A voice drew him back.

Your son will a son of Droma be...

He rolled in coolness, water in his nose, like on many a high-spring morning in the waters of the Gasirad. Eowain had so enjoyed swimming.

How had he come to that place of light and cold?

He'd fallen to a knee after putting his father's spear through his traitor cousin's heart.

Lorcán had found him then. His brother had taken a gash in his fall, a bleeding wound that ran from his scalp into his eyes. "Eowain! Brother!" Lorcán lifted him up in a crushing embrace. Then there were other men. Men of his Company's Horse. "To the king! Defend the king!"

Was it a dream? It seemed much like a dream. Surely, that place of blood and mud, surely that was the dream, and this, floating in the coolness of the Gasirad on a sunny day, surely, that was real and not the days and nights under Annwn's own thunderclouds.

Lorcán and a bare squad of men laid him on his shield with the spear of his father clutched to his chest. "You're going to be alright, little brother."

There was shouting, and the strumming sound of plucked harp strings. One side of his shield tilted, and Eowain's stomach lurched in his chest. "Rally now, lads!" Lorcán's voice was strident and firm. He took Eowain's hand in his three-fingered grasp. "We'll get you there, don't you worry. We'll get you to the shrine on time."

On time? On time for what?

"Eithne's waiting for you, lad." Lorcán gave him a grim smile.

Eowain didn't believe a word of it, and clenched his brother's crippled hand. Lorcán nodded to him. "Alright, lash him to the horses! Drag him out of here! Heave-ho, let's have it, boys!"

"Look out!"

Lorcán let him go then. *Where had Lorcán gone?*

He remembered the day on the river, when the current got hold of Lorcán and dragged him toward the dangerous white-water channel. Eowain had lost sight of him for a moment, only a moment. Then he was alone in the Gasirad, a lad of four and his brother gone and the water up over Eowain's head.

Eowain felt as if he'd been submerged in the coolness and the light. His nostrils rebelled for air. *Am I really on the Gasirad? Am I really just a boy again?*

The pressure on his nostrils broke, light and cold lifted from his moustaches with a snorting spew.

"Quickly. Wrap him in the burial linens. You, girl, fetch the balsam and the yew, chop them. Soak them to a boil in the Cauldron of Tegwedd."

TNÚTHGAL FELT THE warm summer winds from those fabled fields, smelled fertile soil and healthy cattle. He felt the warmth of that shynn-sun on the face of the child into which he hadn't yet been born. For a moment, the spirit of Tnúthgal believed again in Tirn Aill. The hope of being reborn into a new life.

You are nothing but an ambitious pretender, a traitor, the chief failure of your grand-father's declining branch of your clan.

Were those his own thoughts? Tnúthgal couldn't be sure. They seemed more like a whisper from the darkness, the merest allegation of a voice.

Just as he gained a sight of those ripe apple trees and blue, cloudless skies, Tnúthgal was blown away on a dark wind, blown across miles of stern pines. Cold, black blows landed on his face and hands, leathery slaps as of bats' wings. The wintry exhalations of the mountain spirit's guardians sighed down from the heights.

They have grown hoary with age. Tnúthgal didn't understand why he thought so. *The rites have not been renewed. The barriers decay.*

Before he could wonder more at the source these thoughts, he felt himself swept up a steep, deadly mountain pass, into the bleak tundra of the great Ushaam massif. A square fort, assembled from sharpened pine timbers of exceptional girth, stood upon a crag.

Wind and snow swept the dark night of the fort, lit by hearth fires.

Is this the fort of the Narada? The oldest of the eastern tribes, and the most resentful, they ruled a nearly impregnable mountain fastness. Tnúthgal wondered why it was given to him to see such things. Surely, his body in that world lay dead, speared through the heart. Surely he had not flown all this way, many long miles. Surely it was a dream, or a death-vision. *Is that the Lord of Mórraith, King of the Narada, there upon the battlement of his tower?*

Like a bird upon a branch, Tnúthgal found himself among the snowy trees of a mountain marshland of reeds near the Narada tribe's great fort. Forms moved in shadow nearby, hunched and not quite Mannish in their wyrd dimensions.

A wild, yellow-tinged eye rolled out of the darkness to look at him. "Remember: the boy is mine." The figure's other eye was patched with leather, stitched with arcane sworls of small gems.

Somewhere in his heart, the spirit of Tnúthgal felt a sublime sense of satisfaction. A sense of victory. Somehow, something in him had won something.

She will still be mine.

He wondered whose voice it was that echoed in his head. *Not mine, surely.*

The voice whispered back to him from the darkness: *Oh yes. Ours.*

CHAPTER EIGHTEEN

EOWAIN STRETCHED HIS arms and legs. He felt whole and hale. Warm, under the summer sun. He lay on a rock along the lower course of the Gasirad, below the village. Sunning himself. When was the last time he'd indulged himself in such a luxury?

He closed his eyes against the sun in its bright blue sky. A shadow passed across his face.

He rose. It was a woman on horseback. She wore robes of brown, orange, green, gold, and white, the robes of a high-born lady. Surely, the robes of an empress.

She sat astride a dappled white horse with pink ears, a noble beast of the finest stock. Broad in the chest for wind, strong in the haunch for the course. A magnificent steed.

She looked over her shoulder at him. "Aren't you coming, Eowain of Droma?"

Eowain looked at his hands and legs. They were unharmed. There was no pain in his ankle, no wrongness in his knee, no wound in his shoulder. No bloat of poison from Cael's blade, not even an itch after a thousand insects' stings.

"Well?" The woman rode on at a steady pace on her dappled white steed.

Eowain rose. "Wait! My Lady! Who are you?" He trotted after her, and easily overmatched the pace of her steed.

Yet he came no closer to her.

Puzzled, he jogged on after her, and should have easily overtaken that dappled white steed with its flowing grey curled manes. It flickered its pale pink ears at him.

And he came no closer to it.

"Aren't you coming, Eowain? Don't you have someplace important to be?"

He ran after her, yet drew no closer.

He sprinted with all his heart.

Yet drew no closer.

"Aren't you coming?"

Eowain looked to his left. It was his mother, standing in an orchard of trees. She'd died years ago, when he was nine and away in Larriocht for his fosterage. She held two lush red apples in her hands. "Aren't you coming, love? The apples are in bloom."

Ahead of him, the woman in her strange, scintillating robe, astride her pale horse, beckoned to him. "Aren't you coming, Eowain?"

He gave his mother a look, then ran on after the horse. "Yes, I'm coming." Yet he grew no closer to her.

"Never forget, Eowain," whispered the woman to him. "Echraide of Droma is your chief-wife. And I'll have my due of you yet."

THERE WAS SOME argument in the shadows at the other end of the grotto. Corchen scolded one of her novitiates. "Do what I told you. Go prepare for the Rite of the Oracle."

"But Grandmother, I haven't been prepared."

"Go and do it now, Sister Kerridwen. Even you should be able to do this. The rest of us will be along presently."

There was a hissed reply, "Fine, Grandmother," in a tone that told Eithne that the High-Priestess was certainly the girl's grandmother, and it was certainly not fine.

The young priestess left with a thunderous look, followed by two other girls. Corchen emerged from the shadows.

The grotto was twice as long as it was wide. The length of the white marble walls was bordered by a double row of columns on each side, columns of true wood that put out leaves like natural living trees.

Before coming there, Eithne had followed Corchen into an entrance hall in the hillside early that morning. The river flowed there from under a black stone wall at the far end. It burbled through the center of the hall to plunge down through its channel into the valley below. One either side of the channel stood a stout oaken door, banded with black iron. An ancient glyph had been burned into each door.

Corchen had muttered a word under her breath and touched one of the glyphs. "Come, girl," she'd said, and opened the door.

Beyond was an octagonal shrine, lit by four burning braziers. Five women in white robes chanted in a strange tongue before a bronze statue of a tall, beautiful woman holding a sheaf of grain in the crook of her elbow. Behind the chanting priestesses was a stone altar, upon which lay thirteen gem-inlaid wands of hazel wood, arranged in a strange pattern.

From under the altar, the river flowed, bisecting the chamber before its waters frothed out under the wall through which Eithne and Corchen had passed.

Corchen nodded to the priestesses, who never ceased their chanting nor turned to look at them. "They've been praying for your hedge-king's victory." The old woman gestured for Eithne to follow her through an opening in the wall on the left. "This way."

Eithne had followed, through the opening and into a corridor cut from the bedrock of the hill, to a place where a short flight of stairs had been carved, rising up into another wide hall. Four Huntsmen stood guard, two on each side at the top of the broad stairway. Long, fine swords sheathed in leather hung from their belts. On the wall beside the guards on her right, Eithne saw an intricately worked hunting horn of silver inlaid with jet. It dangled on a leather thong from a spike driven into the stone wall.

The guards did not acknowledge Eithne or the High Priestess at all, and Corchen led her past them. "This is the Commemoration Hall." Four tapestries hung from the walls. Two of them depicted a green wreath of mistletoe with red berries, set upon a white field. Another showed a scene of tragedy, a magnificent city drowned by waves. The last showed a white-robed woman arising from a foaming ocean to set foot upon land amid a tumultuous storm. Wooden ships rode the waves behind her. "Here, we are reminded of the Desolation of Samratír and the flight of Thaynú and her people to Iathrann."

In two alcoves on either side of the room stood bronze statues of men. One wore a crown of oak and mistletoe. The other wore a rack of roe-buck antlers.

Set back in the center alcove at the far end of the room was another bronze statue, that of a woman, wearing a ring about her supple neck. Corchen paused to bow to the statue.

Eithne had felt out of place. Sodden with rain, weary from long days in the saddle, anxious for Eowain. "Lady Mother, what of—?"

Corchen raised a hand to still her words, then snapped her fingers. From arched passages to right and left, three young girls in white robes, novitiates of the Goddess of that place, entered the hall. "Go with them. They will see you cared for." She'd looked at the eldest of the girls, with hair as black as night. "Kerridwen, see that she comes to the library when she's been made comfortable."

Once more, Eithne had felt her will was not her own. The girls led her away, gave her a basin of warm water from which to clean and refresh herself, and fresh, dry linens with which to dress herself. They waited discreetly while she changed. Two of the girls gathered her discarded, trail-worn clothes, and the third led her to a six-walled chamber lined with shelves and niches, stacked neatly with books and scrolls. Luxurious black furs covered the floor, and two lit braziers hung from the ceiling. In the center of the room stood a small round table, upon which cups and a pot of hot water for tea had been arranged. Two deep, cushioned arm-chairs flanked the table.

Across the room, a second door opened, and the High-Priestess Corchen entered. "Ah, good to see you refreshed, my dear." She scowled a moment. "A shame about your hair. It's probably quite lovely." She gestured to the girl. "Kerridwen, fetch us a comb, will you?" Then Corchen indicated one of the chairs. "Sit, child. You've had a trying journey."

She and Corchen had sat there a long time, sipping tea and speaking of inconsequential things—her village of Dolgallu, the weather there, the prospect of the spring crops. Kerridwen returned with a comb and began drawing out the tangles from Eithne's hair, as if she were a child. The gentle strokes seemed to gently pull worry and questions away. Corchen took down books from the shelves—local histories, religious treatises, philosophical tracts of interest to any high priestess—and illustrated her words with gestures to charts of various astrological configurations tacked to the fine oak-paneled walls.

Eithne could not recall any more what Corchen had related to her there amid those tomes. Whatever sorcery Corchen had done had given her a sense of calm and well-being. Time seemed to pass as if in a dream. The willow tea was hot and comforting, sweetened with honey and thickened with cream. As concerns for Eowain arose in her heart, they seemed to be pulled away, out of sight, out of mind, as the comb did its diligent work under the girl's nimble fingers.

She'd been there, talking with Corchen much of the day, before she heard some commotion beyond those bookish walls. Soon after, Corchen rose and straightened her robes. "You'll be wanting to see your hedge-king now, I warrant."

With a gesture, Corchen bid her rise, and she did, allowing herself to be led through corridors and down ancient, spiraled staircases of stone, through barrows beneath the hill where, said Corchen, priests, priestesses, and warriors of elder days had been interred under the thick, round stone slabs. They had passed then through an entrance shrine where a clear, unnatural light glowed from the ceiling, and came at last to that large, white-walled grotto.

The stone walls rose up to a cathedral-like height over Eithne's head. At one end of the grotto rose a circular white marble platform, a single step high. Upon it, a yard-wide cauldron yawned. It gleamed with the white glint of a metal that was somehow both silver and gold at once, while forever being neither.

Beneath it, a fire had been kindled, and steam arose from it.

At the other end of the vast hall was a semicircular pool filled with pure, clear spring water. The pool was fully ten yards across and another yard deep. Four more of the tree-like columns with their living leaves lined the pool.

From the center of the spring-water basin, against the wall and up on a pedestal out of the pool, stood a white stone statue. Soft, slender, curved and graceful—the form of a beautiful woman carved in white marble. Ringed around her neck was cunningly twisted torc of silvery metal. The statue seemed fixed in place, as if it had been carved from the living rock. A soft pearly light radiated from it, illuminating the hall.

From the wall on either side of the statue, spring water bubbled and cascaded down into the pool.

Two grim-looking Huntsmen with sheathed swords entered and came to flank Eithne.

In the pool of spring water, nine priestesses in pale robes knelt. There was something floating there between them in the water.

It was Eowain.

Corchen came to her then, from the shadows of those strange tree-like columns. "I'm sorry for this, but it's necessary. Keep silent please." She made a gesture, and Eithne was free again. Two of the Huntsmen took hold of her arms.

Eithne shook the wyrd fog from her head. "What is the meaning of—?"

Corchen raised a finger. "Silence, please."

Eithne felt no more sorcery or glamour then, yet the stillness and strangeness of the chamber—and the stern tone of the High-Priestess's voice—compelled her to silence nevertheless.

Corchen snapped at the priestesses. "Quickly. Wrap him in the burial linens. You, girl, fetch the balsam and the yew, chop them. Soak them to a boil in the Cauldron of Tegwedd."

She watched, restrained by the two Huntsmen, as the priestesses wrapped Eowain's ursine form in long white funereal clothes.

What madness is this? Eithne strained at the Huntsmen's grip, but they pulled her back roughly. *But she said he lived?* Anxiety clutched at Eithne's throat, knotted her guts. She yanked again at the grip of the men, but they were unyielding.

Nine squat, ruddy-visaged brutes in hairs and furs entered the grotto from the two arched passages. They were silent as they passed between the columns, and arranged themselves in a line at the edge of the pool. The priestesses finished their work and lifted the swaddled head of Eowain up out of the pool. One of the brutes took the head and stepped back, drawing more of his body from the water. Two more brutes stepped in and took the shoulders, then two more, and two more again, until the final pair of squat little men took up the feet and together, the nine of them raised Eowain's body over their head.

Her eyes fixed on his wrapped hands. She wished she could hold them to herself. Her own hands clutched the air helplessly.

Corchen began to chant.

> *Bread of the Cult of the Dead in its Place I eat*
> *In the Court prepared*
> *Water of the Cult of the Dead in its Place I drink*
> *A Queen am I, Who has become estranged to the Cities*
> *She that comes from the Lowlands in a sunken boat*
> *Am I.*
> *I AM THE VIRGIN GODDESS*
> *HOSTILE TO MY CITY*
> *A STRANGER IN MY STREETS.*

Corchen raised a silver sickle to the white marble statue of the woman overlooking the pool. "Oh, Spirit, who understands Thee? Who comprehends Thee?"

The dark brutes hefted his body up, carried it with grave ceremony to the silvery cauldron that boiled at the far end of the grotto. The priestesses, their white robes drenched with spring water and clinging to them, rose from the pool and followed after them.

Eithne saw then that the plates of the cauldron had been hammered from within to push out the wyrd metal surface. From the facets of the boiling pot, *coelbreni* runes and curvilinear pictographs stood out in the glow from the statue at the other end of the chamber.

She could see then the ancient image of Karn, god of the forest, on that cauldron. He wore roebuck antlers and sat with goat-legs crossed beneath him. In his right hand, he held a torc, and with his left gripped a horned serpent a little below the head. To the left was a stag with antlers similar to those of the god. Dogs, cats, and cattle surrounded the scene. Some faced the god, others faced away. Between the antlers of the god was the motif of a tree. The antlers of the god reminded Eithne of the massive rack that hung over Eowain's hearth in Dúnsciath. *That seems so long ago and far away now,* she thought.

On another plate was the bust of a torc-wearing woman, flanked by two six-spoked wheels, and what seemed to be two elephants and two fierce, winged gryffins. Beneath the bust of the woman was the image of a terrible lion.

The brutes raised Eowain's linen-wrapped body high in the air. The ancient chants of Corchen and the priestesses rose in a feverish spiral through the grotto.

The cauldron bubbled with herbs and mystic roots. Eithne shrieked a little as his linen-wrapped body sizzled into the scalding water. She had not thought it possible, for those short men to reduce his whole, bearish, war-like body, his whole life, into that cauldron. It seemed not nearly so vast as to contain the man she'd come to love.

And yet they raised him over their heads and folded him down into the waters until he was submerged. His body, wrapped in sodden linens, gleamed with a spring-green pallor in the shadows, as the waters of the cauldron boiled, bubbled, toiled, and troubled.

Then the linen-wrapped form stood up from the cauldron.

Revulsion clutched at her throat.

Corchen spoke urgently: "Now. Get him out of there. Get him upstairs." The priestesses helped him from the waters, the short brutes carried the bandaged body away.

Eithne watched him go and plucked at Corchen's sleeve. "He is alive again?"

She shook her head. "He was never dead. But it was a close thing." She raised her hands in open supplication to the shrine. "The Goddess is restless tonight." She furrowed her brow, as if she listened to some sound lost in the grotto's stones and waters. "The goddess is restless indeed!" Her eyes went wide. "Put Lady Eithne in the novitiate's quarters. Tell the Hunt-Lord to double the guard. Turn all the men out."

"What's happening?" The hands of the robed priestesses closed on her arms, implacable.

"The Dragon is coming. Go now. There is more villainy afoot this night."

EOWAIN PUT HIS hands to his head, squeezed at his firmly shut eyes. *Where am I now?* He wondered what had happened to his swim in the river.

He blinked open his eyes. Candlelight warmed the air. He lay in a narrow cell upon one of two reed mat beds. At the foot of each bed was a wooden chest. In his hand, he clutched a rawhide leather pouch.

Medyr sat on one of the chests, puffing at his clay pipe. He smiled at Eowain. "Well? Aren't you coming, Your Grace?"

Eowain squinted at his old mentor. "Coming where?"

"We have an appointment at the hot-house springs."

Eowain rubbed his head. His hair was damp. "Who is we?"

"Your bridal party, Your Grace."

"Is there going to be a wedding?"

"Yes, Your Grace. Yours, Your Grace."

He rubbed at his forehead. "Oh. That thing?"

Medyr smiled again at him. "Yes, Your Grace. That thing."

"We're still doing that?"

Medyr nodded. "Yes, Your Grace." He sniffed. "We're still doing that."

Eowain rubbed at his face with both hands. "She's said as much?"

"Well, not in my hearing, Your Grace, but I assure you—."

Eowain squeezed his sound, meaty left fist around the pouch in his hand. "Don't assure me. Go find her. I'll hear it from her own lips, or we'll have none of it."

The grave face of his minister looked disquieted. "Aye, Your Grace." Medyr retreated.

Eowain closed his eyes again.

Had it all been a dream? He felt no pain in his leg, no burning in his cheek. *What did they do to me?*

Lorcán arrived to report. He sat close and told Eowain of how he and the men of Droma had finally broken the bandits with their cavalry charge, how they'd found their king slumped over the body of Tnúthgal and borne him up out of the forest.

Then he whispered to Eowain of the nine priestesses that had met them at the top of the pass to the Vale and taken Eowain away into the hill under the circle of standing stones. "That's where you are now, Brother, in the temple complex beneath the sacred hill. They've given over one of the chambers of the priestesses to you."

"What happened? Was I—?" Eowain felt well, better than he'd felt in many a year in fact. But he knew the injuries and wounds he'd suffered had been grave. "Was I dead?"

Lorcán shook his head. "Not quite. That's what the High-Priestess said, though you could have fooled us when we hauled you out of the forest. You were barely breathing, your face was purple. You had a terrible black swelling in your arm, here." Gently, he touched Eowain's left bicep.

There was no mark there from Cael's envenomed blade. Not even a scar. "Then how...? How did they restore me?"

Lorcán shuddered. "I don't know, Brother." His voice was ghastly. "I wish I knew." He clenched his maimed half-hand. "But— I'm sorry, I just don't know."

"What time is it? What day?"

"Evening approaches. It will be Cétshamain Day when the sun sets."

There was a knock on the door, a novitiate priestess with soup and fresh bread for him. Eowain sat up and spooned it hungrily to his lips.

Lorcán rested his hand on his brother's arm as he ate. "But tell me, what happened down there?"

It was easily done, and soon Eowain had told all of it: the swarm of vermin, the burning crock of vitriol, the death of the scout, Corvac. The courage of the merchant, the acolyte, and the Foreigner mercenary. Even the strange matter of the sorcerer rising as from the dead with a hole in his chest where his heart should have been.

Lorcán's eyes grew wide. "Well, the merchant and the acolyte and their Foreigner were still with you in the end. They helped us haul you from wreck of that battle. They're in the room beside this one, in fact, having their injuries tended." Then he shook his head. "And I don't know what that sorcerer was about, but news of him set this hive of women buzzing, I'll tell you what." He leaned in closely. "And I've even heard tell that the Mór-Dára is here."

That was news indeed. The seat of the High-Priest of all Iathrann was in Ard-Cátha, some distance away. It would have taken him at least a fortnight to have traveled to the Vale.

Eowain broke off a chunk of bread. "Medyr says Eithne's agreed to the wedding?" He tried to keep his tone nonchalant, but anxiety tugged at his heart.

Lorcán shrugged. "Aye. So he says."

"You've not heard it either?"

"I haven't seen her since we arrived with you. But she was the one to signal our charge. If not for her, we might have come too late. Even as it was, we still had a hard fight getting you clear of that place. I half-expected her to join us in the charge, so intent on finding you she was. I know I doubted it, but I do think she cares for you, Eowain."

He shook his head. "Maybe so. But after all we've been through, Lorcán? By Gods, I'll hear her say it before I believe it."

His brother's eyebrows rose and fell, his head tilted to the side. "Well... Yes. I can't say as I blame you." Then he shook his head. "But don't be stubborn about this, Eowain. Medyr has assured us she will wed. Ban-Drúmór Corchen herself told him, he said."

"After all we've been through, I will be stubborn about this." He felt anger in his heart as soup and bread brought more life to his limbs.

Lorcán looked unhappy, but drew himself up like a good soldier. "Aye, Your Grace." He rose to his feet. "Unless you need anything else, I should see that our men are billeted in the village. Are you well enough?"

"Aye, well enough. Thank you, Brother." But as Lorcán turned to go, a thought occurred to him. "Wait. You say the merchant and the acolyte are near?"

Lorcán pointed to the wall on Eowain's right. "Right there, Your Grace."

"Are they well?"

He shrugged. "Well enough, I'd imagine. Do you need them?"

"Aye, I think I do. If they're up for it."

"Very good. I'll send them in. Anything else?"

Eowain assured him not, and Lorcán retreated to attend the Shield Company's arrangements.

A moment later, Medyr's acolyte poked his head in. He wore a bandage around his head with a red stain on it.

Eowain waved for him to enter. Behind him came the merchant. His left arm was slung around his neck. "What's your name again, boy?"

Adarc knelt beside the bed. "Adarc son of Triath, Your Grace."

"You'll go and find her for me, Adarc. The Lady Eithne. You'll do this for me, lad?"

The boy looked troubled. "Why, Your Grace, Sir? The Lord-Drymyn, sir, he's gone to fetch her."

"Because I'm not sure I trust your master, lad. Will you do this for me? Yay or nay?"

"Aye, sire. If that's your command."

"It is. Take this merchant lad with you. And his pet Foreigner. Don't let her tell you no. I would see her, will she or nill she."

"Yes, sir." The boy was off like a bolt, no doubt happy to be involved in his master's dark conspiracies at last, Eowain thought. The merchant made a short bow and followed after him.

Eowain waited for her. Yet even with Medyr and his acolyte searching for her, it seemed he lay there many hours of the night before at last she came.

CHAPTER NINETEEN

THE MERCHANT AND the acolyte opened the doors to his little cell.

Through the door, he saw Eithne. Red-haired. Green-eyed. Fair-skinned and freckled. Her eyes grew round, and her shoulders relaxed. She chewed at her lower lip, then looked down and away to the left. Her coppery hair glinted in the candlelight as it fell upon her cheek.

The merchant's Foreigner had a hold on her arm. As he ushered her in, she shook him loose. Her eyes flashed anger at him, then at Eowain. "I do not appreciate being summoned." She sketched an insolent curtsy. "Your Grace." She lowered her eyebrows at him, planted her feet firmly on the stone floor.

"I wouldn't have summoned you if you'd been here."

Out in the hallways beyond his little cell, a tumult arose, as of people crying out in conflict. "I was... a little busy." she said. She glanced over her shoulder. The chords of her throat tensed.

"Too busy to come and tell me what you've decided?"

She turned back and jutted her chin at him. "Yes, maybe." Then she looked down and twisted at the three golden rings on her fingers. "You don't know what's been happening since we—"

"All I need to know is that you haven't yet answered my suit." He pushed himself up. The linen sheets of his bed slipped from his broad, bare chest.

"Didn't Medyr—?"

Abruptly, he tossed the leathern pouch to her. She caught it, puzzled over it. "What's this?"

"A promise fulfilled."

She opened the pouch. Revulsion crawled across her face. She looked up to meet his gaze.

"I swore you'd have the eyes from Cael the Viper's head. The men of Droma keep their word."

"Eowain, I—"

"After all I've been through for you, I'll hear it from your own mouth. Don't play coy with me any longer. Damn it, woman, I'll have your answer."

"After all *you've* been through—?" Her eyes widened.

Outrage rose in his heart. "Yes, in fact. After all that *I've* been through. After all my brother has been through. After all my people have been through, on your behalf, on the scant promise of 'maybe later.'" He levered himself up out of bed, drew himself up to his full height.

She scowled at him. "Listen to me, you oaf. This is not love, this ordering people about." She spat on the ground between them. "I see nothing but boastful pride here before me, not love."

"How dare you—?" He took a step toward her.

She stood her ground and fixed him with the icy stare of her green eyes. "How dare I? How dare you? Love doesn't dishonor others. Love isn't self-seeking, or easily angered. Love keeps no record of wrongs." She pointed a finger at him. "Yet all I see here is a hard mile of accounting."

"Lady, are there no limits to your stubborness?" Eowain pounded his fist against the granite block wall.

"Are there no limits to your damned foolishness?" She put her hands on her hips. "Was that supposed to frighten me, that punch? Am I supposed to cower now like some scullery wench?"

"Damn you, enough of this skirmishing. Let's have it, my lady." He spit in his palm and laid it open for her. "Clap hands and a bargain?"

She stared at his hand. Anger grew like storm-clouds in the greens of her eyes.

"If that's how you woo women in Droma, it is small wonder you find yourself in want of a bride." She curtsied with all due formality. Every line of it mocked him. "Your Grace."

She turned on her heel and walked out, past the obsequious merchant and the shame-faced acolyte.

Eowain stormed from the priestess's cell and shouted after her retreating back: "Who needs the love of such a woman?"

EITHNE DISAPPEARED INTO the press of priestesses, acolytes, and novitiates that came and went. There seemed to be some trouble somewhere, a hushed mumble of panic. Eowain saw Huntsmen among the press with weaponry drawn, directing people to stay calm.

He took the merchant by the collar and watched the color bleed from his olive, Samrabensian complexion. "What's going on out here?"

"Ic ne kunnane," he stammered. "I— I do not know, Your Grace."

Adarc put up a hand to stay Eowain's fury. "My lord, it is the Rite of the Oracle. The Goddess of the Vale herself appeared upon the mound! She took the face of Cátha, Queen of Battles, and pronounced a dread prophecy!"

"What nonsense is this? You and the merchant, fetch me my harness."

He sent them away, then cursed. His head dropped into his hands. *What did I just do?* He sat upon the bed, amid the clean, fresh linens.

Had she really just said no? After all I've been through for her? He hammered his fist against his knee. The knee that was as fit and as whole as on the day he'd walked out of Droma. Had it all been a dream?

He shook his head. He knew it wasn't. He'd seen her, spoken with her. Eithne was real. He'd seen the look in her eyes as they read back each other's missives over their game of fickle. He'd known her heart in those words. Or thought he did.

How dare she? Rage bubbled through him. He'd faced bandits and war-dogs and more bandits. He'd faced sorcery such as he hoped to never see again. And even before all of that, he'd scaled Glúin Hill and fought off Toryn the Stout's wild Cailech-men.

He'd seen and done the stuff of which legends were written and songs were song.

How dare she? Eowain practically spluttered with fury. He could practically hear the bards singing it in the hall of Dúnsciath, back home, among familiar concerns. *Does she not realize that my kingdom has sacrificed cattle and silver, blood and steel, for her bride-price? That I am Eowain the Bear, King of the Droma, who has slain the villain Cael the Viper, the sorcerer Kúlkak, the Cailech hero Toryn the Stout, and my own ambitious cousin, the traitor Tnúthgal?* He imagined friends by the fire on a rare night of peace drinking ôl and *uisce.* The broad rack of the noble Great White Elk of Droma, won by his father, under-lit by the glow of the hearth, shadowed antlers spread up to the stone, timber, and thatch-work of the manor roof.

He'd rise at that feast, with the hero's portion of the hart's haunch in hand. The bards would sing of how he'd faced gloomy mists of shy-nn-midnight, terrible and relentless foes, treacherous villains, and the evil spirits of the mountain itself.

The merchant and the acolyte returned. "Your Grace." They nodded briskly and laid his harness out on the bed. His leather and woolen breeks and greaves. His stout, hard-leathered boots. The tartans of his clan. The mail of iron-rings, stitched to the padded leather jack. Kilt, surcoat, tunic, hose. And then the Foreigner brought his shield, his sword, his belt of knives and tools, and the spear of his father, Findtan.

Eowain dressed with the efficiency of a soldier called to duty from his bed. He knew the buzz of riot when he heard it.

"Tell me, what's going on out there?"

"Sure and no one quite knows, Your Grace." His eyes darted to the merchant, then to the door of the cell. "Some say the Oracle calls for war against the Foreigners. Others say She foretells disaster for all of Iathrann." He shook his head. "Sure and I'm not sure what to believe, my lord."

"Where's your master?"

"Summoned away, my lord. The Great Moot of the Drymyn will begin at any time."

Eowain strapped on his jack of iron-ringed leather, and the bracers for his arms. He hefted his wooden shield, his coif of chain and his round, iron-cap, his sword, and the spear of his father.

"Your Grace?" Eowain looked up. There was a girl, a young novitiate priestess, with braided hair and eyes, and fair, freckled skin. The mercenary and the merchant skulked back from her. She glowed in Eowain's sight. "Aren't you coming?"

With a dizzying lurch, he found himself then upon a forest trail, as if out for a walk. It was high summer time, on the trail that skirted the mound of the Kings of Droma. Ahead of him, there was a woman, dark-haired, fair-skinned, with lips like rose-petals, in robes of ermine and satin, and the green, gold, and white of the Donnghaile. She rode a pale horse.

"Aren't you coming, Eowain?" She turned away from him.

He ran after her in fury, intent upon catching her, but grew no closer, though neither did the dappled-white horse with the pink ears go any faster.

"Haven't you learned by now?" The woman's voice laughed at him, not unkindly.

"Learned what?" Eowain stopped running and stood stock-still.

The woman on the horse grew no closer, but neither did the dappled-white steed go any slower. Yet it marched on. Hooves clopped on the trail, going neither thither nor yon.

The woman astride the horse frowned at him, her brow dimpled. "You must always be chasing us. You must never be having us."

"But after all I've done—!"

She waved a negligent hand at him. "Fluff-and-stuff, you stupid Man. What did you do today, after all? Bashed about a few bandits? Irritated a malignant evil from beyond the næther-realm of Annwn? Risked your immortal soul to hazard a sorcerer? Pish."

"Yes, that's right. That's what I did!"

"Pish, I said. Did you not hear her words? Love does not boast. Love does not dishonor others. Love isn't self-seeking. It isn't easily angered."

"What are you talking about?"

The figure on the horse aged before his eyes, became wrinkled, and stooped. A hump formed upon her back, her spine twisted. Moles and warts grew upon her face, hairs sprouted from her chin. "Damn it, Man. What color are her eyes?"

Eowain couldn't help himself, he goggled at her. Even as he watched, she transformed again, becoming a young fair maiden once more.

The magnificent white shynn-steed continued to prance, never faster, never slower, never coming any nearer, nor growing farther away.

"I don't understand," said Eowain.

"Her eyes, you blasted fool. What color are her eyes?"

Her face appeared before him, fair and lean and hungry. Her eyes glittered at him. "Why, they're the fiercest green I've ever seen."

"And why are you telling me?"

With another vertiginous lurch, he stumbled and sat heavily upon the reed mat in the cell of a priestess beneath the hill. "My lord?" The acolyte looked closely at him. "Are you sure you're quite well, Your Grace?"

CHAPTER TWENTY

EOWAIN FOUND EITHNE in the Commemoration Hall. The granite blocks were centuries old, yet gleamed from long silent years of torchlit vigils. Tapestries hung from the stones, depicting the ancient tale of Thaynú: How she arose from the sea after a great and terrible deluge that drowned all the lowlands. How she came with her sons and daughters, last survivors of an ancient golden empire in the southern seas, to the lands of Iathrann.

This was the place where that miracle happened. Upon this hill. Eowain felt a moment of awe as the brazier-lights played over the particoloured tapestries. Each displayed a different scene in the legends of the Great Mother Goddess Thaynú, and he was surprised to find himself there, under Her hill.

Eithne knelt before a bronze statue of a woman. He came in, girded for war, mailed shirt ringing. She turned about with a small cry and rose to her feet. Her eyes were dark, and the green of them seemed to shine. She looked to him like a hungry wolf in expensive robes with her back up against a stone corner. In one hand, she clutched a sheaf of old, wrinkled parchments, stained and nearly shredded. The epistles he'd sent to her, when she was away in Dolgallu.

Her other hand dropped out of sight. He knew she had a dagger ready there, hidden behind her skirts. The dagger decorated with the dark yellow schorl in the hilt.

He stopped, caught in her fearful gaze. *Will I be stricken to stone?*

"Lady—." His voice stuck in his throat. "Lady. By the Gods, I do attest, no woman upon the Abred has eyes as green and striking and lovely, my lady." He cleared his throat, put his fist sheepishly to his chest, and saluted her.

The fair skin of her cheeks flushed a rosy pink, and freckles like bronze flecks glowed like embers in the firelight. Her lips parted and she gasped, "What?" Her eyebrows rose and the reflected light of the braziers grew from a flicker to a flame as her eyes widened.

He looked down at the floor, pulled at the collar of his mailed shirt. "Your—uhm—your eyes, my lady. They are—" He shook his head. "I mean—" He looked up at her. "How do I start, Eithne? What do I say? Your eyes— They were like sunshine when all I knew was rain. In the darkest moment of my despair, I longed to look into your beautiful eyes, to feel the warmth of their light." His throat closed, then feelings rushed from his tongue in a torrent. "Eithne, the sound of your voice calls me by what I wish to be. It ripples through my blood and melts my heart. In all the chronicles and tales of beautiful ladies and brave warriors, I see now that all the praises of those poets were but prophecies of you." He reached out a hand to her, unsure if he should touch her. He turned over the hand, beseeched her understanding. "Eithne, I want to kiss your rosy lips, and touch your blushing cheeks."

Here eyes went round and she blinked at him, then looked away. Her hair, liquid copper burnished by the ruddy braziers' light, fell again over her face. "Then— This is real now?"

He bent to one knee. "If love is measured by how far one can fall, my lady, or judged by how low one is willing to crawl to save it and make it last, then none have ever loved another so well as I love you." He looked to her face and sought understanding. "Love endures, my lady. It bears a Prince's Truth."

There was a clatter upon the smooth, polished granite floor. The dagger with the yellow schorl in the hilt rattled as it came to rest.

She looked up from it, then away again, tugged at a strand of hair.

"I have endured much tonight as well," she said. Her chin rose as she faced him again. "You've been dead to me, then alive again. And I have—." Her voice went quiet. Her chin fell again. "I have seen things here." Her green eyes met his. "Terrible things." Something haunted lay there.

He did not know what she might have seen, what terrors might still lurk ahead for them. *Who can know such things?* But he reached out and gently touched the epistles still clutched in her hand. "And what of them? Did any one of them tell you I would make a bad husband?"

She scowled at him, the freckles across her nose wrinkled. She cocked her head and put a finger to her chin. A hint of a smile played on her lips. He wondered for a moment what else might bring such a look to her face.

"You know?" she said. "In fact, they didn't." She put her hand to his cheek, his ten-days' beard cleaned and trimmed, the braids re-done. The broad width of his polished ring-mail gleamed in the firelight. She drew him up to his feet.

He looked her in the eye, stepped closer to her. Then he spat in his hand and held it open to her. "Then what say you, my lady?"

Eithne grinned at him, spat in her own hand. "Clap hands, then, and a bargain." She put her hand firmly in his. Her green eyes glimmered, and heat leaped from their hand-fasting like flames from a hearth.

EVEN FROM THE avenue, Kerridwen could see the glow of the great bonfires atop the mound, and the fiery arcs the torches traced against the dark sky. The drums pulsed with a heavy insistence, their beat deepened to thunder as the lads of the countryside competed to toss their torches highest.

Kings and armies might come and go, but the real struggle—sometimes it seemed to Kerridwen the only struggle that mattered—was the one that men waged each year to protect their fields and nurture their crops.

In the distance she heard the lowing of the cattle that had already been driven between the sacred fires and so blessed. She smelled woodsmoke and cooked meat and the sharp fragrance of the mugwort and hypericum from her garland.

"O look," said Achtan, beside her. "See how high they throw the torches? Like shooting stars!"

Keva answered her. "May the crops grow as high as the torches rise!"

They'd brought a bench for Kerridwen to sit on until it was time for the rite of the Oracle. She huddled there gratefully, letting the murmured conversation of the other women eddy around her.

There was a last crescendo from the hill, and then the fires appeared to explode outwards as lads snatched brands from the bonfires and raced down the hill in every direction to bear the sun-power to the fields. The drumming settled to a hypnotic heartbeat. Kerridwen felt the familiar flutter of approaching trance.

It will be soon now, she thought, and then, *whatever comes of this night's work, it will be done.* For the first time in years she had mixed the most powerful trance herbs into the potion, afraid that without their help her own fears might keep the Goddess at bay.

She knew the Mór-Dára was anxious as well, though his face did not show it. He was like a carven image, a shell in which the spirit flickered ever more fitfully. She had seen how much he needed the support of his oaken staff. One day, perhaps soon, he would be gone. There had been times when she hated him, but in the past years they had come to an unspoken understanding. And there was no telling who his successor would be.

But that was a fear she could face once this night was past. The procession was beginning to move now. Kerridwen allowed Keva to assist her to her feet and start up the hill.

The drymyn were chanting; their song pulsed through the warm air.

> *Behold, the holy priestess comes,*
> *Sacred herbs are in her crown;*
> *The golden crescent in her hand...*

There was a moment of surprise when Kerridwen felt the first wave of expectation from the assembled crowd. Then she had a sense of nausea, and a sickening lurch in consciousness as the potion took hold. She fought back a flicker of panic as the world whirled around her. She'd sought after this—whether out of faith or cowardice she was not sure, but this time she wanted the world to go away.

Lady of Life, to You I entrust my spirit. Mother, be merciful to all your children!

Years of practice had given her full control over the techniques of focus and breathing that loosed the spirit from the body. The herbs in the potion aided the process. Her head felt shattered like a broken bowl, and that certain Otherness flooded into her, tossed her consciousness aside like a leaf on a stream.

Her grandmother, the Bándrumór Corchen, appeared before her, undecidable, uncertain. She heard the muttered prayer, watched with limpid curiousity as Grandmother sketched the sign of blessing in the air, where it seemed to burn whitely for a moment, the sharp blue-white fire of the thunderbolt. Kerridwen felt the ban-drymyn priestesses assist her into the chair, and the unsettling sensation of falling even though she knew they lifted her. Her spirit swung between Abred and Ceugant; there was a slight jerk as they set the chair atop the mound. Then she was free.

She floated as if through golden mist. For a time it was enough simply to enjoy the sense of being safe, protected, at home. Suspended in that certainty, the fears she'd left behind her seemed transitory, even absurd. But her body would not entirely release her. Presently, even reluctantly, the mist thinned enough so that she could see, and hear.

She looked down upon the huddle of blue robes in the tall chair and knew it for her own body, dimly illuminated by the embers of the great bonfires to either side. The drymyn and ban-drymyn made a circle with the people behind them, pale robes on one side and dark on the other in two great curves of light and shadow. The great mass of folk who had come for the festival darkened the hillside; points of fire winked from the booths and tents of the encampment that had sprung up around it. Beyond stretched the patchwork of trees. Without curiousity, she noted a swirl of motion in one part of the crowd, and farther off a more regular movement along the trail from the foothills, and the gleam as metal caught the light of the setting moon.

The drymyn priests invoked the Goddess, twining all the incoherent imaginings of the people into a single, mighty image which was at the same time as various as there were people to echo their call. Kerridwen saw the power they raised as a swirl of multi-colored lights and threads. She pitied the fragile form into which it was descending. Now her body was almost hidden. The magick took shape—a female figure, heroic in stature and splendid in form, though the features could not yet be seen.

Kerridwen drew closer, wondered what face the Lady would wear for this gathering.

A whirl of dark-winged shadows fluttered across the circle as a sudden chill wind stirred the fires. The figure in the chair seemed to expand suddenly, then sat bolt upright and threw aside the veil.

"I hear your summoning and I come," she said in the language of the tribes.

The murmur of fright that swept the circle faded to absolute silence. The chair creaked as the figure who sat there leaned forward. In the firelight, Her face and Her hair were as red as a bloody sword. She smiled terribly, and Cétshamain though it was, the wind was suddenly icy, as if the darkness of the Great Queen had killed the sun. The people began to edge backward.

Here ends

The Romance of Eowain,

third tale in the Matter of Manred.

ABOUT THE AUTHOR

MICHAEL DELLERT lives in the Greater New York City area. Following a traditional publishing career spanning nearly two decades, he now works as a freelance writer, editor, publishing consultant, and writing coach. He is also the sole writer, editor, and publisher of the blog *MDellertDotCom: Adventures in Indie Publishing*. He holds a Master's Degree in English Language & Literature from Drew University, and a certificate from the Cornell University School of Criticism & Theory (2009). He is the author of the fantasy novellas, *Hedge King in Winter* and *A Merchant's Tale. The Romance of Eowain* is his first published fiction novel.

About the Cover Artist

Saša Ristović-Ritza is an illustrator and graphic designer living and working in Serbia. His demonstrated skill in epic fantasy and science fiction illustration can be seen at www.dualdesigners.wordpress.com

PREVIOUS WORKS

in the

MATTER OF MANRED SAGA

Hedge King in Winter

A Merchant's Tale

FORTHCOMING WORKS

in the

MATTER OF MANRED SAGA

The Wedding of Eithne

Heron's Cry

Join the mailing list at **mdellert.com/blog/mailing-list/** to receive more information, news, updates, and special promotional offers on these and other exciting new titles coming soon from Skylander Press.

www.ingramcontent.com/pod-product-compliance
Lightning Source LLC
Chambersburg PA
CBHW051947220626
47052CB00004B/837